WILDFIRE

BROKEN BOW

BOOK TWO

ASHLEY A QUINN

TCA PUBLISHING LLC

Copyright © 2020 by Ashley A Quinn

ISBN is 9781733160056

ONE

The hot late-June sun beat down on Tara Miller's neck as she worked on her ancient truck. She knew she should just drive the fancy SUV parked in her garage, but there was something about driving the old Ford that calmed her soul. Life was busy, and the truck made her think of simpler times. When life wasn't so complicated. Or painful.

Her hand slipped off the wrench she used to tighten the bolt on the air filter, and she banged her knuckles on the engine mount.

"Fuck!"

She snatched her hand back and cradled it between her breasts. Straightening, she turned away from the vehicle and looked out over her family's ranch, The Broken Bow. Golden prairie grass waved in the light breeze, birds chirped, and cows mooed. Nestled against the mountain, the ranch had been in her family since the eighteen-sixties. She and all her siblings still lived on it. Some of them—like herself—had left and come back, but they always found their way home again.

She shook her aching hand, then swiped at the sweat rolling down her face with the blue bandana tucked in her shorts pocket. It was hot. Summer had come early this year and hadn't let up.

A red truck with a motorcycle strapped into the bed rolled up the drive, catching her attention. She narrowed her eyes and watched as it made its way to her brother Seb's house.

Great. Jace is here.

The truck pulled up to the house and stopped. The driver's door opened and long, denim-clad legs emerged to drop to the ground, followed by a narrow waist, broad chest, thick arms, a face to die for, and a head of golden hair that begged her to run her fingers through it.

Heat rushed south to flood Tara's core. Why did Jace Travers have to be so damn sexy? And why did her brother think it was a good idea to let the man stay in his house until he found a place of his own?

Shaking her hand again, she turned back to her truck, determined to ignore him and his sexiness. She would just pretend he wasn't a hundred yards away.

She glanced up. Muscles bulged as he lowered the tailgate and hopped up into the truck bed to undo the straps holding the motorcycle in place. He bent over with his back to her and she dropped her wrench at the sight of that tight butt encased in even tighter denim. It clanged through the engine to drop to the stones below.

He looked up at the racket. She ducked her head and prayed he wouldn't come over to see if she needed help.

Tara counted to thirty and chanced another glimpse across the grass. He had mounted the bike and was walking it backward down a metal ramp. Relieved, she crouched down to retrieve the tool she dropped. It had fallen farther back than she thought. Lying down, she scooted on her belly under the vehicle and stretched. Her fingers closed around the cool metal, and she shimmied her way back out.

As she cleared the bumper, she rolled to sit up and found

herself looking at a pair of long, jean-covered legs. She followed them up over strong thighs, a very intriguing bulge, a flat stomach and a well-built chest to a face so handsome it should only be seen on a movie screen.

He arched one perfect golden eyebrow at her and a corner of his mouth quirked. The breeze ruffled his honeyed hair, and those deep blue eyes carried a spark of humor as he stared down at her.

"You need some help?"

And that voice...

It rolled over her like fine wine. So smooth and rich, but with a bite.

She cleared her throat and stood, waving away the hand he offered. "No. I just dropped my wrench." She held up the offending tool.

He gave a slow nod, then looked at the teal Ford. "Car trouble?"

She shook her head and blew a piece of hair out of her eyes that had come loose from her ponytail. "Just routine maintenance."

"Like an oil change?"

She nodded. "Among other things."

"You know how to do all that? I thought you were a chef."

"I grew up on a ranch. I can take apart the tractor and rebuild the engine in the middle of the pasture if I have to."

"With just dental floss and a hairpin?" He flashed a teasing grin.

She rolled her eyes and crossed her arms, tapping her foot and ignoring the MacGyver reference, no matter how accurate or funny it was. "Did you have a reason for coming over here, or did you just feel like bugging me?"

His smile faded, and she thought she saw a flash of hurt in his eyes. Her conscience niggled at her, but she shoved it back into its box. He was dangerous to her sanity and needed to leave.

He held up his hands. "Just thought you might need a hand. My mistake." He backed away. "See you around, Tara." With a brief wave, he turned and jogged back to Seb's house.

Tara turned back to her truck and tried not to watch that perfect ass of his flex as he ran. Focusing on the air filter, she tightened the cover and lowered the hood. It closed with a bang and she tossed her wrench into the toolbox on the ground.

Scooping it up, she walked into her garage and deposited it on the workbench before going inside, stripping off her clothes and stuffing them straight into the washer. Naked, she walked to her bathroom and turned on the shower. She might be a grease monkey, but that didn't mean she wanted to smell or look like one.

After a brief shower, she dressed in a pair of mint green capris, a sleeveless white blouse, and brown leather sandals, then headed outside to her truck. She had time for a quick trip into town before she had to be at the restaurant to prepare for dinner. She needed a latte and a dose of Macy's craziness to banish the image of Jace Travers from her brain.

Windows rolled down, she savored the breeze as she drove the ten miles to town, letting it wash away some of the tension. She needed to find a way to cope with his presence since he would be her next-door neighbor for a few weeks at least.

It wasn't that she didn't like him—she liked him too much. The man was sex on a stick. And he was nice. Any single woman in her right mind would love to have him hanging around. But she had sworn off adrenaline junkies and men who looked like they could break her heart. She'd had enough heartache.

That old, familiar pang stabbed her in the chest as she

remembered her husband, and she took a steadying breath. No, she never wanted another man like that again. She couldn't handle it.

She cruised into Silver Gap and headed straight for Peppy Brewster, Macy's coffee shop. She tucked her vintage truck between two SUVs and shut off the engine.

"Yikes." A peek in the mirror revealed the wind did a number on her hair. At least it was dry now. She scraped it up into a messy bun and stepped out of the vehicle.

Inside the shop, the scent of fresh coffee assailed her. She took a deep breath of the heavenly smell.

"Hey, girl. What brings you to town?"

Tara smiled at Macy and walked up to the counter. "I needed a latte before work and to clear my head. Jace arrived."

Macy's grin was wicked. "Ooo, yum! That man is so hot." She grabbed the filter for the espresso machine and packed it full of coffee grounds, then affixed it to the machine. "You want your usual?"

"Yeah, but iced. And hot or not, he still irritates me."

Macy giggled and scooped some ice into a plastic cup and poured milk over it. "Yeah, because he gets you all hot and bothered. Would it hurt to give into that? It might lighten you up a bit and get you to relax."

"I don't have time to relax." Her phone dinged, and she opened her purse. It better not be her old editor again. He kept calling, but she'd yet to listen to his messages, read his texts, or call him back. She wasn't interested in that life anymore.

Finding her phone, she turned on the screen to see a message from her assistant manager, Cassie, groaning as she read it. Her produce shipment was late.

"Case in point." She sighed and showed the message to Macy. "I have to go straighten out this mess now and hope I have enough stuff to come up with *something* for the menu."

"Go talk to Rayna. See what she's got that might tide you over for today." She dumped the two shots of espresso into the milk and gave it a stir.

Tara's face brightened. "Hey, that's a good idea."

Macy smiled and stuck a lid on the drink, then handed it to Tara. "Duh." She flipped her hair and batted her eyes.

Tara laughed. "Thank you. I can always count on you to turn my mood around." She passed her friend her credit card and took a sip. "And this." She moaned in delight. "I can always count on this too. I don't know how you do it. Mine never turn out this good." She had an espresso machine at the restaurant, but her lattes never tasted as good as Macy's.

Macy shrugged and handed her back her card and a receipt. "Magic."

"Sure." She narrowed her eyes at her friend. "One day, you're going to tell me where you get your coffee beans."

"Trade secret." She leaned on the counter and grinned.

Tara tipped her cup toward Macy as she backed away. "One day."

Macy laughed.

Tara grinned. "Thanks for the tip about Rayna. I'll drive out there now."

"Sure. I hope she has some things left for you to use. Her farm market's been going gangbusters lately. That greenhouse she put up has already paid for itself."

No kidding. Rayna was one of the few locals who grew vegetables year-round, and she was the only one who grew on such a large scale.

Tara waved and left the café. Hopping back into her truck, she backed out of her space and headed toward the ranch. Rayna's family owned the property that bordered The Broken Bow to the east. They ran cattle, but Rayna had also turned a section of the ranch into a profitable vegetable and herb farm. Tara just wished it was bigger. She would buy all her fresh produce from the Nyderts if she could. But Rayna ran that part of the ranch alone, and what she cultivated was as much as she could handle.

The breeze blew through the cab, and she sang along to the radio in a much better mindset than when she left her house. She knew it wouldn't take much. She just needed a good laugh. And coffee.

She picked up her cup and took another drink. No more golden boy clogging up her mind. Thanks to Macy's magic latte and the frantic text from her assistant, she could focus now and switch gears to plan a new menu for tonight. Thankfully, her meat delivery had arrived. She just had to worry about sides. Rayna's greenhouse grew food all year, so if she had any produce left after today's market, she would have some decent choices.

She passed the entrance for the Broken Bow and continued down the highway another three miles before she reached the turnoff to the Nydert's ranch, the Double Moon.

Bumping down the dirt road, she headed for the greenhouse where Rayna's SUV sat outside. As she pulled to a stop, Rayna came out to greet her.

"Hey. Macy called and said you needed a hand."

Tara stepped out of her truck and shut the door. "Yeah. I ran into a minor snag. My produce delivery didn't arrive. I need whatever you've got."

Rayna blew out a breath and swept a hand over her hair and down her ponytail. "That's not much. But come on in and take a look."

Tara followed her inside to a set of tables laden with crates. She peered over the edge of the first few, then looked up at her friend.

"Wow. I'm both happy and sad. Happy for you, but sad that I'm going to run out of side dishes tonight."

Rayna laughed. "I do have some other things I haven't

harvested. They're on the edge of ripe, so I was going to pick them for tomorrow's market. Don't worry, we'll get you enough to hold you. Grab a crate." She pointed to a stack of empties on the floor.

They walked down the aisles of plants, and soon, Tara had enough produce to last the night.

She loaded the last crate into her truck and shut the tailgate.

"Thank you so much. I will cut you a check once I get back to the restaurant."

Rayna shrugged. "I know you're good for it. And you've saved me from hauling all this to market tomorrow. I don't mind a slow day." She leaned against the side of the truck and sent a coy smile at Tara. "So. Macy also said you had a run in with a certain hunky detective."

Tara rolled her eyes and groaned. "It was nothing. He moved into Seb's house today. We said hello."

She waggled her eyebrows. "Really? Is that all that happened?"

The image of his butt in those jeans popped into her head. "Yes."

Rayna pushed her tongue into her cheek. "Uh-huh. Okay."

"What? What do you want me to say? He came over and said hello, then he left. As far as I'm concerned, he can stay away."

An eye roll was Rayna's response. "Oh, come on. You know you find the man attractive."

"Of course I do. Have you seen him? But I'm not ready for a relationship, especially not with a man who rides a motorcycle and looks like the sun god himself."

"Those are the best kind of men. And Tara, it's been three years since Sean died."

"There's no timeline on grief, Rayna."

Rayna straightened and moved closer to lay a hand on Tara's arm. "I know that, sweetie, but you aren't grieving. You aren't even really living."

Tara glanced away, her mouth set in a firm line. "What are you talking about? Of course I'm living. I opened my restaurant."

Rayna shook her head. "No, that's a distraction, and it keeps you from thinking about things. From feeling."

Tara shifted, uncomfortable with the turn in the conversation. She wanted to say Rayna was wrong, but deep down she knew her friend was right. But it was easier to stay busy and stuff her feelings down where they would never see the light of day than to deal with them.

She shrugged and opened the truck door. "Yeah, well, it's how I deal. Look, I need to get going. Thanks for helping me out."

Rayna sighed and nodded. "Anytime. Remember what I said, though. Think about it at least?"

Tara nodded and climbed inside. The door closed with a creak. She had no intention of doing any such thing. That particular can of worms could stay right where it was. But she offered Rayna a genuine smile. "Have I told you lately how much I appreciate you? Thank you for looking out for me."

The other woman beamed. "You're welcome. Now go. Make something delicious."

Tara pulled away with a wave.

Dammit. She picked up the now tepid latte and took a sip. Its magic was gone, though. But it wasn't thoughts of Jace that wouldn't leave her mind now. It was thoughts of another man who was never coming back.

Two

Moisture beaded and dripped down the side of Jace Travers' neck. He didn't have much to unload, but it was enough to make him sweat carrying it all in. He picked up the last box, which was full of books, and headed inside, where it was blessedly cool. He deposited his load on the floor near the lone chair and went to the kitchen to get a drink. Gulping down a glass of water, he looked out the window over the sink at the mountains surrounding the ranch. It was so beautiful here. Haskell was flat and covered in prairie grass. It also held a lot of bad memories he would rather forget. He hoped by moving here, he would finally be able to move on.

The image of the dark-haired beauty who lived next door entered his mind. She sparked his blood with her deep, dark eyes and tall, curvy figure, but she wanted nothing to do with him, it seemed. He didn't know why, either. From the moment they met, she took an instant dislike to him, even though he was nothing but nice. It was baffling.

He'd find out why, though, and change that. She didn't know it, but her attitude was like throwing down a gauntlet. He would wear her down until she came to like him.

Pushing back from the counter, he decided that even as hot as it was, to take a stroll and explore his new surroundings. He was here several weeks ago, but had been so busy helping Seb with the serial killer investigation, he didn't get a chance to see much of the ranch.

He stepped out the front door and automatically looked to his right at Tara's house. That vintage truck of hers was gone. It still shocked him she knew how to fix cars. Most of the women in his acquaintance couldn't do more than change a flat. He found it extraordinarily sexy that she liked engines. He did too. He'd built the engine on his motorcycle. When he came upon her earlier, he'd wanted to get a look at the truck, but her standoffish demeanor kept him from hanging around.

Turning left, he decided to go say hello to Tara's parents, Lee and Jenny Archer, and let them know he'd arrived. His boots crunched on the gravel as he walked, adding to the sounds around him. He looked up as a hawk cried overhead and heard a horse whinny in the distance. The one thing absent was the sound of traffic. In Haskell, his house was in the city. Out here, it was just nature, and it was a welcome change.

His footsteps echoed on the wooden porch as he ascended the steps and knocked on the door. He saw Jenny come around the corner to answer his knock and waved at her through the glass.

She pulled open the door, a bright smile on her pretty face. "Jace. You made it. Come in. I just made some sun tea." She pushed out the screen door and motioned him inside.

"Tea sounds great. It sure is warm." He followed her inside to the kitchen.

"Yes, it is. This is about as hot as I can remember it being this early in the summer. And there's no letup in sight."

"I heard it isn't supposed to rain much, either."

She shook her head and took a pitcher of tea from the

fridge. "No. We're going to have some drought issues and we're in for a bad fire season, I'm afraid."

"Wildfires?"

She nodded as she poured two glasses of tea. "With these temps and no rain, it's a recipe for lots of them."

He took the glass and spooned some sugar into it from the bowl on the counter. She handed him a spoon, and he gave it a quick stir before taking a sip.

"This is good. Thank you."

She added sugar to her glass and smiled at him. "You're welcome. Let's go in the living room and sit."

He followed her, then took a seat on the couch opposite the chair she chose.

"How was your drive?"

"Long." He smiled. "Mostly because I was anxious to get here."

"Well, we're glad to have you. Seb, especially."

He nodded. "I just wish the job offer had come under better circumstances."

Her smile faded as the conversation took on a more somber tone. "Yes. What happened to Deputy Bering was tragic. But at least the man responsible is dead." She glanced out the front window, a sad smile on her face. "I still can't believe it was Ryan. He was a staple in this community and no one ever suspected what he was."

"Some serial killers are very adept at hiding their true nature. I'm just glad we stopped him before he could hurt London. How's Adelaide doing, by the way? She was in pretty rough shape when she escaped."

Jenny looked down at her hands and swiped a drop of condensation off her glass with her thumb. "She's doing okay. She's seeing a therapist, and she's been going to church. I've really been impressed with how she's turned herself around. London's had a big part in that. She took that girl under her wing and refused to let her slide into a depressed funk. I'm not saying it's been easy, or that she won't have setbacks, but she's going in the right direction."

"That's good. I'm glad. So, do you know what's going to happen with the hardware store?"

"Ryan didn't have any family left, so all his property went to the state. The store and his house are both up for sale, but neither have sold yet."

He nodded at that bit of information, then looked around at the comfortable room. The walls were a soft gray. Tan furniture, with light green and peach accent pillows, sat clustered around a television on an off-white farmhouse stand. A cream-colored rug with swirls of green and gray covered part of the warm wood floors. Pictures of the Archer siblings lined the built-in shelves surrounding a brick fireplace. His eyes landed on one that looked like it was of Tara. She held a magazine in her hands, showing the cover, and had a huge smile on her face.

"So, what are you up to this afternoon?" Jenny asked. "Moving in?"

He shook his head. "I already did that. I didn't bring much with me. Didn't seem like there was much point until I find my own place. I think I'm just going to explore some. Get a feel for the ranch."

Her smile was quick. "That sounds like a wonderful idea. It's too bad Tara has to work. She loves to go out and take pictures whenever she can. She knows this place better than her father, I think."

"I would love to have her show me around. I don't think I'm her favorite person, though."

She waved a hand at him. "Don't let her get to you. I think you make her want to break out of the box she put herself in."

He frowned, not quite sure what she meant. "She put herself in a box?"

Jenny nodded. "Tara's just been going through the motions of life the last few years. Her husband died, and it changed her. She plays it very safe now, and I think she sees you as the opposite of safe."

Shock rendered Jace speechless for a moment. Tara had been married? "What happened?"

"Sean—her husband—was a SEAL. He died in combat."

Holy shit. He'd met a few of those guys when he did his short stint in the Army. They were a different breed. Fearless, bold, determined. He couldn't see uptight Tara with a man like that. But, from the way it sounded, she wasn't always that way.

"I'm sorry to hear that. Losing a loved one is never easy." Pain lanced his heart at the truth of his words.

Jenny noticed the pinch to his features. "You speak from experience."

He nodded. "I was married once too. And I had a daughter. They died in a boating accident five years ago, along with my parents."

She gasped. "Oh my goodness! That's terrible. I'm so sorry."

"Thank you."

"What happened, if you don't mind me asking?"

Jace took a deep breath and rolled his glass between his fingers. That familiar lump appeared in his throat, but he pushed past it. "A freak storm came up while they were on the lake, and the boat capsized. They all drowned."

She covered her mouth with her hand, her eyes wide. "That's just awful. How old was your daughter?"

"Four. Haley was four." His voice was raw as he thought about his little girl. He missed her bright smile and that little laugh that was so contagious. His heart ached every day for what he'd lost.

Uncomfortable with the direction of his thoughts, he

drank the last of his tea and stood. "Thank you for the tea. I should let you get back to what you were doing."

She rose too. "I'm sorry if I pried."

He gave her a small smile. "You didn't. I'll never be over their deaths, but I have learned to live with them. It still makes me sad, though, to talk about them, especially Haley."

"Well, I'm still sorry for bringing up such a painful subject."

He handed her his glass. "It's okay. Thank you again for the tea. I'll see myself out."

Thoughts gloomy, and his heart aching, he left. Once outside, he paused to take a breath of the clean mountain air before turning and heading for the horse barn. He hoped to find Brady and talk him into letting him saddle a horse so he could go for a ride.

Instead, he found Lee, who was tending to one of the yearlings.

"Jace, hi. Good to see you." Lee reached over to shake his hand before going back to using the currycomb on the colt.

Jace took his hand. "Yes, sir. Just got in a little while ago. I was already up at your house and said hello to Jenny."

"Good. So what brings you in here? Just exploring?" Lee asked, running a currycomb over the young horse's back.

He nodded. "Yep. Needed to stretch my legs a bit. I don't suppose you'd mind if I saddled a horse and went for a ride, would you?"

The older man arched a dark brow. "Well, that depends. Can you ride?"

"Yes. My parents owned a farm. I had a horse growing up, and I rode quite a bit even up until the last few years."

Lee stepped back from the yearling. "Okay, then. Let's get you saddled up."

Jace followed him deeper into the barn to a tack room, where Lee picked up a saddle and handed it to him. "Here.

You're about Seb's height, so you can have his saddle. You can ride his horse, too." He picked up a set of bridle and a saddle blanket, then exited the tack room and led Jace out of the barn to a fenced pasture where several horses grazed.

Lee gave a sharp whistle, and the horses looked up, then came trotting over. He ducked between the rails and walked up to a tall, gray gelding whose coat was so shiny it gleamed like silver in the sun.

"This is Pike." Lee patted the horse on his neck. He stuck a hand in his pocket and pulled out a chunk of carrot, which he offered to Jace.

Jace set the saddle on the ground and took the treat, then stepped forward, offering it to the horse. Pike lapped it up and nudged his hand for more.

"That's all I've got, buddy." He held his hands up for the horse to see, then slid one palm up and over Pike's face to scratch him between the ears. The horse whinnied and pushed his head into Jace's hand.

"Pike's a good horse. Steady. You won't have any problems on him. And if you get lost, just let go of the reins; he'll bring you home. He's very food motivated and knows where his treats come from," Lee said with a chuckle.

Jace grinned. "Sounds good."

"Grab that saddle. I'll help you get him ready." He led the horse toward the barn.

Together, the two men had the horse ready in a few minutes. Jace swung up into the saddle, and Lee handed him the reins.

"If you head further into the hills, there's a nice trail, and it opens up into some pretty meadows. The river's that way too." He pointed behind them, past the houses.

"I'll do that. Thanks."

"Not a problem. When you get back, dress him down and put some fresh hay in his stall."

"Will do."

Lee stepped back, and Jace led Pike out of the barn. Once they cleared the doors, he could feel the suppressed power vibrate through Pike's muscles as the big animal tamped down his urge to run. Jace nudged his sides and let him loose.

They took off through the grass, past the houses and deeper into the Broken Bow's land. The wind rushed by, taking some of Jace's heartache with it as he reveled in the freedom of being on a horse again.

He rode up into the hills, slowing once the buildings were out of sight. Pike snorted, catching his breath after the run, but still continued a steady pace as they wove their way higher.

Jace admired the beauty of his surroundings as he rode. It was so wild here. No roads or houses. No towns in the distance. Just nature. He made a mental note to look for a house outside of town when he started searching. Some place that had a porch or a deck, so he could sit out there in the mornings with a cup of coffee and soak up the solitude. He already felt more at peace.

He went around a bend, and the landscape opened up into a giant meadow. Wildflowers in full bloom set the field ablaze with color. Cattle milled around, grazing lazily in the warm sun. He steered Pike through them to where the river cut through. When he reached its banks, he hopped off and let the horse drink while he walked forward to get a closer look at the water. It babbled over rocks and around logs. Small sandbars dotted the expanse, a resting spot for birds that wanted to take a dip, while fish swam in the crystal clear water.

Taking Pike's reins, he swung back up into the saddle and walked the horse along the edge of the river, enjoying the quiet until his stomach rumbled, reminding him he'd skipped lunch. He led the horse back across the meadow to the trees, circling around the way he'd come. One day soon, he'd get one of the Archer siblings to take him on a longer ride and show him all the spots he would never find on his own.

As they crested the hill and the ranch buildings came back into view, Jace could feel Pike's excitement build back up as his pace quickened.

"You want to run again?"

Seeming to understand him, Pike tossed his head and danced forward. Jace laughed and gave the horse his head. He took off, and they barreled down the hillside. Going full-bore, they didn't slow until they reached the clearing surrounding the houses and barn.

Jace pulled up on Pike's reins, a huge smile on his face. "Whoa, Pike."

The horse dropped to a walk, and Jace led him into the barn and out to the corral, where he walked him a couple laps to cool down his muscles before heading back inside.

As he ran a soft brush over the horse's back while Pike munched on some fresh hay, a noise down the corridor drew his attention.

He paused, listening. That hadn't been a barn cat. Unless it could knock down heavy tools and close a door. He set the brush down, then clipped a rope to Pike's halter and looped it around the doorpost before making his way out of the stall, leaving the door open. He kept his steps light, doing his best to keep his boots from making a sound.

A shovel leaned against the wall, and he picked it up. It was probably just one of the Archers, but something kept him from calling out. He'd seen no signs of anyone when he rode into the barn, nor since.

He peeked into each stall as he passed, but kept moving toward the supply and tack rooms at the back of the barn. The noise hadn't been in a stall; he'd have heard a horse make some sort of sound.

When he reached the rear of the building, the supply

room door was open like it had been when he rode in, but the tack room door was shut, and Jace had left it open after he put Pike's saddle away.

Heart thumping, he wished he had his gun, but it was locked up in Seb's house. He muttered a curse and grasped the knob, giving it a quick twist and shoving open the door. He stepped into the doorway, brandishing the shovel, only to be met by an empty room. A pair of hoof trimmers laid on the floor, though.

Lowering the shovel, he stepped into the room and picked the tool up off the floor, then put it back on the workbench. He glanced around, but nothing else was out of place. With a frown, he backed out of the room, leaving the door open, and walked back down the aisle to Pike's stall to finish grooming him.

The back of his neck tingled, and he glanced around. The barn was empty, but he couldn't shake the feeling he was being watched.

THREE

Tara wiped her hands on the towel tucked into her apron. The supper rush was in full swing, and her kitchen was running like a well-oiled machine. "Cassie, I'm going to go make the rounds of the dining room," she told her assistant manager.

The younger woman nodded, sparing her a quick glance as she worked.

She paused in the staff restroom before going out to make sure she didn't have some random ingredient splattered all over her face—it had happened more than once—then pushed through the swinging doors that led to the dining area.

Noise assaulted her as she stepped through. The bustle of nearly a hundred people filled the space and echoed through the cavernous room. She smiled, loving it.

Cooking was something she'd loved since she was a girl. It had been a challenge to see what ingredients she could combine to make something spectacular. For a long time, her dream had been a restaurant like this. Then, her parents bought her a camera for her fifteenth birthday and she'd had a new passion. And a talent for taking pictures that captured every emotion the subject expressed, whether they wanted it seen or not.

Tara attended the University of Colorado on a full scholarship for photography. It was there she fell in love with photojournalism. It offered an adrenaline high that rivaled any she'd ever felt on any of the stupid, life-threatening escapades she committed as a teen. For almost ten years, she traveled the world, covering some rather harrowing world events.

It also led her to the man who stole her heart, Navy SEAL Sean Miller. For five years, she'd had everything she ever wanted. An exciting career, the chance to see the world, a man who loved her beyond reason, and the start of a big, happy family of her own. Then, in an instant, her world shattered into millions of tiny pieces. Sean's team was ambushed, and he'd been killed. Tara's passion for photojournalism died with him. Her passion for anything adrenaline-inducing.

She'd come home because she didn't know where else to go. After a year of grieving, she'd known she needed to decide what to do with her life. She'd also known going back to the career she'd loved wasn't an option. She still loved to take pictures, but the thrill of doing it in some of the most dangerous locations on earth no longer appealed to her.

It was her mother's idea for Tara to open a restaurant. She surmised that maybe Tara needed a completely different direction for her life.

She'd been so right. Bit by bit, the joy seeped back into Tara's life. She wasn't healed yet, but she was getting there.

Tara stepped out past the bar to wander amongst the tables, talking to her guests and making sure everything was to their satisfaction. She prided herself on providing a stellar experience for everyone who visited, and she'd built her reputation on that. It showed in the packed house she hosted almost every night.

She rounded a column and stopped short. Jace sat at a table a few feet away, nose buried in a menu.

"Great," she muttered under her breath. She'd managed to shake all thoughts of him. Now, here he was in all his golden glory to bring them all back. Dammit.

She heaved a sigh and stepped forward, pasting a smile on her face. She'd be damned if someone saw her not be nice to him, though. Her reputation would not suffer because this man made her lady parts wake up and take notice against her will.

"May I suggest the eight-ounce sirloin and house vegetables?" she said, walking up to his table.

He looked up to spear her with those deep blue eyes that reminded her of the Mediterranean. Tara's insides quivered.

"Steak sounds good." He closed the menu and smiled. "What are the house vegetables?"

"Yellow squash and carrots—locally grown—in a brown sugar glaze. Or we have a house salad, also locally grown, if you'd prefer."

"Squash and carrots work for me. Are you my waitress?" He leaned back in his seat, draping one arm over the back of the chair, and grinned up at her.

She lifted one imperious brow, ignoring the sight of his broad chest stretching his clay-colored t-shirt and the hint of ink on his muscular arms. "No. I just came out to check on my diners."

He pouted, and Tara had the insane urge to suck that full lower lip between her teeth and bite it.

She stifled a groan. Why did her long-dormant hormones decide to wake up around this man?

"That's too bad. You'd certainly make dinner interesting. How about you join me instead?"

"I'm working."

"So take a break. I have a feeling you work all the time. Sit down for a bit."

"I can't. It's the dinner rush. I really only stepped out to check on things."

He held his arms wide. "Everyone looks like they're enjoying themselves. I'm betting the kitchen's running well or you wouldn't be out here." He kicked out the chair across from him. It skidded to a stop next to her legs. "Sit down."

She huffed, indecision warring in her head. She knew she needed to keep her distance from him if she wanted to maintain her sanity, but her body had other ideas. It overruled her brain, and she sat.

"Happy?" She folded her arms on the table.

He leaned forward and mimicked her pose, that grin still on his face. "Yes."

She stared into those blue eyes of his and couldn't help but think she'd lost her damn mind. Why was she sitting here?

"So, tell me about the pictures," he said, motioning to the walls. "I noticed them the last time I was here. There are similar ones at Seb's house, too. He said you took them all."

She looked up at the photograph closest to them. It was of her dad on a tractor, tilling a hay field as the sun rose to his right. Golden clouds streaked across the sky, and the mountains cast shadows in the distance. Her entire restaurant was decorated with pictures she'd taken of the area.

"I did. What do you want to know?"

"What was your inspiration for them? And why use them in the restaurant?"

She shrugged. "I wanted this place to be somewhere welcoming. Where people felt at home. Silver Gap—Boone County—is home to me. No matter where I was in the world, this place was *always* home. When I started thinking about names and décor, the idea for this series of photos popped into my head. I already had a few that would work. Like that one."

She pointed at the picture of her dad. "So, I went out and took more and blew them up to various sizes."

"Seb said you were a photojournalist, so why are you running a restaurant? I mean, you're a seriously amazing photographer."

She sat up, pain lancing her heart as she thought about her past life. It was not a topic she liked to discuss.

Before she could answer, the waitress assigned to this section walked up. Tara stood, relieved.

"I'm sorry, Ms. Miller. I can come back," the girl said.

Tara waved a hand. "It's fine, Ainsley. I need to get back to the kitchen." She glanced down at Jace to say goodbye, only to find him looking up at her with a knowing look in his eyes. She had a feeling she would be answering that question in the future. He didn't look like he was going to forget it.

She gave him a nod and hurried away. She'd just have to avoid him and he wouldn't be able to ask, she decided.

A cool breeze blew through the open window of Tara's truck as she drove home, ruffling her sweaty hair. She couldn't wait to get into the bathtub. Her feet hurt from being on them all night, and she was grungy from being in the hot kitchen. She was going to strip naked, grab the wine from her fridge, and fill her tub with some of Rayna's special bath oil concoction and relax before she fell into bed.

She parked in her drive and made her way inside. Like she did that afternoon before she left for town, she took off her clothes and threw them in the washer before strolling through her house to the bathroom, stopping only to get the wine. The bottle was a little less than half full, so she didn't even bother with a glass. She kind of wished there was more. It might help her get Jace Travers' handsome face out of her head.

Tara turned on the sound system wired into the bathroom, and music filled the room. Singing along, she filled the tub with steaming hot water and reached onto the shelf above the toilet for her bath oil.

Her hand closed around the bottle, but something about where it was made her pause. She spent several evenings a week in the bathtub, soothing tired muscles and letting the stresses of her day wash down the drain. She had decorated the bathroom with that in mind and kept it looking nice. There were wash cloths stacked in a wicker basket and all her various bath oils, scrubs, and soaps in decorative bottles arranged in a particular way on either side of it. She *always* put them back in the same place. The bath oil went to the right of the basket on the outside. But it was on the inside.

Frowning now, she looked over the shelves and noted a few other slight discrepancies. A succulent moved over, a small inspirational sign tilted a little bit the wrong way. She hadn't touched some of the items since she dusted in here last week.

Alarmed, she turned off the tub faucet and opened the linen closet. It, too, looked messed up. Nothing terrible, just a few things out of alignment or turned wrong from the way she remembered.

She shut the door and stared at it, her mind whirling. Why would someone search her bathroom? Had they searched anywhere else?

That thought propelled her into the hallway and to her bedroom. Again, there were small things. A couple pillows on the bed had been rearranged and some of her shoes moved.

Her skin prickled as a rumble of fear shot through her. She reached for a shoebox on the top shelf of the closet and ripped the lid off. She took out the ring box and flicked it open, sighing with relief when her wedding set stared back at her.

She looked through the rest of the box, which was mostly pictures, but didn't find anything missing. Replacing the box on the shelf, she snagged a robe off a hanger and pulled it on, then wandered out to the living room and kitchen, running an assessing gaze over both rooms.

It was the same as the bathroom and bedroom. A few things had moved. Not enough to be noticeable at first, but for someone like her, who was a bit of a neat freak, it stood out in glaring relief.

She bit her lip, debating what to do. The house was empty, so she wasn't in any immediate danger. But would she really be able to sleep if she didn't let someone else know what she suspected?

Her eyes strayed to the clock on the wall. It was nearly midnight. Seb was sound asleep at London's, and she didn't want to pull him out of bed for this.

But Jace is right next door.

Tara cursed her subconscious. It would have to remind her of that. She glanced around her living room again, debating what to do. All the little places where things weren't right jumped out at her.

She huffed. "Fine." Spinning on her heel, she marched back to the bathroom to shut off her music, then continued to her bedroom. If she was going to go over there and wake him up, she wasn't doing it in just a silk robe.

Careful not to disturb the things out of place, she gathered some clothes and dressed in a sports bra and t-shirt with a pair of cotton shorts. She stuffed her feet into some canvas shoes and walked out the door before she could change her mind.

The night air hit her, thick and wet. Dew dampened the grass, soaking her shoes as she walked between the houses. She reached the front door of Seb's darkened house and banged on the wood, then crossed her arms to ward off the chill. She should have grabbed a sweatshirt. The daytime might be sweltering, but it was still early enough in the year that the nights still had a bite.

Within seconds, the living room light snapped on. She could see Jace's silhouette through the curtains as he moved from the bedroom to the door.

The porch light came on and she heard the lock click. He threw the door open, and Tara stood mute at the sight before her. He had on a pair of loose sweats that rode low on his hips and nothing else. His skin glowed as gold as his hair in the low light. The tattoos she glimpsed at the restaurant earlier were now on full display. A twisted, gnarled tree wound up his right arm. His left had a line of text running down the inside. Dark blonde hair dusted his perfect chest and abs, narrowing to a vee and disappearing beneath the waistband of his pants. She clenched her fists so she wouldn't reach out and touch him to find out if it was as soft as it looked.

"Tara?"

His sleep roughened voice pulled her out of her stupor, and she brought her eyes up to his face. That beautiful hair was mussed and hanging over his forehead. Sleep still showed in his eyes, even through his frown.

She swallowed and dropped her arms. "I'm sorry to wake you. I didn't want to drag Seb out here so late, but I wasn't comfortable going to bed unless I showed someone first."

"Huh? What's going on?"

She knew she wasn't making much sense, but his bare torso had scrambled her brain. "It's easier to show you. Can you put on a shirt and some shoes and just come over? Please?"

He stared at her a moment, then stepped back with a nod. "Yeah. Hang on a sec."

Tara bit back a moan as he turned away, and she got an unobstructed view of his back. It was every bit as well-defined as his front, and there was a tattoo of a raven in flight between his shoulder blades.

She slapped her hands over her eyes and tipped her head back when he was out of sight. "Why, God? Why him?"

Why couldn't the first man she was attracted to since her husband's death be someone safer? Like a balding accountant or a schoolteacher with a serious dad bod? Why did it have to be a motorcycle-riding, tattooed cop who looked like he modeled for GQ in his spare time?

The soft thud of tennis shoes on the wood floor brought her attention back to him. A black t-shirt now covered his delectable body, but the memory was burned onto her eyeballs.

She turned and led him off the porch and through the grass.

"You want to elaborate on what's wrong?"

She glanced over at him. "I got home and went straight into the bathroom to take a bath. I was filling the tub and went to add some bath oil when I noticed it wasn't in the same place I left it."

"Where was it?"

"It was still on the shelf, but the bottles were out of order."

"Your bottles have an order?"

She sent a cross look his way. "Yes. When I was embedded with military units overseas, I quickly figured out that I needed to be able to bug out fast, so everything had a place and I *always* put things back in their place, so I knew I had everything."

Tara pushed open her front door. Jace followed her inside and closed it.

"When I moved home, I never shook the habit." She'd needed the structure to help her deal with the intense emotions. "Anyway, I started looking around the room and noticed a few other things a little out of place, so I searched the rest of the house. Some pillows on my bed were rearranged and my shoes messed with. Out here, a few of the books were moved, and in the kitchen, someone rifled through my cupboards."

As she talked, the lines on his face deepened, and the corners of his mouth drew down.

"And you just noticed all this tonight?"

She nodded. "I know there isn't really anything you can do, but it's got me a little freaked out."

He propped his hands on his hips and glanced around. "I wish I could tell you differently, but you're right. I can check all the locks for tampering and make a report in the morning, then have someone come check for prints. I'm betting we won't find any that don't belong, though."

"I know. I just couldn't go to bed without letting someone else know what I suspected. I swear, I'm not crazy, Jace."

"I believe you. I think someone was in the barn earlier. I went riding, and when I came back and was cooling Pike down, I heard something drop in the tack room and the door shut. When I looked, there was a pair of hoof trimmers on the floor. None of your family or any of the hands would drop a tool and not put it back."

Her eyes widened. "What the hell is going on?"

He shook his head. "I'm not sure. I think tomorrow, though, we should talk to the rest of your family and have them look at their houses to see if they notice anything out of place."

She wrapped her arms around herself, disturbed by the idea that someone might target her family. She couldn't imagine why. They were just a normal ranching family.

Jace wandered away to check her door locks. Tara sat on a barstool and waited, strung tighter than when she walked in a little while ago. Even if she drank the wine and took the bath now, she still wouldn't be able to sleep. Every creak and bump she heard would make her wonder if it was someone in the house.

"Everything's locked up tight. I think someone picked the lock on your back door, though. It's got some scratch marks I wouldn't attribute to keys."

She nodded and brushed her hair back with a shaky hand. She'd figured as much, but to have him confirm it made it worse, somehow.

He noticed and stepped forward, wrapping a hand around one of hers. "Whoever it was is long gone. Do you want me to stay? I can bunk on the couch." He pointed at her tan, microfiber sofa with its pillows that weren't where they were supposed to be.

Oh, how she did! But she wasn't sure it was wise with the way he sent her hormones into overdrive. But she would get no sleep if he didn't.

"Yes. I know it's crazy. I've slept in worse places under scarier circumstances, but this feels different."

"It's because you aren't expecting this kind of thing to happen in your home. When you're in a war zone—well, you know bad things are possible."

She narrowed her eyes at him. "That sounds like you have experience with it."

He nodded. "I spent four years in the Army right out of high school. Did two tours. One in Afghanistan and one in Iraq."

Shadows in his eyes told her all she needed to know about those tours. She said nothing. Didn't have to, because he knew she understood.

After a moment, he looked away and ran a hand through his hair. "Let me go get my service weapon. Do you have an extra pillow and blanket?"

She nodded. "I'll get those out while you're gone. Thanks, Jace. I appreciate it."

"Anytime." He took two steps back toward the door, turning. "I'll be right back."

When he left, Tara went into her spare bedroom, which she'd turned into her home office, and took a pillow and blanket from the closet. She grabbed a pillowcase from the hall closet and covered the pillow, then took everything out to the living room. She set the items on the couch and removed the accent pillows, piling them in the armchair.

Unsure what to do with herself while she waited, she wandered the room, moving things back where they belonged. She was in the kitchen, fixing the stuff in the cupboards when the door opened and Jace stepped through. He had his holstered gun in his hand, along with a bottle of whiskey.

He shut and locked the door before walking to the kitchen. She watched him come, his stride smooth and graceful, like a predator.

"I thought you could use this." He put the whiskey bottle down on the counter next to her. "Got a couple glasses?"

She thought about the wine waiting in the bathroom and decided the liquor was a much better option to calm her nerves. She turned and took two tumblers from the cabinet to the right of the sink and handed them to him. He put a splash in both and pushed one toward her.

Tara picked it up and raised it to her lips, knocking back the amber liquid in one swallow. It burned down her throat, spreading a pleasant heat in her belly.

Jace drank his and set his glass down. "Want another?"

She shook her head and put her tumbler in the sink. "No. One's enough. Thank you. I have wine in the bathroom, but the whiskey's better."

He screwed the cap back on the bottle. "Good."

She stared at him for a moment, her eyes roving over his gorgeous face, pausing on those full lips, before she gave herself a good mental shake and pushed away from the counter. "I should get to bed."

"Yeah. Me too." He picked up his gun and followed her out of the kitchen.

She glanced at him over her shoulder as she entered the hallway. "Goodnight. And thanks again."

"You're welcome. Get some sleep."

Tara nodded and turned away, forcing her feet to carry her down the hall. She had a feeling sleep would be elusive now for an entirely different reason.

FOUR

Jace walked into London's B&B, The Lilac Inn, the next afternoon, looking for Seb. When he left Tara's just after dawn, he went back to Seb's and checked the locks. They, too, looked like someone picked the lock. Whoever this was had no fear—or was very desperate—if they were willing to break into the sheriff's house.

He nodded to the inn's long-term guest, Doug Brown, who sat in the living room, reading. Jace couldn't help but wonder what was up with the man. He'd been on their suspect list in the serial killings last month before Seb cleared him. He was still up to something, but they hadn't figured out what yet. As he wandered through the inn, looking for his new boss or London, he made a mental note to see if Seb had uncovered anything else on the man.

He found London first, upstairs, cleaning one of the guest rooms. She looked up and smiled when he stopped in the doorway.

"Hi. I heard you made it in safely. You get settled into Seb's place all right?"

"I did, yes."

"Good. So what brings you by? Just stop to say hello?"

"Kind of. I need to talk to Seb. Is he around?"

"He's out back, working on the mower. It was running rough."

"Awesome. Thanks." He gave her a wave and went back downstairs, crossing the living area and entering the kitchen to go out the back door. Seb stood by the shed, hunched over the lawn mower.

"Hey. Need some help?"

Seb looked up and smiled. "Hey." He stepped toward Jace and extended a hand. The men shook hands, then Seb turned back to the mower.

"What's wrong with it?"

Seb tightened a nut with his wrench and straightened. "Oh, it just needed a tune up. I'm going to change the oil in it and it should be good to go." His eyes narrowed as he looked at Jace. "But I'm guessing you didn't come here to hear about London's lawn mower or just to say hello." He crossed his arms. "What's up?"

Jace sighed and shook his head. It would take some time to get used to how perceptive his new boss was. He ran a hand through his hair. "Something weird is going on out at the ranch."

Seb's face turned serious. "How so?"

"Your dad let me take Pike out for a ride yesterday. When I got back, I thought I was alone in the barn, but then I heard something drop and a door close. Someone dropped a pair of hoof trimmers on the tack room floor, then fled. Later, Tara woke me up around midnight to tell me she thought someone had been in her house. She said things had been moved. I checked all the locks and I think someone picked the back door. She was pretty freaked, so I slept on her couch. When I went home this morning, I checked the locks there and someone's been in your house too."

Seb's face grew darker as Jace talked. "Did you talk to any of the others?"

Jace shook his head. "No. I wanted to run it by you first."

"This doesn't make any sense. Why would someone search buildings on the ranch but not take anything?"

"I'm not sure, but you may want to have a chat with your family. Have them check their houses and see if they can think of a reason someone would want to search the place."

Seb sighed. "And here I thought we were past all the craziness now that Marsters is dead. All right. I'll stop by after I finish the yard. Thanks for telling me."

"Yep." Jace said. He stuffed his hands in the back pockets of his jeans and rocked back on his heels, staring out at the lawn toward the trees. There was something he wanted to ask Seb, but he wasn't sure how to bring it up.

Seb bent to slide an oil pan under the mower. When he straightened, he noticed Jace still standing there. He cocked an eyebrow. "There something else you needed to talk about, or are you just bored and want to watch?"

Jace laughed. "The former." His smile disappeared, and he frowned, perplexed. "Is there a reason Tara doesn't like me? I mean, even last night when I came over to check things out for her, she was standoffish."

Seb picked up his wrench and squatted to remove the bolt for the oil reservoir. Once he had it open, he rested his arms over his knees and looked up with a grin. "According to London, she doesn't hate you. She hates what you do to her."

"Huh?"

"She finds you attractive."

"That's a bad thing? I find her attractive too."

"It is for her. Her husband died a few years ago. She hasn't let herself get close to anyone since."

Jace crossed his arms and looked away in thought as he

pondered that. "Your mom told me about him. That's rough. Was she over there at the time too?"

"You know about her time overseas?" Seb looked up, shock in his eyes.

"She mentioned it, yes." He frowned at his new friend. "I take it she doesn't talk about it much?"

Seb shook his head. "No. She's been pretty mute about her former career since she's been home. I think it makes her sad because she equates it with Sean."

He got that feeling too. He knew how painful it was to even think about his wife. It had only been in the last year or so he'd been more comfortable with it—with talking about her. And Haley.

"I wouldn't worry too much about it, though," Seb continued. "She'll come around."

Jace wasn't too sure about that. He didn't think Seb understood just how much she didn't want to be around him. He was going to do his damnedest to get her to relax around him, though. It had been a long time since he'd felt this level of interest in a woman. He wasn't about to let that go.

Tara walked into her parents' house for a family meeting still clad in her chef's coat. Sweaty tendrils of hair that escaped her ponytail clung to her neck and forehead. She'd come straight from the restaurant—and would go straight back.

"Geez, Tara. You couldn't have wiped the sweat off before you came over?"

She stuck her tongue out at her twin, Thomas, who looked at her with his nose wrinkled. He stood with their brother, Brady, near the fireplace.

"I still smell better than you do when you're at work." As

the local vet, Thomas often came back from a farm call smelling like manure.

Brady laughed. "She's got you there."

Thomas made a face, but had no comeback. Instead, he crossed his arms and changed the subject.

"Do you know why we're here? Seb just said we needed to talk about something that concerned all of us."

She nodded. "I do, but let's wait until he's here." She didn't want to have to explain more than once. It was disconcerting to think about it at all.

The door opened and Seb, London, and Jace walked inside. Tara's gut clenched at the sight of Jace. Would it ever not do that?

His eyes found hers, and heat suffused her body. She looked away, smiling at her soon-to-be sister-in-law. London stepped over to stand next to her just as the back door banged. Footsteps in the hall heralded the arrival of Tara's youngest sibling, Maggie.

Seb moved into the center of the room, while Jace found a section of wall and leaned against it.

"We're all here, so let's get started."

Conversation died as everyone turned to Seb.

"We might have some trouble brewing on the ranch. Someone's been prowling around and searching the buildings. Jace thinks someone was in the barn yesterday, and Tara had someone break into her house and search it. Nothing was missing, but she said things were moved. Jace checked her locks and those at my house, and I checked the locks here just now. There's evidence at all three places that someone picked the locks."

A murmur went through the room.

"Someone's been in our house?" Lee said, his brow furrowed.

Seb nodded. "It looks that way. You need to look around

and see if you notice anything missing or out of place. Brady, Thomas, Maggie, you need to do the same. Tomorrow, I'll file reports on the break-ins and have the CSI team come out and dust for prints."

"Why would someone search the property and not take anything?" Brady asked. "That just seems weird."

"Agreed," Seb said. "And I don't know. We need to keep an eye out too. If anything seems even a little off, report it to either me or Jace. The smallest thing could give us a clue who is doing this and what they're after."

"Do you think it's a guest from the restaurant?" Tara asked. "We get a lot of the public out here."

"It's possible."

"Maybe we should look into adding some security cameras past the restaurant," Brady said. "We have some extra poles. We could mount them on those."

"That's a good idea, son." Lee turned to Seb. "Could you look into that?"

Seb nodded. "Of course. We probably should have added some security when the restaurant opened."

"It's not like Silver Gap is a hotbed for crime, though," Tara said.

"No, but we weren't expecting your restaurant to draw people from other parts of the state the way it has. I know a guy from my FBI days who installs security systems. I'll give him a call and have him come assess the place. Until then, let's set up some trail cams just to keep an eye on things."

Brady pushed away from the wall. "I'll go see what we've got."

Thomas followed him. "I'll help you."

Tara watched her brothers leave and sighed. She hoped they could find out what was going on, and that it wasn't related to her restaurant. She hated to think that her business was putting her family in danger.

"You okay?" London asked, laying a hand on Tara's arm.

She looked up at her friend. "Yeah. This is just crazy."

"I know. You'd think after everything we went through with Marsters, this wouldn't be such a shock. Maybe it's because it's so stealthy."

Tara nodded. "Yeah. It was very unnerving to think someone was in my house and went through my things. I don't think I would have gotten any sleep last night if Jace hadn't stayed."

London's eyes widened. "Jace stayed at your house?" Her voice had dropped to a loud whisper. She cast a glance at the man where he stood next to Seb.

Tara cursed under her breath. It was a testament to how tired she was that she let that little nugget slip out.

"Yes. It was late when I discovered someone had been in the house, and I was freaked out. He offered to stay, and I knew I wouldn't be able to sleep if he didn't. I still didn't sleep great, but I did at least get some rest."

"Is he staying again tonight? And where did he sleep?" She gave Tara a wicked grin. "In your bed?"

"No!" Tara flushed and lowered her voice as the others turned to look at her. "No. He slept on the couch. And I think I'll be fine tonight."

London just arched a brow. "If you say so."

Tara rolled her eyes. "I do. I need to get back to the restaurant. Can you tell Seb to let me know if there's anything he needs from me for the police report?"

She nodded. "Yep."

"Thanks." She stepped away and waved at everyone before making her escape.

FIVE

Tara snapped awake. She stared up at the ceiling, unsure about what woke her up. Motionless, she laid there, listening.

A chair scraped on the floor in the kitchen.

She sat up and stared at the door, her heart thundering in her ears.

Someone was in her house.

Without a sound, she flipped the covers back and swung her legs over the side of the bed. On her tiptoes, she crossed to her closet and took out her shotgun, quickly loading several shells. She reversed direction and slowly opened the bedroom door.

It must have made a noise, because she heard a whispered curse, then the sound of footsteps running on the tile floor.

Not bothering with stealth now, she rushed forward as the back door banged shut. She ran toward it and yanked it open. Standing in the doorway, she scanned the yard and property beyond, but it was too dark to see much. She cast a glance at the moonless sky.

"Dammit," she whispered. Lowering her weapon, she

backed into the house and locked the door. Her hands shook as she laid the shotgun on the counter, the adrenaline making her heart race. She walked over to the fridge and pulled off the sticky note stuck there with Jace's number scrawled on it in his bold, masculine handwriting. She'd almost taken it down and thrown it away when she found it yesterday. She had no desire to talk to him in person or on the phone. But the memory of why he'd been in her house had kept that little yellow square right where he left it.

She picked up her shotgun and walked back to her bedroom. She propped it against the bed and picked up her cell, entering the number on the note. It rang several times before Jace's rough voice came over the line.

"Travers."

"Jace, it's Tara. I just chased someone out of my house."

"What?" The sleep was gone from his voice now.

"I heard a noise and went out to investigate. Someone ran out my back door. It was too dark for me to see where he went. Or even what he was wearing."

"I'll be right over."

The line went dead. Tara held the phone away from her ear and stared at it a moment before standing. She wandered back out to the living room and flipped on some lights.

A quick scan of the room revealed that whoever had been inside went through her things again. Only this time, he wasn't as subtle. The chair she heard move was crooked, and the books and decorative items on her bookshelves were rearranged. Several cabinets were also open, some of their contents on the counter.

She jerked at the sound of Jace pounding on her front door and let out a soft shriek. Heart thumping, she put a hand on her chest, hurrying over to the door to let him in.

~

Jace fought the urge to bang on Tara's door again as he waited for her to open it. There was no reason for this frantic, edgy feeling coursing through him, but he'd be damned if he could make it go away. Her phone call sent his adrenaline spiking into the stratosphere, and his rational mind was struggling to stay in control.

The door swung inward, but his relief was short-lived as another emotion put him on edge. Tara stood in the doorway, her dark hair down around her shoulders, tousled from sleep. Miles of creamy skin glowed gold in the light coming from inside thanks to her miniscule gray cotton pajama shorts and lightweight pink camisole. The latter clung to her full breasts, doing little to hide what was beneath.

Jace knew he was staring, but he couldn't seem to help it. She was a beautiful woman, even fully clothed. In that tiny outfit, with her hair a mess, she looked like a pinup model.

She frowned at him as he continued to stand there. "Are you going to come in?"

He cleared his throat. "Um, yeah." He took a step forward, thankful he'd yanked on a pair of jeans this time. They helped hide his reaction to her state of dress.

His eyes darted around the room as he brushed past, doing his best not to look at her. He noted the chair askew from the table and the open cupboards.

"You said he went out the back door?" He glanced at her, then immediately wished he hadn't. She'd raised her arms to run her hands through her hair, which only tightened her already snug top and raised it a few inches to show off her toned midriff.

Jace's blood rushed south again, and his mouth went dry. Tara's eyes met his, widening as she finally realized she was practically naked.

She dropped her arms and crossed them over her breasts. Her face flushed, and she looked away.

"Um, yes. He did. You can go look. I'm going to go grab a robe."

He didn't have a chance to reply before she darted around him toward the hallway and out of sight.

Dammit. Jace pulled a quick breath through his nose and blew it out, trying to clear his mind. She hadn't called him over to ogle her.

With his mindset a little straighter, he walked over to the back door and unlocked it. Drawing his pistol, he opened the door and stepped out into the night. Inky darkness greeted him. Without the moon, he could only see a few feet in front of his face. He strained to see through the dark, but it was no use. Lowering his gun, he stepped back into the house.

Tara stood by the sink, twisting the sash of her lightweight silk robe in her fingers. "Did you see anything?"

He shook his head. "No. It's too dark. I think whoever it was is long gone."

Her body seemed to deflate. She sagged into the counter. Moisture shimmered in her eyes, and Jace stepped forward.

"Hey. It's okay. You're safe. I'll bunk on the couch again tonight."

She turned her watery brown eyes on him, and all the air left his lungs as the fear and weariness on her face sucker-punched him in the gut.

"For tonight, I'm safe. What about tomorrow? What's going on? Why does someone keep breaking into my house? What do they want?"

Against his better judgement, he shuffled closer and laid a hand on her bicep. "I don't know. But we're going to figure this out."

She nodded and sniffed, raising her hands to wipe at the tears in her eyes. "God, I'm a mess. This is ridiculous."

"You're allowed to be upset and scared, Tara."

She dropped her hands. "I know. But I shouldn't be. I've

been through worse." She took a deep breath and blew it out, gaining a little more control of herself. "Have you called Seb?"

Jace let her change the subject without elaborating on what she meant by that. "Not yet. I wanted to check things out first." He reached for his phone in the back pocket of his jeans and called her brother.

Seb picked up after two rings, grumpy. "'Lo?"

"Hey, it's Jace. Someone broke into Tara's house again. This time, she was here. He ran when she went to investigate the noise."

"What? Is she all right?"

Jace glanced at Tara, who leaned against the counter, hiding in her robe. "She's fine. Shaken up, but okay. He's probably long gone, but we should still conduct a search." He heard rustling over the line and the soft sound of London's voice as Seb told her what was going on.

"I'm on my way. I'll call the others, so expect company." He hung up.

Jace tucked his phone back into his pocket and looked at Tara. He didn't like the blank expression on her face. He much preferred the tears. At least then, she wasn't locked away inside her head.

"Seb's going to call your family. They should be here soon."

Her head bobbed, and she pushed away from the counter. "I'm going to get dressed." Expression still closed, she walked away.

He stared after her, frowning. Her earlier comment about having been through worse echoed through his mind. He had a feeling her shuttered emotions had more to do with whatever happened in her past than tonight's intruder.

～

Tara leaned against the wall by the bookshelf, listening to her family chatter around her. Only sheer will kept her upright. The adrenaline left her an hour ago, making her even more tired than she was when the intruder woke her up. All she wanted to do was fall into bed and forget tonight ever happened.

She stared at the back of Seb's head and willed him to send everyone on their way. He, their brothers, and Jace had already searched the area around the houses. They found a few footprints, but no other signs and no idea where the guy went when he fled her house.

A yawn cracked her jaw. She tried to hide it, but her mother noticed and nudged Seb. She murmured something to him, and he looked back at her. A frown pursed his lips, and he nodded, then let out a sharp whistle. Conversation ceased as everyone turned to look at him.

"I think it's time we wrapped this up for the night. We need to make some changes to living arrangements, though. Until we figure out what's wrong, I think Tara and Maggie should move into the main house with Mom and Dad, and Thomas, Brady, and Jace should bunk together."

"We don't have enough beds for that," Jenny said. "Remember? I turned the girls' room into a sewing room. And there's only a king-size bed in the boys' room now."

"I can stay here with Tara," Jace said. "Maggie can stay with you, and Thomas and Brady can stay together."

Tara's eyes widened. Before she could protest, though, her mother agreed to Jace's plan.

No! No, no, no!

She resisted the urge to cover her face with her hands and sink to the floor. An image of him in nothing but those sweats with all his tattoos on display popped into her head. The last thing she wanted was Mr. Greek God in her house all the time. It was all she could do now to resist him. If she had to trip over him night and day—well, he wouldn't be on the couch for long.

Even while her hormones rejoiced at that idea, she had no desire to get involved with a man like him. She didn't really want to get involved with any man. It hurt too much when it all fell apart.

Maggie noticed the grimace on her face and gave her a wicked grin. "How about you stay with Mom and Dad? I don't mind having Jace at my house."

Jealousy reared its head. Tara glared at her younger sister. "I'm not staying with Mom and Dad." She looked at her parents. "No offense. My hours are crazy and I don't want to disturb you when I come in at midnight or later every night. It's just best if I stay here."

Jenny nodded, accepting Tara's flimsy excuse without question. "That's settled, then."

The gleam in Jenny's eyes told Tara her mother saw right through her. She narrowed her eyes. She hoped her mom didn't have any ideas about setting Tara up with Jace. It would go nowhere fast.

Jenny smiled at Tara, then tugged on her husband's arm. "Come on, dear. Let's get going. Hopefully, we can still get a few more hours of sleep." She looked at her youngest. "Are you coming home with us, or will we see you tomorrow?"

"I'll see you tomorrow. I doubt anything else will happen tonight with all the activity."

One by one, Tara's family said their goodbyes until only she and Jace were left. She closed the door behind Seb, then slowly turned around. He stood near the couch, his hands tucked into his back pockets.

She let her gaze drift over his tall frame before coming to rest on his face. Twin sapphire pools stared back at her, questions lurking in their depths.

Not up for answering anything, she broke eye contact

and looked at the clock on the wall behind him. "You can go home too. Maggie's right. Nothing else will happen tonight."

He shook his head and sauntered toward her, stopping when only a couple feet separated them. One perfect brow arched.

"Do you really think you'll be able to sleep without me here?"

"Yes," she bit out, knowing full well it was a lie.

His mouth slashed into an amused half smile. "You're lying." He spun on his heel, heading for the hallway.

Tara frowned, perplexed. "Where are you going?"

"To get my blanket and pillow."

She sighed and let her head hang, too tired to argue with him. To her horror, she felt tears well in her eyes.

What the hell is wrong with me? Why couldn't she keep her emotions in check? What was it about this man—this situation—that had her so discombobulated?

She dashed the moisture away with the backs of her hands and followed him down the hall. It was just stress and exhaustion. She was overworked, and it was getting to her. Nothing a good night's sleep wouldn't cure.

Even as she thought it, another part of her brain called her out for lying again.

"Which room do you keep them in?"

She shoved the door closed on her thoughts and looked at Jace. He stood in the hallway between the doors, motioning to the rooms.

Tara sighed, resigning herself to his continued presence. He *did* make her feel safer.

She pointed to the office. "They're in the closet."

He walked into the room and opened the door, stepping in to take a blanket and pillow from the shelf. Tucking them beneath one arm, he turned and made his way back to her. She moved to the side to let him pass, but he stopped in front of her and just stared.

"What?"

Brow wrinkled, concern shone from his deep blue eyes. "You want to tell me why this has you so out of sorts?"

It was her turn to frown. "Someone broke into my house. With me in it."

"I know, but you seem like you're pretty resilient. So, why are you having trouble dealing with this?"

She crossed her arms and cocked out a hip as she stared him down. "What makes you think you know me?" she countered.

He shrugged. "Past experience. You didn't bat an eye when a serial killer abducted your friend. No, you attacked that situation head-on. So, why aren't you doing the same here?"

"That was different." She barely wanted to admit to herself how vulnerable the break-in made her feel. She certainly wasn't going to clue Jace into that fact.

"How so?"

She rolled her eyes and dropped her arms. "It just was. I'm going back to bed." She spun on her heel to go to her room, but he grabbed her arm to stop her. An electric jolt shot up her arm, and she jerked.

She turned and leveled a glare on him. "What?"

Her death stare had little effect. He continued to hold her arm in a gentle grip. The jolt turned into a steady hum.

"You're not alone, you know. Your family, me—we're all here for you."

She nodded, shifting her weight. Tara could feel her heartbeat quicken as the heat spread outward from his touch on her arm. He needed to let go. Her emotions were already in a blender, and the feel of his hand on her wasn't helping. She tugged against his hold, and he released her.

"I know." She backed up a step, eager to put some space between them so she could regain her equilibrium.

"Do you?"

Tara frowned. "What do you mean? Why wouldn't I?"

He shrugged. "You just act like you need to deal with everything by yourself. Don't take what your family offers for granted, Tara. They love you and want to help you in any way they can. Be thankful you have them."

Twin pops of red bloomed on her cheeks. "I am thankful for my family. They have done more for me in the last three years than I ever expected or asked them to. You'll have to forgive me if I don't want them to sacrifice even more for me. I don't need you to stand here and lecture me, so how about you butt out and maybe focus your efforts on your own family? I'm sure they probably miss you since you moved away."

A pinched expression came over his face, before a flintiness appeared in his eyes.

"I don't have a family anymore."

Tara's mouth dropped open at his admission, her eyes wide.

"I'm sorry if I overstepped. It won't happen again." He whirled on his heel, leaving her staring after him, stunned.

He was in the living room before she gathered herself enough to go after him.

"Wait." She ran down the hall and slid to a stop at the edge of the living room. He turned to look at her, his face closed off.

"What do you mean, you don't have a family anymore? What happened to them?"

"They died."

She resisted the urge to roll her eyes. "I gathered that."

His chest heaved with a harsh sigh. He threw the pillow and blanket on the couch, then rested his hands on his hips and stared at the floor. When he looked back up at her, there was a haunted look in his eyes.

"I'm an only child. My parents died in a boating accident five years ago." He swallowed hard. "Along with my wife and my four-year-old daughter."

Tara gasped and covered her mouth. Tears welled in her eyes. "Oh, Jace. I'm so sorry. I had no idea."

He nodded, looking away. "Yeah, well, it's not something I broadcast. Seb doesn't even know." He ran a hand through his golden hair. "Look, I'm sorry I snapped at you. Allie and Haley have been on my mind a lot with my move. It's brought back a lot of memories and feelings I thought I'd dealt with."

She moved closer. She wanted to touch him—offer comfort—but she didn't dare. He short-circuited her brain just standing there. "If anyone should be sorry, it's me. I haven't been as nice to you as I could be. You remind me of my husband. Not in your looks, but in your attitude toward life."

"That's a bad thing? From what Seb and your mother said, he was a good guy."

"He was, but he was a daredevil. And it got him killed. When I needed him most, he wasn't there because he was dead." She sucked in a breath and pushed back the grief. Going into that rabbit hole wouldn't help anything. "I'm sorry I've been such a bitch. Like you, I'm dealing with feelings I thought were long buried. I will strive to do better and at least be civil. How about we start over?" She held out a hand. "Hi. I'm Tara Miller. It's nice to meet you."

A slow, sexy grin spread over his face. Tara's breath caught in her chest as it transformed his already handsome features into stunning. He really did look like the sun god, bright and shining, and gorgeous beyond measure.

His hand closed around hers. She swallowed against the onslaught of fire that raced up her arm and returned his smile.

"Hi, Tara. I'm Jace Travers. It's nice to meet you too."

He continued to stare, and her smile faded as awareness crept in. The fire turned to a full conflagration and her body awakened. Her eyes strayed to his mouth, and she couldn't help but wonder what it would feel like on hers.

He tugged on her hand, pulling her in until they were only inches apart. She could feel his breath fan over her face as he looked down at her. He raised his free hand to brush at a lock of her hair with one finger. Goosebumps erupted where he touched her, and her eyelids fluttered.

"You're so beautiful."

His whispered voice rolled over her nerve-endings. She looked up at him as he lowered his head. The reality that he was about to kiss her sent a shock wave through her brain, jolting her out of her desire-induced fog.

With a gasp, she stepped back. He gave her a confused look.

"I'm sorry. I can't." She spun around and hurried away, willing the tears not to fall until she reached her room.

Once behind the closed door, she leaned against it and let go. She knew Sean was dead and never coming back, but it felt like such a betrayal to lust after another man, even after three years. He'd been her everything. Why couldn't she move on from that?

Tara sniffed and dashed at the tears on her face before pushing off the door and climbing into bed. She was past crying over her husband. It did nothing but leave her puffy-eyed and give her a headache.

Six

Jace walked into the horse barn on a mission to find Tara. After their near-kiss the night of the break-in two days ago, she'd made herself scarce. He'd seen her when she came home from work around midnight each night, but she'd done little more than say goodnight to him before retreating to her room. During the day, he hadn't seen her at all. He even stopped into the restaurant to eat after work both evenings, but she'd stayed hidden in the kitchen.

Jenny told him she was taking a break today, though. That she'd decided to saddle up her horse, Brandywine, and go for a ride. Jace didn't like the idea of her going anywhere alone with what had happened. He also wouldn't mind seeing more of The Broken Bow. He hoped he could convince her to let him tag along.

He slid his sunglasses up on his head as he entered the dim interior. A woman's voice echoed through the barn, singing a soft, soulful song. He followed the beautiful sound and found Tara standing inside a stall, brushing a rich chestnut-colored mare, singing to her as she worked.

"Is there anything you can't do?"

She shrieked. The mare, startled, whinnied and side-stepped, knocking Tara onto her butt in the straw.

Jace walked into the stall and up to the horse, grasping her halter and running a calming hand on her neck to keep her from stepping on Tara.

"Easy, there, girl." He glanced down at Tara, who was pushing herself up and dusting off her rear. "You okay?"

She nodded, blowing a strand of hair out of her face. "I'm fine. What are you doing out here beside scaring the daylights out of me?"

"Your mom said you were planning to go for a ride. I was kinda hoping you'd let me come along."

"You want to go on a trail ride?"

He nodded and stroked Brandywine's face. "Yeah. The short one I went on the day I got here wasn't enough. I'd like to see more of the ranch. What do you say? Can I tag along?" He tried not to look too hopeful while she thought about his request.

She chewed on her lip as she went back to brushing her horse. Jace continued to stroke Brandywine's face, waiting for her to answer.

"I guess it would be okay if you came. I should warn you, though, I'm planning on taking a long ride. Several hours."

"That's fine. I really do want to see more of this place."

She looked at him then and gave him a curt nod. "Okay. You can take Pike again. Do you remember where everything is?"

"Yep." He backed away and left Brandywine's stall before she could change her mind. He gathered Pike's gear and saddled the horse in record time. If he held her up, she wouldn't hesitate to leave without him.

He heard the clack of Brandywine's hooves on the barn floor as he pulled the last cinch on Pike's saddle. He buckled on the horse's bridle and led him from his stall and out into the pasture behind the barn.

She looked over at him as he stopped beside her. "I grabbed you some water from the stash in the workroom. I'm not sharing my snacks, though."

Jace's lips twitched, but he held back the smile. "Fair enough. I won't starve before we come back. You ready?"

She nodded and turned back to her horse, mounting the mare in one swift, graceful motion. He followed suit. Pike danced beneath him, ready for a run once again.

Tara looked at him over her shoulder and tossed him a wicked smile. "Keep up, will ya?"

Before he could reply, she nudged Brandywine's sides, and the horse took off.

Pike danced faster, wanting to go after her. Jace gave him a soft squeeze, and he shot forward. Wind rushed past Jace's face and through his hair. He leaned over Pike's neck and urged the horse to go faster. Exhilaration made his heartbeat quicken. Seb's horse was incredible. He'd been fast when Jace took him out a few days ago, but now that he had something to chase, he flew.

In moments, he was pulling past Tara on the way to the pasture gate. Her laughter echoed behind him. He glanced back to see her hunch lower on Brandywine. The mare, sensing she was losing, kicked it into a higher gear. Pike was larger, though, and easily kept his lead.

As they neared the gate, he pulled up on the gelding's reins. The horse came to a halt a few feet from the post.

Pike snorted and stomped one hoof. Jace patted the animal's neck. "Easy, boy."

Tara came to a stop next to him, grinning from ear to ear. Her dark eyes sparkled, and a flush colored her cheeks from the excitement and exertion. "Where did you learn to ride like that?"

"My family owned a farm. My parents raised dairy cows. We had a couple horses too. I rode every chance I had."

"You grew up on a farm? How did you end up becoming a cop, then?"

Jace moved Pike closer to the gate and opened the latch. He gave the gate a push and motioned Tara through. He followed behind and closed it.

"As much as I loved growing up in the country, I did not like farm life. Being tied to the place all the time, never getting a day off—I wanted to see more of the world than just our little corner of Nebraska. So, I joined the Army. They assigned me to an MP unit, and I loved the policing aspects of it. Wasn't overly fond of the overseas tours in the Middle East, but then few people are. I did four years, though. Enough to get college paid for."

"What happened to the farm?"

"My parents sold the dairy operation while I was away. They were both older—I was a late in life baby—and Dad had a heart attack about two years after I left home. He decided it was time to retire at that point. They sold everything except the buildings and the acreage they sat on. All the pastureland, animals—except my horse—and machinery went to a neighboring operation." His mouth turned down. "They used some of the money to buy the boat they were on when the storm came up."

"I'm sorry." Her soft voice carried over to him on the breeze.

"Thanks." He cleared his throat, shaking off the sudden melancholy. "So, where are we going?"

Her face blossomed into a pretty smile, catching him off guard. His reaction to this woman still threw him for a loop. He shifted in the saddle and focused on her words.

"It's a secret."

He arched a brow. "Secret? And you're sharing it with me?"

She laughed. "I guess it's not that much of a secret. There's a spot in the back acreage that only the family goes to."

"Okay." He drew the word out, frowning. "Again, you're sharing it with me?"

She rolled her eyes and nudged Brandywine forward. "Yes. I know we've gotten off on the wrong foot a bit, but I realize you're here to stay. And you helped rescue London. That alone makes you part of the family."

"I didn't do anything any other cop wouldn't have."

"But you aren't any other cop. Would you stop arguing with me and just say thank you?" she growled.

He couldn't hold back the grin at the annoyed look she cast back at him. "Thank you."

"Better. Come on. We better pick up the pace or we'll be riding back in the dark."

Jace gave Pike a nudge. "How far away is this place?"

"An hour or so."

Which meant at least two hours in the saddle. His legs were going to hate him later. It had been years since he rode a horse. His ride the other day had only been a little over an hour, and he'd felt it the next day.

Resigning himself to sore muscles and bowed legs, he and Pike fell into step beside her as she led them into the hills.

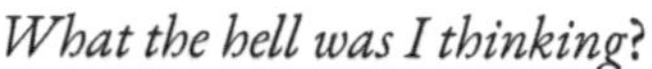

What the hell was I thinking?

Tara tried her best not to look at Jace as he rode beside her. His tall frame sat straight in the saddle. The breeze ruffled that gorgeous, sun-streaked hair of his, giving him a rakish appearance that only added to the magnetism he exuded.

It was that damn promise she made to herself. She knew

she should have continued to treat him like a pariah. She wouldn't be in the middle of nowhere with him and no chaperone in sight if she had.

She let out a sigh and did her best to focus on her surroundings. The Broken Bow was beautiful. Flat grasslands gave way to rocky outcroppings and tree-studded hillsides. Right now, they were in the hills, but she knew it would eventually open into a valley where the cattle grazed around a small lake.

That's where they were headed. It had been a while since she made the trek, but she needed the solitude and peace the lake provided. It spoke to her in its seclusion and allowed her to think. When she first returned home, she spent many hours sitting on the lakeshore just thinking and grieving. It had helped her come to grips with the fact her life would never be the same and that Sean wasn't coming back.

She cast a surreptitious glance at Jace, wondering how he had coped with the death of his wife—of his daughter and his parents. Tara couldn't imagine losing all of her family at once. She would be a blithering mess.

They rode in silence for several more minutes before curiosity got the better of her.

"Jace?"

He turned to look at her, his face relaxed.

She almost chickened out, not wanting to upset his mood. In the end, though, she *had* to know how he dealt with so much loss. Some days, she felt like she was barely treading water. She could use some insight on how to handle days like that.

"How did you cope? Losing your family so suddenly? And all at once?"

The lines around his eyes deepened, and his mouth flattened. "I didn't. Not at first, anyway. Losing a child—" He broke off and looked toward the horizon. "Well, it's not something you're ever prepared for. And to lose my wife and my parents at the same time—I spent a lot of time holed up at home with a bottle of whiskey.

"Thankfully, I had a few good friends in Haskell who staged an intervention. They came over one day and took all the alcohol out of my house, threw me in the shower—literally, and with my clothes on—then made me talk. They made me get out everything I was feeling. All the pain and grief. Without that, I'm not sure I would be where I am today. It allowed me to see a little sliver of light. That maybe I would one day be able to take a breath without my chest feeling like it was going to crack wide open. Each day, the light got a little brighter and the pain a little less. It's still there, but it doesn't bring me to my knees anymore." He looked back at her then, a crooked smile on his face. "Usually."

She offered him a small smile, but it didn't reach her eyes. She'd thought she was at that point until he showed up. Rayna was right. Tara hadn't fully dealt with all she'd lost. She'd gotten to a point where the grief was manageable, then just buried the rest. Her reaction to Jace forced her to deal with it. Her body wanted to move on, but her heart and her mind needed to catch up.

"I'd tell you you're lucky because you only lost a spouse and not a child, but there's no winner there. Losing a loved one hurts no matter who they are to you."

To her horror, she felt tears spring up in her eyes. She turned her face away and sniffed quietly.

Jace's leg brushed hers. "Tara?"

The muscles in her thigh jumped when he touched her. She steered Brandywine a few steps to her right. She couldn't deal with her attraction to him when she felt like this.

"Hey. Are you okay?"

She sniffed again and turned to look at him. Her head jerked with a nod. "I'm fine."

Concern shone from the depths of his blue eyes. "No, you're not. I'm sorry. What did I say that upset you?"

Tara took a shaky breath and pressed the back of her hand to her mouth to hold in the sob that wanted to break free. Her gaze caught his, and she opened her mouth to speak before slamming it closed and frowning so hard her eyebrows touched. Could she tell him? Better yet, why did she *want* to tell him?

She stared at him a moment longer, a war waging in her mind. No one but her mother knew what really happened. Why she had *needed* to move home.

In the next second, she scoffed at herself and brushed away her tears and gathered herself. Confiding in Jace was a ridiculous idea. She could barely stand to be around the man. Why would she tell him something so personal?

Because he could understand.

Tara ignored the voice in her head. "Don't worry about it. I'm fine. Let's keep going." Not waiting for him to reply, she gave Brandywine a squeeze. The mare sped up to a trot.

She knew she was running away, but didn't care. Letting Jace get to really know her would be disastrous. She had enough trouble resisting him now. If she let him in, she wouldn't stand a chance. Although she had a feeling she didn't, anyway.

SEVEN

Jace lifted his face to the sun and closed his eyes. The trill of a red-winged blackbird and the occasional bellow from one of the cattle wandering the grassy plain were the only sounds intruding on the silence in the valley Tara led him to. It was like an entirely different world here than what he'd come from. Nebraska had its wide-open, isolated spots, but nothing compared to this. He felt like he'd been transported to an alternate universe. A beautiful one, but foreign nonetheless. Isolated didn't begin to cover how this picturesque landscape felt.

He opened his eyes and stared out over the water from his perch on a boulder near the shore. The conversation from earlier ran through his head. Tara hadn't said more than a handful of words since then. He knew he'd upset her, but he didn't understand how.

He also didn't understand his insane urge to know more about the woman. She'd stuck her nose up at him at every turn. But he couldn't seem to take a hint and maintain the distance she was determined to keep between them. He'd never chased after a woman before—never had to—but Tara made him want to. And not because she wanted nothing to do with him. She intrigued him. There were a lot of layers to her, and he knew he'd only scratched the surface. Her surly attitude was designed to keep him from getting too close. He wanted to smash through those top layers and find the real woman underneath.

Jace sighed and ran a hand through his hair. Jesus, he sounded like a sap. Allie would laugh her ass off if she could hear his thoughts. She'd always accused him of being the least romantic man on the planet, and she wasn't wrong. He was a bit too rough around the edges for all the hearts and flowers shit. He'd brought her flowers on her birthday and their anniversary, but she most definitely hadn't married him for his ability to wine, dine, and sweet talk her.

He glanced up at the bright blue sky. Puffy clouds drifted lazily overhead, belying the turmoil of his thoughts.

"What am I doing, Al? Why can't I get her out of my mind? I don't want anyone else. Not like that. And especially not a woman who can barely stand the sight of me." He hung his head and pressed his fingers to his eyes. "God, I wish you were here." He sighed, lifting his head, heart aching. Needing to move, he bent and picked up a rock. He ran his fingers over the smooth surface. Standing, he tossed it at the water, skipping it several times over the glassy surface. He rested his hands on his hips, watching it skitter over the water, then sink.

"You're pretty good at that."

He looked over his shoulder at the woman responsible for his current emotional state. He dropped his hands and turned around, striding toward her. "It was a favorite hobby as a kid."

"For me too."

He cocked an eyebrow. "Oh, yeah?"

She nodded.

"Care for some friendly competition?"

Her mouth spread into a slow grin. "Sure." She brushed

past him and crouched near the shore, picking through the stones.

Jace followed and stood just behind her, crossing his arms over his chest. She rose and took her stance, then whipped her arm forward. The rock skipped across the water six times before it sank beneath the surface.

The grin she leveled on him sent his pulse into overdrive. The joy in it transformed her entire face.

"If I recall, yours only skipped four times."

He let his arms fall back to his sides and walked toward her. "That was just a warm-up."

"Yeah?"

"Yeah." He looked at the ground, scanning it for a suitable stone. A flat, round rock about two-and-a-half inches across caught his eye.

He scooped it up and turned back to Tara. "Look out." He shooed her away so he could stand closer to the water.

She rolled her eyes, but took a couple steps to the side.

Jace turned the stone in his hand a few times, finding the perfect grip, then let it loose with a quick flick of his arm and wrist. It skipped half a dozen times across the water, then dropped.

"You still didn't beat me." She sauntered past him to pick up another rock from the shoreline. She let it fly, and Jace counted eight skips before it sank.

Tara dusted off her hands, a smirk lifting her mouth. "You should know, my brothers never beat me. Maggie came close once. We tied. But I'm still the champ because I was the champ before she matched me."

He took three long strides forward until they were toe to toe. A challenge gleaming in his eyes, he leaned forward to whisper in her ear. "I'm not your brothers." When he straightened, their gazes met, and Jace realized he'd made a grave error. His stomach flip-flopped as desire punched him in the gut.

Her smile died as he stared down at her. "No." Her voice came out breathy. "You most definitely are not."

He couldn't have backed away if he tried. Her gaze drifted down to his mouth, and he was lost. One hand snaked out to wrap around the back of her neck, and he kissed her. She froze for only a moment before her hands landed on his chest and she kissed him back.

A million strobe lights went off behind his eyes at the feel of her lips sliding against his. He wrapped his hand in her ponytail, angling her head, and deepened the kiss. She let out a little whimper that went straight to his groin. It was enough to shock him out of their embrace. He broke the kiss, staring down at her a moment before letting her go and stepping back.

What the hell was that? Jace ran a hand through his hair and spun away to stare out at the lake, trying to make sense of the intense desire coursing through his body.

Shaken, he headed for where the horses grazed. "We should probably head back. I have an early morning tomorrow." It wasn't a lie, but he didn't need to go to bed before the sun set. He did, however, need to get a little distance from the woman who'd just tipped his world on its axis.

He could hear her moving behind him, grateful she wasn't arguing with him for once. When he reached Pike, he checked the saddle to make sure it was still tight, then looped the reins over the horse's head and climbed on. Leather creaked as he settled into his seat.

From the corner of his eye, he could see Tara mount Brandywine. As soon as she was settled, he turned Pike back the way they'd come.

This was not what I meant when I asked you what I should do, Allie. He rolled his eyes heavenward, knowing she was probably up there, delighting in his discomfort. He wouldn't doubt that she'd somehow had a hand in putting Tara in his path. They'd talked once, not long after they were married, about what they would do if either of them died. Both had urged the other to find someone and live a full life.

He wasn't sure he was ready for that, though. No matter how much Tara's kiss made him burn.

Why, God? Why him? Tara wondered again as they rode back toward the barn. She stared at his broad back. Why did the first man since her husband's death have to be someone just like him? Why couldn't she fall for someone like Brady's rancher friend, Knox? The most dangerous thing he did was wrangle a stubborn cow. And he was easy on the eyes.

Her gaze wandered over the man in front of her. His powerful thighs gripped Pike's sides, and his strong hands held the reins with a gentle touch. She shivered as she remembered the feel of those long fingers wrapped around the back of her head and tangled in her hair.

Because Knox would never make her lose her mind with just a kiss; that was why.

Maybe she should just stop fighting it. Didn't they always say that relationships that burned hot never lasted? She should just sleep with him. They could get it out of their systems and move on with their lives as, if not friends exactly, then as pleasant acquaintances.

Her fear, though, was it wouldn't just be her body he set on fire with his touch. That kiss touched something deep down. A place that hadn't seen any light in three years.

Tara sighed. The one thing she knew was until she could digest that little nugget of information, she needed to stay the hell away from his lips. Any more kisses would just confuse her further.

She looked away from Jace and out over the landscape,

doing her best to concentrate on where they were. It was unlikely they would get lost—Pike knew the way home—but on the off chance he took a wrong turn, she wanted to know before they got too turned around.

The miles passed in a blur—faster than she thought they would—and soon the ranch buildings came into sight. Both horses sped up, eager for the hay they knew was coming their way.

As they passed a stand of trees at the base of the hill, Jace pulled Pike to a halt.

Tara looked over her shoulder and turned her mare around. He stared at the copse of trees.

"What?"

"I don't know. I saw something in the trees, I think." He turned his horse toward them.

She followed, curious.

"What did you see?" she asked, stopping beside him.

He peered up into the branches as he spoke. "It was like a reflection. Like light on a mirror or something." He swung a leg over the horse and hopped off.

Tara frowned and glanced up, then dismounted as well.

Jace rounded one of the trees and came to a halt. "What the hell?"

His tone made her hurry over. She looked up to where he pointed, and her eyes widened. Part way up the tree, a camera sat attached to the trunk.

"Why is there a camera in the tree?"

"That's a good question. I'm guessing it's not one your family set up?"

She shook her head. "If they did, they didn't tell me. And it doesn't make sense for it to be up there. It would be on a fence post with an unobstructed view."

He handed her Pike's reins and stepped toward the tree.

"Well, let's find out then, shall we?" He grabbed a low-level branch and began to climb.

Tara stood below with the horses and watched as he made his way up to the camera. It was pointed at the houses and had a telescopic lens attached. Jace straddled a branch and unsnapped the buckle on the band securing it to the tree. It slid free. He made quick work of securing it over one shoulder, then climbed down. Once on the ground, he set the camera down, then picked up a twig to turn off the motion activation switch.

She stared down at it. Brandywine nudged her sleeve, and she reached up to absently pet the horse. Some of the fear she felt the other night when she caught the intruder in her house returned. Did this have anything to do with the break-in?

She looked up at Jace. "Now what?"

He bent and lifted it by the strap, moving to the saddlebag she'd put on her horse, stowing the device inside.

"Now we go home. I'll take the camera into the station and check it out."

"That's it?"

He nodded and took Pike's reins from her. "It needs to be checked for prints and logged as evidence before we watch the footage." He mounted his horse.

His argument—while logical—did little to assuage her need to figure out what the hell was going on. Frustrated and worried, she did her best to shove it aside. For now, she was safe, and so was her family.

She blew out a breath and climbed back on Brandywine. Turning the mare around, she led them down to the barn, trying not to think about what might be on that camera. Trying, but failing miserably.

EIGHT

Tara stepped into the restaurant kitchen and smiled, a bit of contentment smoothing over her frayed nerves. She took the day off to get a break from the demands of running a business before all hell broke loose this weekend with the town's Fourth of July celebration, but after their discovery, she needed a bit of normalcy to help calm her mind.

It was just past the dinner rush, so the din in the kitchen was low as the staff dealt with the slower pace and cleaned up from the earlier influx.

"Hey, boss. What are you doing here?"

Tara looked over at her assistant manager, Cassie, and smiled. "I got bored at home," she fibbed. "How'd the rush go? Any problems?"

Cassie shook her head. "No. It was smooth as butter."

Her phone dinged in her pocket and she dug it out. She frowned as her editor's name flashed on the screen with another text message.

"Everything okay?"

Tara hit delete without reading the message and looked up at Cassie's question. She shoved the phone back in her pocket and forced a smile. "It's fine." She glanced around the room again. Everything appeared to be running smoothly. Cassie had it all under control. The woman was gold, and Tara was lucky to have her.

"I think I'll go make a round through the dining room, then check on a few things for Pioneer Days. Double-check we have everything."

Cassie smiled and nodded. Tara returned her smile, then walked through the kitchen to the doors leading to the dining area, pushing through them.

The sound of happy diners greeted her. Conversation flowed with an occasional laugh breaking through. She paused at the edge of the bar to take it all in. It still astounded her to see a packed house most nights. She'd opened with high hopes, but knew that because of the restaurant's rural location she would likely have to reduce the number of days and hours The Heartwood was open. That hadn't really been the case, though. She'd made a couple adjustments a few months after she'd opened, but mostly, business stayed steady. She was thankful. This place had saved her sanity. She was counting on it to do it again.

With a smile on her face, she wandered the dining room, stopping to speak to the customers and make sure they had everything they needed. On the outdoor terrace, she noticed a lone man and made her way over to him.

"Hi, Doug." Doug Brown, London's long-term renter, was one of her most frequent customers. No one knew why he was really in town, but he seemed nice enough. The waitresses loved him. He was always polite and left a big tip.

He looked up at her greeting and smiled.

"Hey. I thought you were off tonight. Kaylee said you needed a break."

She scrunched her face up and looked out at the trees for a moment. "I did. I went horseback riding."

He frowned. "And you didn't have a good time?"

The memory of Jace's mouth pressed against hers flooded her brain, and she fought the blush that wanted to break free. "It was fine. It was what happened when we got back that wasn't so great."

"Oh?" He leaned back in his chair, draping an arm over the back as he turned toward her. "What happened? I heard you guys had some trouble out there. Everything all right?"

She sighed and pulled out the other chair to sit across from him. "I don't know. Jace—the new chief deputy—went with me. When we were riding back, he noticed something in one of the trees. The sun hit it just right, I guess. Anyway, we rode over to investigate and found a camera aimed at the houses."

"Really?" He reached for his water glass and took a drink. "Any idea who put it there?"

She shook her head. "Not yet. Jace called Seb and disappeared with it. I'm sure they're dusting it for prints and looking to see if there's any footage stored on it. It's just crazy, you know? I mean, who would want to break into our houses and spy on us? My family is boring."

Doug shrugged, fiddling with the silverware on the table as he talked. "You all think you're normal, but the Broken Bow is worth millions. Maybe someone's trying to get their hands on it."

She narrowed her eyes at him. One of Seb's theories about Doug was that he was a land developer. In fact, he'd told everyone he was here looking at property before Seb discovered that particular part of his identity was fake. They all knew he was up to something, but no one knew what. Seb had concluded he was likely a private investigator, but didn't know what he was investigating. He'd been rather tight-lipped about that. It was all rather strange.

"How do you know what the ranch is worth? And who would want to take it?"

He sat back and held up his hands. "I'm just making an observation. An operation that size is worth a lot of money. There are probably quite a few people out there who would want it."

She frowned as she considered his words. That was true. She knew her parents had received several offers over the years. But if that was the reason for all their trouble, how far would this person go to get his or her hands on the Broken Bow?

Jace walked into the station and headed for Seb's office. After he and Tara settled the animals into their stalls, he called Seb and asked to meet him. He'd been a little cryptic on the phone because he didn't want to discuss the case around Tara at the moment. She'd seemed a little rattled by the discovery. He didn't blame her. It looked like the lens was pointed right at her house.

He rapped his knuckles on Seb's door, then entered as Seb looked up.

The other man's eyes immediately fell to the camera in the ziploc bag Jace carried.

"What's going on?"

He set the bag on Seb's desk. "I found that in a tree on the south side of the houses on the ranch."

Seb frowned and looked in the bag. Surprise lit his face. "A camera? How did you find it?" He pulled some gloves from his pants pocket and put them on before taking the camera from the sack.

"Tara and I went out for a ride, and when we came back, the sun hit the lens just right, and I saw it out of the corner of my eye. I went to see what flashed and found that." He pointed at the matte black camera in Seb's hand.

"Did you look at the memory card yet?" Seb turned the

camera over in his hands, looking for the card slot. Once he found it, he removed the card and set the camera down.

Jace shook his head. "No. I wanted to bring it in here so you can put the card into evidence if need be."

"Well, as far as I know, none of us put up this camera, so that's probably where it will go. We have others we put up occasionally to watch for predators, but they're just trail cameras and don't look anything like this." He sat down at his desk and took a card reader from a drawer and plugged it into his computer. Jace walked around to stand behind him.

"Let's see what we have." Seb pressed some keys, and a folder opened. Hundreds of images popped up.

They were all of the back of Tara's house. More than one of them featured the woman herself. One particular shot made Jace's blood boil. It was a clear shot through the kitchen window, and Tara was naked.

Seb muttered an oath.

Jace straightened and looked away. He swallowed hard and shoved his emotions back into a tight vault in his mind. "Why would someone spy on your sister?"

Seb's frown was deep. "I don't know." He continued to scroll, but there weren't any images of anything other than Tara and her house. He blew out a breath and ejected the card, then pushed back his chair to stand.

"Come with me. Let's go visit the crime lab and see if we can get them to dust it for prints quick." He picked up the camera and led Jace from the room.

They went out the back door of the station and crossed the parking lot to the building next door. Inside, they quickly signed in and went through the door on the left, which led to a long hallway, and headed for the lab at the end.

As they passed the offices lining the hall, a door opened and the lead crime scene investigator, Katie Mitchum, stepped out.

She saw them and the object in Seb's gloved fingers and groaned. "Seriously? I was this close to being out of here." She held up two fingers only millimeters apart, then heaved a huge sigh. "What is that, and what do you want?"

"I found it out at the ranch," Jace said. "It has pictures of Tara and her house."

Katie's eyes widened.

"Can you dust it for prints?" Seb asked.

She nodded and turned down the hall toward the lab. A skeleton crew sat scattered around the room for the night shift on duty for emergencies and to work on the backlog.

Seb and Jace followed her across the room to her workstation. She dumped her bag on the floor, then pulled on a pair of latex gloves and picked up a jar of fingerprint powder and a brush.

"Let me see it." She held out a hand for the camera. Seb passed it to her.

She set it on the table and dipped her brush in the powder, then ran it lightly over the camera.

Jace crossed his arms and watched her work, impatient for some results. It bothered him to think someone had been keeping tabs on Tara. And not just because she was his boss's sister. The woman had him thinking and feeling things he hadn't in a long time. Not since his wife.

Katie set her brush down and peered at the camera with a magnifying glass, a smile quirking one side of her mouth. She straightened and looked at them. "Well, he or she isn't a very smart criminal. This thing is covered in prints." She took one of the special cards they used to pull fingerprints off objects and stuck it to a print on the power button.

"How fast can you run that?" Seb asked.

She looked up at him like he was a little stupid. "How long have you worked with me?" She flipped a hand at him and turned away to put the card on a scanner. A few taps on her keyboard and it was running through the fingerprint database.

With a grin, she spun around to rest against the counter and readjusted her translucent pink glasses, then crossed her arms. "Hopefully, it won't take too long. I ran it through our database first. If I don't get any hits, it'll flip to a statewide search, then national."

No sooner were the words out of her mouth than the computer dinged. She spun around, and Seb and Jace stepped forward.

"What's it say?" Seb asked.

"Hmm. That's weird."

"What?" Jace asked.

She looked up at them. "It came back to those prints you had me run when you investigated that murder case last month."

"Which ones? You ran several for me," Seb said.

"The ones you took off that guest of London's. Doug Brown."

"What?" His voice rolled like a clap of thunder through the room.

Jace's face matched Seb's. What did Brown want with Tara?

"Run it statewide," Seb said. "I figured out his company is a shell, but before I could dig deeper, we discovered the killer's identity, and I let it drop."

She turned back to her computer and tapped a few keys. "This will take longer than the local search. It might be tomorrow or longer before we know anything."

He gave a curt nod. "As soon as you know, call me."

She nodded.

"How about we go ask the good Mr. Brown while we wait?" Jace said.

"Good idea. Let's go."

Jace spun on his heel, leading the way back through the building. They signed out and headed for the police lot. They made a quick stop to get Seb's things and then were heading to their trucks.

"Do you think he's at the B&B?"

Seb paused. "Maybe. He usually goes out for dinner."

The men looked at each other, the answer to where hitting them both at the same time. They split apart, running to their trucks.

"I'll call London and find out if he's at the B&B. If he's there, I'll call you."

Jace nodded and climbed into his vehicle. He had a feeling the answer to that question would be no. Doug Brown was more than likely at The Heartwood Grill, spying on Tara.

"I talked to London," Seb said, as he climbed from his vehicle. He closed the door and jogged toward Jace, who'd beat him there by thirty seconds. "She hasn't seen him, but said she'd keep an eye out. I sent Gentry over too."

"Good. I don't want him to slip through our fingers."

They reached the front door, and Jace pulled it open. The mouth-watering aroma of grilled meat and spices hit his nose as soon as he stepped inside, reminding him he'd skipped dinner. Depending on how their visit panned out, it could be awhile yet before he ate.

Seb waved at the hostess, then led him through the room to the kitchen. In here, the smell of food was much stronger, and Jace's stomach grumbled. He ignored it and scanned the room, looking for Tara, and frowned when he didn't see her. She said she was coming here.

He glanced at Seb and noticed a similar frown on his face,

but he stepped toward one of the other chefs before Jace could say anything.

"Cassie."

The woman looked up from her workstation and smiled. "Sheriff. Hi."

"Hey. Is Tara here?"

She nodded and pointed toward a door at the back of the kitchen with her chef's knife. "She's in the office."

"Thanks."

The two men wove their way through the tables. Seb knocked, but didn't wait for an answer, turning the knob.

Tara glanced up from the desk, an expectant look on her face, which quickly turned to a frown as she caught a glimpse of Jace beside her brother.

"What are you two doing here?"

Seb stepped inside, and Jace leaned on the doorjamb.

"Is Doug Brown here?" Seb asked.

Tara's frowned turned curious. "He was. He left about half an hour ago. Why?"

Seb looked back at Jace, who held up his hands in supplication. He was already on her bad side after their kiss. Seb could upset her this time.

He sighed and turned back to his sister. "We found prints on the camera. They belong to Brown."

Her eyes widened, and her mouth dropped open. "What?" The word came out on a scant breath and she looked away, thinking. "Oh my God." She turned her gaze back to the two of them, something else riding alongside the surprise now. "I told him what we found."

"Why would you do that?" Jace couldn't help himself. Shock loosened his tongue.

She glared harder at him. "He's always been nice to me and my staff. He knew I wasn't supposed to be here tonight and asked why I was. It was an innocent conversation. And I was frustrated." She propped her elbows on her desk and buried her face in her hands. "Hell. I tipped him off."

Seb pulled out his phone. "You sure did." He looked at Jace. "I'm going to put out a BOLO on his car." He squeezed past Jace to go out and make the call.

Jace watched him go, trepidation in his gut as he was now alone with Tara and expected to console her. He suspected that was Seb's plan. The bastard.

He stepped into the tiny office and stood next to her desk. He crossed his arms and cocked a hip, then uncrossed them and stuffed his fingers in his front pockets.

She turned her eyes on him, still glaring. "You going to berate me for being an idiot?"

"No. You had no idea it was him. He was a sympathetic ear when you needed one."

She blew out a breath. "What a mess."

He laid a hand on her shoulder. She tensed, then pushed back from the desk and stood. "Did you manage to get into the footage on the camera?"

Jace stiffened. He nodded, but remained silent.

She arched a brow at him. "Well? What was in it?"

His jaw worked. He didn't want to tell her, but he knew she would find out, eventually.

He hung his head, then blew out a breath and looked at her. "The camera was aimed at the back of your house. All the images were of your place. And you." He left out the naked part. She could find that out another way.

"What?" Disbelief made her eyes wide. "What the hell is going on?"

He shook his head. "I don't know."

Tears shimmered in her eyes, and Jace couldn't stop himself from touching her again. He hated to see her hurting. Reaching out, he took her hand and squeezed it. "I'm going to find out, though."

Seb picked that moment to walk back in. Jace bit back a groan as the man grinned at the sight of their entwined hands. Any ground he'd gained with Tara had just been erased.

She yanked her hand free and crossed her arms, then looked at her brother.

"BOLO's out. I also put in for a warrant to search his room at the inn. I'm waiting on a signature from the judge."

"Sounds good. I'll follow you back."

Seb frowned. "It might be a good idea for you to stay here." He looked at Tara. "Did he tell you what we found on the memory card?"

She nodded.

He looked back at Jace. "Someone should stay with her until we find Brown and figure out what this is all about."

"I'll come to the inn with you. There isn't much for me to do here, and I don't feel like sitting at home twiddling my thumbs with him staring at me." She pointed at Jace. "I'll hang out with London while you two search."

Seb's lips twitched, but he held back the smile. "Okay. I'm going to head to Judge Brandt's house to get the warrant. I'll see you two at the inn." He backed out and walked away before either of them could protest.

Tara implored him with a look. "I don't suppose you'd let me drive my own truck to London's?"

Jace shook his head. He hooked a thumb over his shoulder where Seb stood only moments before. "And risk his wrath? No."

She grimaced but didn't argue. "Fine." She put away the files she'd been working on and picked up her purse, turning off the lights as they exited. Waving at Cassie, they left the building.

Tara hugged the door of Jace's truck as he drove them to London's B&B. She stared out the window at the darkening scenery, not caring that she couldn't see much. She just didn't want to have to make conversation.

But she could feel his eyes on her and sensed the silence wouldn't last.

"Has Brown ever said anything to you about what he was doing here? Ask you anything that seemed... nosy?"

She turned her head to look at him. "I don't think so. Most of our conversations were innocuous enough. He'd ask where I got the idea for a dish or what I had planned for the menu for a certain day. We'd talk about things happening around town. He expressed sympathy for what happened to London and Adelaide. Nothing I wouldn't talk about with anyone else. And I only asked him what he was doing around here once when he first arrived in town. He said business. I didn't press the issue because he seemed reluctant to talk about it."

"Yeah," Jace muttered. "Now we know why."

Tara looked out the windshield, eyes seeing nothing as she was lost in her thoughts. "I can't believe he was spying on me all this time. Why?"

"If he's a private investigator like Seb thinks, someone hired him. We just need to figure out why."

"That's just it. What is there about me—about my life— that someone would hire someone else to spy on me? I'm boring. I get up, go to work, come home, sleep, repeat. Throw in a few girls' nights and family parties, and you have my life."

"I don't know, but there's something there. We just have to figure out what it is. And Seb's right. Until we figure this out, you go nowhere alone."

"I don't have time for this," she groaned. "The Pioneer Days celebration starts in two days. I'm setting up an outdoor restaurant in the park. We're doing everything the old-fashioned way. I have three different trucks coming in tomorrow to deliver all the food, and I have to start the meat. I don't have time to wait on someone to show up and shadow me every time I need to make a trip from the ranch to town."

"Well, then, I guess you have a new chef."

She stared at him, eyes wide as his meaning sank in. "What? No. You're not cooking in my kitchen."

"Why not? Besides the fact it will eliminate the need for you to wait around for an escort, it sounds like you could use an extra set of hands."

"Do you even know how to cook?"

"Yes. My mama made sure I could fend for myself. And Allie didn't like to cook all that much, so we shared the kitchen duties."

Jace turned into London's drive, saving her from answering. It would be a cold day in hell before she let him cook alongside her. As soon as he parked the truck, she was out the door and headed into the house.

Aaron Gentry, Seb's youngest deputy at a mere twenty-two years of age, sat on the couch in the living room. London's niece, Abigail, sat across from him, smiling at the handsome rookie with stars in her eyes.

Tara smothered a smile. Abigail was too young for Aaron, and they both knew that, but it didn't stop the girl from admiring a handsome boy when he was near.

London poked her head through from the kitchen and motioned her inside. She heard Jace come in and close the door, but didn't spare him a glance as she made a beeline for her friend.

As soon as she waltzed through the doorway, London slid the pocket door closed.

"Chocolate. I need chocolate."

London giggled and slid a plate of brownies across the counter toward her. "Lucky for you, I made those today."

Tara grabbed one and stuffed a bite in her mouth. She moaned as the sweet taste of fudgy milk chocolate hit her tongue. "Oh, that's good."

"So, what's got you craving the nectar of the gods besides our dear Mr. Brown?" She waggled her eyebrows and gave Tara a wicked smile. "Does it have anything to do with the handsome hulk of a man who walked in behind you?"

Tara groaned, then stuffed another bite of brownie in her mouth and glared. "No," she mumbled around her food. She could feel her cheeks heat with the denial.

London laughed. "Oh, this sounds good. What happened?"

"Nothing."

"Your red face tells me otherwise. Spill."

Tara rolled her eyes and finished her brownie. "He kissed me and it was toe-curling and we both freaked. End of discussion."

London's eyes widened. "No. Not end of discussion. When did this happen? And why did he freak out too?"

"It was earlier today when we went out riding. Before we found the camera. And I'm assuming it has something to do with the fact he was married once. She died in a boating accident." Tara swallowed hard and blinked a couple times. "Along with their young daughter and his parents."

London gasped. "Oh my goodness! I didn't know that. That's awful."

Tara nodded. "He said he doesn't talk about it much. Only if the topic of family comes up and someone asks."

"So, you think he wigged out because of her? Like it was a betrayal to her or something?"

Tara shrugged. "I have no idea. He backed off, and we rode home. We haven't talked about it." She moaned and took another brownie off the plate. "My life is such a mess."

London laughed again. "No, it's not. There are worse

reasons to shove your face full of chocolate than being attracted to a blonde god."

That there were. And she had another good one. "Let's talk about the other, then, shall we? Brown hasn't been back since he left my restaurant?"

The other woman sobered. "No. Unless he slipped in before Seb called. I was upstairs in the apartment, so it's possible I missed him. I don't remember hearing anyone come in, though. Seb will review the security footage, I'm sure. He's loving the new system he had put in."

Tara grinned. "Did he drive you crazy with all the technical garb?"

"Yes." London rolled her eyes and smiled. "But he looked very cute doing it. I didn't learn much, but he appreciated my appreciation of his enthusiasm."

"Oh, yuck! No sex talk about my brother." She needed more chocolate—probably even some wine—if that was going to be on the docket. She could use some of that, anyway.

The pocket door slid open and Seb stuck his head in. "Who's talking about sex? And why?"

"I was just telling Tara how much I appreciated the security system you put in."

Seb's grin was predatory as he looked at his fiancée. "Oh, yeah. That was a good afternoon."

Tara waved her arms and stood. She walked over to the fridge, the jars in the door clinking together as she yanked it open. "No details, please." She took the bottle of wine off the top shelf and closed the door. "I take it from the fact you're here, you got the warrant to search Doug's room?" she said, changing the subject. She rummaged through the dishwasher for a clean glass, not caring that it was a water glass. Yanking out the cork on the bottle, she poured a healthy dose of the crisp white wine into the tumbler and took a gulp.

"Lush." Seb said, stepping into the room.

Tara stuck her tongue out at him. "Stop talking about your sex life in front of me and maybe I won't have to drink to forget. Now answer my question."

He chuckled. "I'll try."

She could tell by his tone he wouldn't and narrowed her eyes at him, but stayed silent.

"And yes, I did. I just came in here to get the key, so I don't have to bust down the door."

London pulled a key ring from her pocket. "Please don't." She walked over and handed it to him.

He took the keys and bent to press a kiss to her lips. "Thanks, babe. I'll come find you when we're done."

"Seb." Tara took a step toward him, and he looked at her.

"I want to know what you find. No matter what it is. I deserve to know what kind of information he's been gathering about me."

Expression serious, he nodded. "Hang tight. I'll be back."

Tara took another swallow of her wine and watched him leave, both dreading and anticipating what answers his search would bring.

"You get the key?" Jace asked Seb when he walked back into the living room.

Seb nodded and held up the key ring. "Yep. Let's go." He didn't stop and led the way to the staircase on the other side of the room.

Both men took the steps two at a time to reach the second floor of the inn.

"What took you so long? Everything okay in there?" Jace asked once they were out of Abigail's earshot.

Seb sighed and found the key for Brown's room as they reached his door. "Yeah. I hope you're prepared for drunk

Tara, though. She was downing a glass of pinot grigio. And there was still more in the bottle."

"Honestly, I was kind of expecting it. I'm amazed she's held it together as well as she has."

"Yeah, well, my sister's pretty tough. She's been through some really rotten shit." He inserted the key in the lock and opened the door.

"I know. But it's still been a rough day, and finding out someone you've come to view as, maybe not a friend, but not really a threat, either, is spying on you and breaking into your house is upsetting."

"True. Let's see if we can figure out why." He motioned Jace inside.

Brown's room looked like a bomb had gone off in it. Papers, clothes, and other miscellaneous things were scattered over every surface. Jace glanced over at Seb, who's look of shock mirrored his own.

"I take it that it doesn't always look like this?"

Seb shook his head. "No. He's usually immaculate. He must have come back after he left The Heartwood, and London didn't see him. Let's find out what he left behind."

Jace took the far side of the room. He donned his gloves and started leafing through the papers scattered on the desk. A lot of it was notes about Tara's movements. Places she visited, how frequently, what days—a detailed look at everywhere she'd been for the last three months. He couldn't believe how much data the man had. It was more than one person could collect. Especially considering he knew there were times Brown had been somewhere other than where Tara was.

"Hey, Seb?"

"Yeah?"

"When we get back to the ranch, we need to check your sister's vehicles for trackers."

"Are you serious?"

Jace looked over his shoulder and waved a sheet of paper at him. "He's been following her. Everywhere."

Seb cursed. "Okay. Yeah, we need to find those and make sure they're deactivated so he can't continue to do it."

"We should check everyone's cars, just to be safe."

"Agreed."

"You find anything yet?"

"No. Just a bunch of empty pockets." He threw down the pair of pants he just rummaged through and picked up another.

Jace turned back to the papers. Buried beneath the reports on her whereabouts, he found a slip of paper with a phone number on it. He took a quick picture of it with his phone, then dialed the number.

"What are you doing?" Seb walked up behind him.

Jace held up a finger as the call rang. It rolled to a message telling him the number was no longer in service, and he hung up. "I found that beneath all these reports. It's disconnected."

Seb took out his cell. "I have a contact at the FBI who might be able to tell us something about that. Let me get him on it. Keep looking. My side is a bust. It's just a bunch of clothing."

He started shuffling through the papers again while Seb made his call, but it was more of the same. Glancing down, he noticed several slips of paper on the floor and in the trash can. He kneeled down and picked them up. They all had a date and time written on them. Maybe times Brown was supposed to meet whoever hired him. Jace laid them on the desk and made a mental note to ask Tara where she'd been at those times. It could be data that hadn't made it into the reports yet.

He turned to the rumpled bed and shook out the bedding. Other than a t-shirt and a sock, there was nothing. He opened the nightstand drawer. It had a phone charger and some lip balm.

As he turned his head away, something caught his eye behind the headboard on the floor. He turned on the flashlight on his phone and shined it into the crack. There was something there. It looked like more paper.

Jace set the phone down and pulled the bed away from the wall to find a file folder.

"What's back there?"

He straightened with the folder in his hand. "This." He flipped it open, and a picture of Tara wrapped in the arms of a tall, dark-haired man stared back at him. A ripple of jealousy rolled through his belly.

"Is this Tara's husband?" He turned the folder around for Seb to see.

Seb stepped closer and frowned, nodding.

Jace turned it back and kept flipping. He heard Seb talking on the phone, but didn't hear what was said. He sank onto the bed, unable to believe Brown left this behind.

"Seb. We have a problem."

NINE

Tara paused mid-sip and looked over the rim of her glass at her brother and Jace as they walked into the kitchen. Seb's brows were drawn so far down they touched. Jace's mouth was a thin, grim line.

She lowered her glass as her stomach sank. She was not going to like what they had to say.

"What?"

Seb motioned to the table, a file folder in his hand. "Have a seat, T. We need to talk."

Tara gulped at the serious tone of his voice. Something they found had them extremely concerned. "Oh, God. I know I said I wanted to know, but now I'm not so sure. Did he have a bunch of naked pictures of me or something?"

"We found those on the camera," Jace muttered.

Her step faltered on her way across the kitchen and she stumbled into the table, sitting down harder on the chair than she intended, and it skidded several inches before she came to a rest.

"Jesus, Tara. How much did you have to drink?" Seb asked, sinking into the chair across from her.

She blew her hair out of her face and turned annoyed eyes on him. "I just refilled my glass before you two walked in. Now, tell me what you found besides naked pictures. Did he sell them too?"

Seb sighed and flipped the folder open. "No. But we found this."

He turned the folder around and Tara looked down to see a picture of her husband in uniform.

Her eyes darted back up. "What's going on? Why does he have Sean's picture?"

Seb glanced up at Jace, who stood beside them with London. Tara glanced at him. His mouth was still set and concern shone in his eyes.

"The rest of the file contains details about Sean's last tour in Afghanistan. Whatever Brown's here looking for isn't about you. It's about Sean."

Tara sat back in her chair, eyes wide, and looked away, stunned. That was the last thing she expected to hear. "Why?" She looked back at her brother. "What could he think I have or know about Sean's military career? And after three years?"

"I'm not sure, but I'm going to make some calls. See what I can find out about the information in this folder. I may not get very far, because I'm guessing a lot of the stuff in this file is need-to-know. How Brown got it is anybody's guess, but if we catch him, it's going to be more than me he answers to."

She scrubbed her hands over her face, unable to process all she was hearing. "This is nuts. Let me see that folder. I was with the unit for his last tour, so maybe it'll jog something." She reached for the file, but Seb pulled it back.

She looked at him with a frown.

"You need to let this soak in first. You're so shocked right now only part of your brain will pay attention to what you're reading. It's late. Go home, get some rest, and we'll start fresh in the morning."

"Seb, I have a million things to do tomorrow. The festival starts Saturday. We need to do this now."

"I know you're busy. We are too." He motioned to himself and Jace. "But I guarantee you'll miss something if we don't wait. You need to take a step back first."

Her sigh came out as more of a growl, but she nodded. "Fine. But it's going to be first thing. I don't want this hanging over my head all day."

"That's fine. I'll leave the file with Jace. You two can go over it before you head to work. But," he paused and looked at both of them, "you will wait until morning." He turned stern eyes on his new deputy. "Don't let her turn those dark eyes—or other parts of her—on you and get you to show it to her sooner. You probably should sleep on top of it too. I wouldn't put it past her to sneak out of bed in the middle of the night and read it."

"Hey!"

"Don't even start. Mom had to lock your Christmas presents in a trunk in the attic and wear the key on a chain around her neck because you wouldn't stop trying to look."

"Thomas did it too," she grumbled.

"Well, you two did share a womb, so there's that." He stood up, closing the folder and scooping it off the table. "Tomorrow morning. Sunrise. No earlier."

He held the folder out to Jace. "Take her home. And keep an eye out. I don't know if Brown will try to get to her tonight or not. It'll depend on how desperate he is to get whatever he thinks she has."

Jace nodded and stepped forward, holding out a hand. "Come on, Tara. Seb's right. Let's go get some rest."

Tara stared at the long, tanned fingers he held out to her, her brain struggling to catch up. So much had happened in such a short amount of time. She just wanted answers. The set to her brother's jaw told her she would have to wait, though.

And as much as she didn't like it—and hated to admit it—he was right. She was in no condition to give any sort of critical thought to what was in that file, both because of her emotional state and the half bottle of wine she drank.

She sucked a steadying breath through her nose and put her hand in Jace's, letting him pull her from her chair. Giving London the best smile she could muster, she let him lead her from the room.

Jace double-checked the locks and shut off the lights in the kitchen on his way to the bathroom to get ready for bed. It was only nine o'clock, but after the day they had, they were both ready to get some rest. Tara had immediately gone to take a shower and put her pajamas on while Jace ate a sandwich and checked the property.

Grabbing some clean clothes, he showered off the day and brushed his teeth. As he exited the bathroom and turned to go back to the living room, noise from behind Tara's closed door caught his attention.

What was that?

He dropped his clothes on the hall floor, but kept his gun. On light feet, he crept across the hallway to listen. It only took a moment for him to register what he heard. He thumbed the safety back on his weapon and lowered it to his side.

Giving the knob a twist, he gave the door a gentle push. The sight that greeted him about broke him. Tara laid on her bed curled up like a baby, sobbing into a pillow. She looked at him for a brief moment before melting back into the mattress, the stream of tears never faltering.

Jace was across the room before his brain registered his feet were moving. He laid his gun on the nightstand and sat down behind her, then scooped her onto his lap. She turned her face into his chest, and he soon felt the wet heat of her tears through the fabric of his t-shirt.

He let her cry. He knew sometimes you just needed to get it out. Let all the pent-up pain and anger flow away with the tears. So, he sat there on her bed with her in his arms and stroked her hair, murmuring soft platitudes in her ear. Slowly, she calmed until the gut-wrenching sobs turned to soft hiccups and sniffles.

Her fingers released his shirt, and she sat back to look at him. Even with her red, puffy eyes, she was the most beautiful woman he'd ever laid eyes on.

"Thank you," she whispered.

"Anytime. Do you want to talk about it?"

She sucked her bottom lip between her teeth, chewing on it a moment before blowing out a breath. "Not really, but seeing as I just blubbered all over your shirt, it would probably be the polite thing to do."

He smiled down at her. "You don't have to talk about anything. I have lots of t-shirts."

That made her grin. "We keep finding surprises like the one tonight and we'll probably go through them." She patted the damp spot on his shirt.

Jace covered her hand with his, and her smile faded. He cleared his throat and looked away, knowing if he didn't, he was going to kiss her again. It didn't feel right after she'd just been crying over her dead husband, no matter how much he wanted to.

She shifted off his lap to sit beside him on the bed. He mimicked her pose and drew his knees up to his chest, looping his arms around them.

"I thought I was all done with crying over him. It seems kind of pointless. It won't bring him back."

"No. But sometimes the grief builds up. We don't even

know it, but it does, and then it needs a place to go when something makes that dam with the slow leak overflow."

"Do you still cry over your wife?"

"I haven't in a while, but I used to all the time. She'd kick my ass if she saw me crying over her still after all this time." He smiled, then continued. "I still cry over Haley, though. I don't think that will ever change. I think it'll get less and less frequent —it already has—but I think there will always be something that makes me cry about all the things I'm missing out on with her."

Tara leaned her head against his shoulder. "What were they like?"

Realizing they were in for the long haul on this conversation, Jace scooted up against the headboard and pulled her up beside him, draping an arm over her shoulders and tucking her into his side. She turned into him and laid an arm over his stomach.

"Allie was a lot like you, actually. Headstrong, determined, ambitious, smart, pretty—" He cast a sideways glance down at her. "Sassy."

She looked up at him and stuck her tongue out, making him grin.

"She was quieter than you, though. She'd wait and bide her time, gathering as much information about an issue as she could, then tackle it with everything she had. You're more impulsive, but no less able to come out on top."

An image of his wife standing in the kitchen scolding him for not taking the trash to the curb for the second week in a row materialized in his head. "She wasn't afraid to yell at me, either, but it was usually because of something I forgot to do, not just for being me."

Tara rolled her eyes. "I've gotten past that. Mostly."

He chuckled. "You'd have liked her, I think. She would have fit right in with you and London and your girlfriends."

"She sounds nice."

"She was. We met in high school, but we didn't start dating until after I came home from my time in the Army. She was a couple years younger than me and working at the local grocery store while she went to college for teaching. My mom sent me to the store to pick up some whipped cream for Thanksgiving dinner at the last minute before they closed, and she was the cashier on duty. I remembered seeing her in there a few times since I'd returned, but for some reason, that night I was just blown away by this beautiful girl. I asked her out, and she said yes. We got married right after she finished her degree in the spring."

"What did she look like?"

"She had blonde hair and brown eyes. Tall, but not as curvy as you. I have a picture in my wallet. Hang on." He got up to retrieve his clothes from the hall and pulled his wallet from his pants pocket as he walked back in. Flipping through it, he located the picture and handed it to her, then dropped his things on the floor and climbed back up beside her, tucking her back into his side.

"She was beautiful," Tara said, staring down at the photograph. "And your daughter is just adorable."

A wistful smile crossed his face as he looked at the picture alongside her. "Yeah. Haley was stunning. Inside and out. That picture was taken about a month before they died." He cleared his throat as emotion clogged it. "You'd have liked her too. She was a ball of energy with a smile that lit up the room and a wit far beyond a child her age. Even at four, she would come up with these one-liners that left us in stitches." A tear leaked from the corner of one eye, and he swiped at it with his thumb. "I miss her," he said on a broken whisper.

"I'm so sorry, Jace. I didn't mean to drudge up old memories."

He sniffed and blinked a few times, getting himself back

under control. "It's all right. The pain of losing a child never really goes away. Sometimes it's the good memories that hurt."

Tara's lip wobbled. "I know," she whispered.

Jace nodded. His mind on his daughter, it took him a moment to register what she said. When he did, he looked down at her wide-eyed. "What?"

She took a shaky breath and met his gaze. "I said, I know."

He frowned. "I don't understand. You don't have any children, and no one's ever mentioned any."

"Because no one knew. Except Mom. When Sean died, I was pregnant. I lost the baby the same week I moved back to the ranch." Her brown eyes watered as she stared up at him. "So, I know exactly how you feel. I may not have lost my *entire* family on the same day, but I lost two of those most precious —and the one thing that held me together after Sean died— within the span of about two weeks."

"Christ, Tara. I'm sorry."

She nodded and looked away, wiping at the tears trickling silently down her face.

"How far along were you?"

"Nineteen weeks."

Astonishment made him look like a fish, he was sure, but he didn't know what to say.

That must have been written on his face, because when she looked at him again, she smiled. "I know. How did I hide that? Why?"

He nodded.

"I was still overseas on assignment with Sean's unit when it happened. He got a rare weekend of leave and we took off for Athens for a night. A month later, I finally realized I was late. I didn't want to be sent back to the states while he was still in the Middle East, so I kept it a secret—even from Sean. He only had a few months left on his tour, and I was determined to stay with him as long as I could. I finally told him when I couldn't hide it from him anymore, which was at about twelve weeks. I begged him not to say anything. That he was so close to being done, and we'd go back to San Diego and I'd find a job stateside."

"He agreed to that?"

She nodded. "He knew I could take care of myself, and that I was careful. I knew the risks of being a woman in that part of the world, and I'd been living there for years by then. He trusted me to take care of us."

"So, why hide it from your family? Your parents would have been thrilled to have a grandchild."

"I didn't want to tell them while I was still in the Middle East. My mother would fret until I came home. She already worried about me being over there, and I didn't want to add the extra burden. Sean and I had it all planned. Since I was going to be so close to the midterm ultrasound when his tour ended, we were going to find out the gender and surprise them when we came to visit."

"Why did you keep it from them, though, once he died?"

She shrugged. "It felt wrong to be so joyful when I felt so sad. And it was winter, so I could hide my condition with bulky sweaters and coats. I just didn't feel like celebrating and having people tell me how lucky I was to still have a piece of him with me. All I could think about was how my baby would never know how wonderful her daddy was. I didn't want anyone reminding me of that with what they perceived to be helpful comments."

"And then you miscarried."

She drew a deep breath through her nose and blew it out. "Yeah. After the funeral in Denver where Sean's family is from, I came back to the ranch, only intending to stay for a week or two before I went back to San Diego to pack up our house and start looking for a new job. I needed to get back on my feet and make a home somewhere for my baby. But first, I needed some time to heal, and this ranch is the best place I know to do that." She shifted and wiped at her wet face.

"Anyway, a couple days after I was here, Mom and I were in the kitchen, baking, when I felt some cramps, but it wasn't the first time, so I didn't think much of it. Mom saw my face and asked if everything was okay, then said she knew about the baby. That I wasn't fooling her with the baggy clothes. I was about to tell her I was fine, when a terrible pain shot through my belly, and my water broke. And it was bloody." She paused to collect herself.

Jace tightened his arm around her and stroked her hair with his other hand. Fierce pride burned in his chest for this woman and how she'd come through the other side of such tragedy as the woman she was today.

"She rushed me to the hospital, but there was nothing they could do. The baby was already gone. I was bleeding so much, they had to do an emergency c-section." She wiped at her face again. "I had a girl. They said she'd died the day before. The placenta was malformed. She looked more like she was about fourteen weeks than nineteen."

Her breath shuddered out and Jace took an unsteady one of his own.

"I named her Lucy. It means light, because she was my light in the darkness of my grief. When her light went out, I wasn't sure I'd ever see again."

Moisture made Jace's vision swim. God, how he knew how she felt. Some days, he missed Haley so much it was all he could do to get up in the morning. He blinked a few times to clear his eyes.

"But you did, though," he said softly.

She sniffed and nodded. "It took a while, but yeah."

"Why doesn't your family know about her now?"

"At the time, I didn't want more sympathy. I'd had enough of people fawning all over me. I just wanted to mourn in peace, so I made Mom promise not to tell anyone. I think she told Dad. I didn't really expect her not to, but she told the others I'd just come down with a sudden illness. Appendicitis. They bought it. By the time I recovered enough from losing Lucy to be ready to talk about her, six months passed, and it felt really awkward to just tell all my siblings that the illness I'd had was actually a late miscarriage, and that their niece's ashes were buried up at the lake."

Jace froze, frowning. "Wait? The same lake we were just at?"

She nodded.

"Why didn't you tell me to buzz off, then, when I asked to go riding with you?"

"Because, honestly, I didn't want to go up there and wallow in my grief anymore. I wanted to talk to her and tell her I missed her, but not descend into that bone-aching grief I've been trying so hard to dig my way out of. I knew having you along would make me keep my visit short and that there was enough space up there for me to wander off and visit her grave without you seeing."

"So, you used me," he joked, trying to lighten the moment.

It worked, and she gave a short laugh. "Yeah, pretty much."

"I'm sorry you went through all that. If it makes a difference, I admire what you've built since then."

She looked up at him, a tremulous smile on her face. "It does. Thank you."

"Anytime."

He paused for a moment, then changed the subject, knowing they both needed to get out of that particular head space. "So, tell me more about Sean's military career. Maybe we can figure out a place to start looking for whatever Brown was sent here to find out."

Tara blew out a breath. "I don't know where to start. Let's see. We met on my very first overseas assignment. He was brand new to the teams and could sweet talk the sugar out of a candy bar. Everyone called him Sweets. Anyway, his commander assigned him to PR duty, and it was his job to show me around, give me sound bites, keep me out of trouble —that sort of thing."

"Let me guess. You didn't take well to having a handler."

She laughed. "How did you guess? No, I didn't. He quickly figured out he couldn't charm me. It didn't stop him from trying, but he started to look at me differently. I wasn't just the hot journalist anymore. Now, I had a brain and some scruples. Once that happened, he opened up more and started to show me not just the real Sean, but what was really happening in the area. The first article I wrote cemented my presence over there. My editor refused to consider anyone else for my job. I stayed with the SEAL teams there even after his tour ended. When he shipped out, he asked if he could keep in contact, and our relationship grew from there.

"He was in and out of the Middle East after that, and it was all more of the same for him. They were hunters. He and his fellow SEALs roamed the mountains looking for Taliban and Al-Qaeda. He lost a few friends, got injured a few times. It wasn't unlike what any other SEAL or Ranger experienced over there."

"Except he had his girlfriend, then wife, tagging along."

"Our situation was unique, yes, but other than some ribbing from his unit, we didn't catch much guff. Both my editor and his commander explained the rules to us in explicit detail, and we stuck to them. Neither of us wanted to be separated, so we did our best not to make any waves. Most people didn't even know we were a thing unless someone told them."

"Did he ever have a mission that went sideways? Maybe where something he did impacted someone else?"

"The only mission they had that went absolutely wrong was his last one. I'm not just saying that because he died. Their intel was solid—at least that's what the commander told me. They were going after a regional war lord they'd been trying to get for three years. Mohammed Al-Aziz. They got info from a villager he was going to be at a house deep in the mountains north of Bagram.

"They made it to the compound and inside without inci-dent. Then something happened, but no one's sure what. Their video feed cut out. The Navy thinks someone jammed the signal. When it finally came back on, it was to Sean's unit leader, Jared Fetter, holding his helmet in his hand, blood all over his face as he gave a sitrep."

"Was your husband the only one killed or were there others?"

"Just Sean. Jared said when they entered Al-Aziz's bedroom, he was waiting for them. Sean was the first in, and the guy shot him with an automatic rifle." She broke off to swallow back the tears. Jace stroked her silky, dark hair and gave her a reassuring squeeze.

"He was shot eight times. Two of the bullets hit arteries. One in his thigh and one in his arm. His teammates took a couple minor shots, but Sean's body blocked most of the others. They grabbed him and pulled him out, but by the time they were able to get out of the house, he died of blood loss."

Her story made Jace sweat as memories of his own tour there surfaced. He'd cleared buildings a few times. Every time, his biggest fear had been going around a corner to find an insurgent ready to blast him with a rifle or blow him up with a grenade. He'd been shot once doing it, but the bullet had been a through and through of his left flank.

Something about the story bothered him, though. "What happened to the warlord?"

"Sean's team killed him."

"What about the guy's men? Surely, he wasn't alone in that compound."

"They killed several on their way in and a few more on their way out."

"But the guy knew they were coming, right? So why didn't they get mowed down on their way out? Or why didn't Al-Aziz just flee before they ever arrived?"

Tara frowned, contemplating his questions. "I'm not sure. I didn't ask too many questions. That's the story his teammates told me and what I gleaned from the official report. The version I was allowed to see, anyway."

Jace hummed and stared at a point on the wall over her head. It still sounded off. Maybe there was something about that mission someone wanted to know, and that's why Tara was being targeted.

But what could a dead man know that the living didn't? And why did it matter now, three years later?

Ten

Pain lanced through Tara's head as she came awake.

Ugh. Too much crying, not enough water.

She tried to sit up, but a weight over her middle kept her pinned to the mattress. Opening her scratchy eyes, she looked down to see a tanned forearm dusted with blonde hair wrapped over her side and tucked between her breasts.

Eyes wide as her memory kicked in, she sank back onto her pillow and closed them again. Embarrassment made her cheeks hot. What *was* she thinking?

She wasn't; that was the problem. She'd had just enough wine last night to loosen her tongue and keep her from caring that she spilled her guts to him. But now, in the light of day—and sober—she couldn't bear to look into his eyes and see the pity of all she'd revealed.

God, what a mess.

Maybe if she could get out from under him, she could go take a shower and delay the inevitable a bit. She picked up his hand and gently lifted it from where it sat. He inhaled sharply, and she looked back to see those indigo eyes blink open. *Crap!*

Eager to get away without a discussion, she started to sit up, but his arm tightened and he pulled her closer.

"Not yet. The file can wait a few more minutes."

"I wasn't—" she broke off and frowned. She hadn't even thought about that file yet. "I was just going to go take a shower."

He made a noise, acknowledging what she said, but made no move to let her up.

Tara stared at the wall and toyed with his fingers. She wasn't sure she liked not being able to see his face. But if she turned around, it put those lush lips of his in kissing range. Considering their location, that probably wasn't the best idea. Especially since they both had a full day.

"Did you sleep okay?" he asked. "Once you fell asleep, that is."

She nodded. "As well as could be, I suppose." Truthfully, she had one of the best night's sleep she'd had in years, even if it was a little short. Maybe there was something to be said for unburdening one's soul.

"Good."

His voice rumbled through her, waking her up more than any shower ever could. She glanced over her shoulder, which was a mistake. Those intense blue eyes stared back at her. Awareness shimmered in their depths.

She swallowed hard, but couldn't look away.

He brought his hand up from where it rested to stroke her face.

"You make me feel again. Things I thought were dead and gone with Allie."

Her eyes widened at his admission. Whatever was happening between them wasn't one-sided.

"Yeah," she breathed. "Same here."

His thumb brushed her lip, and her heart beat a staccato in her chest.

"Jace. This isn't a good idea," she warned, trying to preserve her sanity.

"Why not?" He inched closer.

She stared up at him for a moment, a blank look on her face. She hadn't expected him to contradict her, and his nearness was messing with her ability to form a coherent sentence.

"What? No answer?" The smile he leveled on her was downright naughty. "Good." He swooped down and covered her mouth with his.

Tara knew how it felt to kiss him thanks to their interlude at the lake, but it was still a shock to the system. Kissing Jace was like stepping into a wildfire without a fire shelter. The heat blindsided her, consuming her in its wake. It made her forget why it was a bad idea to do this. That they both needed to get up and get ready for work. That she didn't want a relationship, which burned hot again with a man who took chances with his life every day. Her only focus was the fire he stoked with his big hands as he ran them down her sides to hold her hips, and his soft lips as he plundered her mouth.

The blare of her alarm pulled them apart.

Tara groaned while Jace cursed. She rolled away to turn it off, sitting up to punch the off button.

What the hell am I doing?

All the reasons for not starting anything with Jace still rang true. She couldn't handle another man who put himself in the line of fire. One who did dangerous things. Her heart couldn't take it.

She scrubbed her hands over her face, then ran them through her hair. No matter how nice he was or how much he understood what she'd been through, and no matter that his kisses left her breathless and aching for more, she couldn't let it go any further. If she did, and she fell for him, and then something happened to him, it would break her. Utterly and completely in a way that she wasn't sure she would ever recover from. Hell, she hadn't even totally recovered from Sean's death. What would adding Jace's do to her?

The bed bounced and then the mattress dipped as he came up behind her on his knees. When he reached around to wrap his arms around her, she shot up.

"I'm going to go take that shower now." Without looking back at him, she walked into her closet and grabbed some clothes. After a quick stop at her dresser for underwear, she breezed into her bathroom and closed the door.

Once locked in the bathroom, she let out a long breath. She wished she had time to take a bath and let it melt away some of her stress, but the day was waiting, and it was going to be a busy one.

Jace's eyes widened as he got his first look at the downtown area where the festival would take place. Canvas tents and covered wagons lined the street, each one housing a different aspect of pioneer life or offering goods for sale. Vendors scurried around, arms and wagons full as they set up their areas.

He walked down Main Street, looking in tents and waving at people as he passed. They really went all out here for this. When Seb mentioned the annual Fourth of July celebration, Jace pictured a few demonstrations and some food trucks. Maybe some fireworks after dark. Not this pioneer town that had sprung up.

At the end of the block, the right side of the street opened up into the town park. A larger tent sat in the middle of the grassy area with picnic tables under and around it. He saw the tall figures of Brady and Thomas Archer moving through the tent loaded down with boxes. Their mother stood off to the side, directing them where to go.

His eyes roved over the rest of the tent, looking for Tara,

but he didn't see her. She'd barely said two words to him this morning. Once she got out of the shower, she told him she would be around her kitchen staff all day and he could report to Seb for a duty assignment. When he asked her about the file on Sean, she said she put it in her bag and would read it at work. Then she gave him a quick wave and left.

To be honest, he was more than a little peeved at her. After all they shared last night, she still wanted to hold him at arm's length. He'd be damned if he was going to let her. Not now that she'd cracked open the door to the feelings he'd stowed away. They didn't want to be locked away again, and he didn't really want to close them up anymore. It was nice having them out in the open again.

That in mind, he jogged over to the tent.

"Jenny," he called as he got closer.

She looked over at him, then smiled. "Jace, hi. Seb send you over here to help?"

"No. I was just patrolling through town and saw all the activity. I thought you might need another set of hands."

"Sure. Follow the boys. They'll show you what needs done."

"I'll do that, thanks." He glanced around once more, looking for Tara's dark head.

"She's not here, honey. She went back to the restaurant to get another load."

He gave her a sheepish grin. "I was that obvious, huh?"

She smiled. "Only to me. I've prayed and prayed Tara would find someone who made the light come back in her eyes. You did that, even if she is glaring at you most of the time. Just be patient with her. Life hasn't been good to her the last few years. She's getting there, though."

Jace took a step closer. "I know. We had a long talk last night. She told me about Lucy."

Jenny's hands flew to cover her mouth as she gasped, her

eyes wide with shock. A tear spilled over as she dropped her hands.

"She told you? You're doing better than I thought. Not even her siblings know about her."

He wished he had her confidence. Every time he thought he made some headway, she shut him down again. "That's what she said. I'm learning Tara's a very private person and doesn't like to show her true feelings."

"No, she doesn't. Some of that comes from growing up with four brothers and sisters. Thomas, especially, was relentless about teasing her when she cried. Then when she went to the Middle East, showing emotion there could get her killed, so she just shoved everything down further. Sean was the only one she really talked to. When he died, she lost that outlet. I tried to fill it, but it wasn't the same."

Surprise made him stiffen when she stepped forward and enveloped him in a quick hug.

She released him and stepped back, wiping at her tears. "Oh, I'm so glad you showed up. Don't you dare give up on her."

He cleared his throat and glanced around. His gaze connected with Thomas', who was coming their way. He looked back down at Jenny. "I won't. I should go help Brady and Thomas," he said, motioning toward her son. "I'll see you later."

She smiled up at him, waving him away. "Okay. Make sure Tara gives you your costume tonight. Seb said he was going to send it home with her."

"Costume?"

She just grinned at him, then turned away when someone called her name.

"Everything okay?" Thomas asked, reaching him.

Jace looked away from Jenny, a frown still on his face. "Yes. But what's this about costumes?"

Thomas grinned and laid a hand on Jace's shoulder. "It's Pioneer Days. We all like to play the part."

Jace had a sudden vision of himself in chaps and spurs with some sort of fancy ascot tied at his throat. "I see. So what kind of costume do the men wear?"

Thomas dropped his hand and shrugged. "Depends on their job. Mine won't be much different from what I'm wearing now." He gestured to his jeans and short-sleeved Oxford plaid shirt. "The pants are a little different and I have a vest. You get a tin star since you're a cop. Seb has an awesome duster he wears every year. Makes him look more like the town villain than the town sheriff."

"What about your mom?" He glanced back at the woman directing staff with military precision.

"She's the schoolteacher."

Jace laughed. He could see that. She had the command needed to control a wily bunch of kids.

"You here to help?" Thomas asked.

He sobered and nodded. "Yep. Unless I get called somewhere." He tapped the radio clipped to his belt.

"Come on, then," Thomas waved him toward the edge of the tent. "Cassie's waiting in the parking lot with a truck full of table settings."

Jace followed him out of the tent. The sun immediately blasted down on his head, making him wish he'd worn a hat. He was thankful there was a pleasant breeze or it would be unbearably hot.

"So, you sure everything's okay? I saw the hug Mom laid on you. And it looked like she was crying."

He looked over at Thomas. Concern pinched the man's brows together.

"It's fine. I told her about a conversation I had with Tara yesterday. It just made her happy."

"What did you talk about? You ask her to marry you, or

something?"

Jace chuckled. "No, nothing like that. Just some stuff about our pasts. Your mom's happy she's opening up."

If possible, Thomas' frown deepened, and he stopped walking. "Wait. Did she tell you about—No. She wouldn't. No one knows about that."

Suspicion made Jace narrow his eyes. "Tell me about what? You mean, what happened when she came home after Sean's funeral?"

Thomas stared at him hard for a moment. "When she was in the hospital?"

Jace gave a succinct nod.

"Fuck me, man." Thomas spun away and removed his hat to run a hand through his hair.

Arms crossed, Jace watched the man pace a few steps. Tara hadn't been as adept at hiding her condition as she thought.

Thomas turned back and speared Jace with a look that could wither flowers. "Why would she tell you and not us? We're her family. She's known you a month."

"Before we go any further, I need you to tell me exactly what it is you think she told me. Because if I tell you and it wasn't what you thought it was, she'll never speak to me again."

The other man ate up the distance between them. When he spoke, his voice was low and pain filled his eyes. "About her baby. She told you about her baby."

Jace sucked in a sharp breath. It was one thing to suspect Thomas knew, but quite another to hear him say it. "Okay. Yeah. She told me about Lucy."

"Lucy? She had a girl? And she named her?" Anger colored Thomas' face red. "Why the hell did she tell you and not us?"

Jace sighed. It was a day for revelations, it seemed. "Because she isn't the only one who's lost a child. I lost my four-year-old daughter five years ago. Along with her mother and my parents."

Thomas' eyes widened and some of the anger left his face. "Hell, man. That's rough. What happened? Car accident?"

Jace shook his head. "Boating accident." He waved a hand through the air. "But we're not talking about me. You know about Lucy? How?"

Thomas sighed. "We all know. We just don't know any of the details. You can't hide a belly like that, even with the baggy clothes she favored. Any time we hugged her, we could feel it."

"Why didn't you say anything to her, then?"

"We thought she'd tell us when she was ready. Tara's always been a private person. Sean's death really dealt a blow to her. She withdrew into herself and kept everything bottled up even more than usual. I still don't think she's really let it all out." He cocked his head. "Though maybe she's starting to now that you're around." He shook his head. "I still can't believe she told you."

"I think you should tell her you know. That you all know. Lucy's buried on the ranch. Up at the lake. I think it would be good for Tara to know that you all mourn her daughter too."

"Even though she never told us about her?"

Jace nodded. "She said she didn't want the sympathy. That she was tired of being fawned over. Once she got past that, months had passed and the time never felt right. Now, I think she's afraid you'll all be mad at her for keeping such a huge secret for so long."

"I am. We are," Thomas growled. "But we also understand. And we love her. All any of us ever wanted was to be there for her, but she shut us out."

Jace opened his mouth to speak, then closed it again, frowning, before trying again. "All I can say is cut her some slack. I can tell you from experience, that kind of pain—it's hard to deal with. And it's hard to share. I spent a few months in the bottom of a bottle before some of my friends hauled my ass out and forced me back into life."

"But you share what happened. She doesn't."

"I think that's more because what happened to my family was public knowledge. Tara was the only one who knew about her pregnancy. I'm not sure I would share what happened if others didn't already know. It's hard to think about even now. I've talked more about my family in the last few days than I have in years."

Thomas' mouth flattened, and he stared off into the distance. "Yeah, I guess I get that." He looked back at Jace, sizing him up. "I hope you're ready for what's coming."

Jace gave him a quizzical look. "What do you mean? She won't be mad at me. You already knew."

One corner of Thomas' mouth quirked. "I'm not talking about that. Although, I'm sure she'll find a way to lay blame on your head. What I mean, is I hope you're ready for life with her. I've seen the way she looks at you and how you look at her. Coupled with her willingness to confide in you, I think you're stuck with her."

Jace smiled. "I know. And I don't plan to let her push me away forever. If there is any woman who can make me want what I had with my wife again, it's your sister."

Thomas gave him a short nod. "Good." He inclined his head toward the parking lot. "Now that we've got all that out in the open, how about we go unload more stuff? Mom's going to come after us soon if we don't get a move on. I think she brought the ruler that goes with her costume."

Jace laughed. "I'm sure she'd use it too. Okay. Let's go."

As they picked their way across the grass to where Cassie waited with the truck, Jace felt something shift in his mind. That door opened a little wider to let in possibilities he'd shuttered when Allie died. Glancing around the park, he realized this place was starting to feel like home.

Eleven

"Tara, I don't think this is going to work," Jace said, stepping out of the bathroom at her house the next morning. When they got back last night, she handed him a bundle of clothes to wear today, but he was too tired to try them on before he went to bed. He should have. There was no way he could wear these pants all day.

He stepped over the threshold of her bedroom, tugging at the pants, trying to loosen them. They clung to his butt and thighs in ways he didn't know pants could cling.

She paused from fixing her hair into a braid and looked over at him. Mirth sparkled in her eyes, and she rolled her lips inward as she took in his appearance.

"How did you even get into those things?"

"They've got some stretch." He tugged at the crotch. His balls felt like they were being strangled.

She secured her braid and rose from the seat at her vanity. The skirt of her pioneer dress swished as she walked toward him. "You know, I knew you were more muscular than Seb, but I didn't think it was quite this much."

He tugged at the pants again as they rode up his butt once

more as he shifted. "Me neither. I guess I should skip leg day every once in a while."

She glared at him. "Don't you dare."

Fire lit in his eyes. "Maybe I should just suffer and wear these then." He leaned a little closer.

Her eyes landed on his lips for a moment before her cheeks colored and she took a step back, giving a little laugh. "No. I fear what would happen to everything south of your belt if you have to walk around in those things all day. Do you have a pair of khaki-colored jeans you can wear?"

He nodded.

"Wear those." A slight frown marred her face, and she looked at his shoulders and chest. "What about that shirt? It looks a little snug too."

He quit tugging at the pants to swing his arms across his chest a few times. The shirt was a little small, but he wasn't popping any seams. "It's a little tight, but so long as I don't have to button the neck, I should be fine."

"Are you sure? I can call Brady and see if he has an extra, since he's bigger than Seb."

Jace stretched his arms across his body again, then raised them over his head. The shirt pulled, but he could still move. "No, this one's okay. I'll just keep the sleeves unbuttoned and rolled up. It's hot out, anyway."

"Okay." She looked down at his sock-covered feet. "You do have boots, right?"

He nodded. "I need to run next door and grab them. I'll do that when I go get my jeans."

"Sounds like a plan."

"Good. I'm going to go peel these things off." He spun on his heel to go back to the bathroom to change.

"Mmm-hmm."

He glanced back over his shoulder at the distracted note in her voice to find her staring at his ass as he walked away. A smile threatened, but he bit it back and continued to the bathroom. He could have just told her the pants were too tight, but he'd wanted to see her reaction. It had been worth every uncomfortable second. She wasn't immune to him, and he wanted to keep it that way.

Beads of sweat dripped down Tara's temple as she sliced tomatoes and peppers. She wiped the side of her face on the shoulder of her dress and blew a tendril of hair out of her eyes. She loved Pioneer Days, but she hated the outfit. The long, heavy skirt restricted airflow, and the tight bodice over the bustier kept the heat trapped against her torso. What she wouldn't give for shorts and a tank top right now.

Maggie walked up next to her, an empty tray in her hands, looking equally hot and miserable. "Remind me again why we do this every year?" She fanned herself with the tray.

"Because it's fun?" Tara quipped, scooping the tomato slices into a bowl.

Maggie gave her a droll look.

"Oh, come on. When else do you get to pretend you're a woman of the eighteen-sixties? Or see all the men in town dressed in chaps?"

The younger woman giggled. "I guess there is that." She nudged her sister. "I saw Jace when I took my break earlier. He looked mighty-fine in those chaps."

Tara's cheeks reddened as she thought about how good he'd looked in the too-tight pants that morning. His ass was perfection. "I haven't seen him since he left this morning. He hadn't donned the chaps yet." She cleaned off her knife and stowed it back in its sleeve, then reached for the plastic wrap.

"Hmm." Maggie cast a look at her askance. "The lunch

rush is done. You should go walk around a bit. See if a certain chief deputy is still wandering the festival."

"I'm fine. There's other stuff I need to do now that it's slow." She tore off a piece of the wrap and covered the bowl. "Besides, I shouldn't be walking around by myself." She wouldn't mind a break, but wasn't about to go get lost in the crowd where Doug could come from anywhere and get to her.

Maggie frowned. "I hadn't thought of that."

Tara pushed away from the table with the bowl and walked over to one of the refrigerators they'd set up for the food. They might look like they lived in the eighteen hundreds, but the food preparation was definitely twenty-first century. She put the tomatoes in the fridge and turned back to her sister.

"You're welcome to take a break again. I could use one of Macy's iced lattes."

Before Maggie could answer, the flap at the back of the kitchen area lifted and Jace walked in. Tara's breath caught. Maggie hadn't been kidding. Those chaps did something for his legs that even those tight pants hadn't been able to do. It showed off the thickness of his thighs and framed his very masculine hips. Sweat beaded at her hairline again, but it had nothing to do with the heat in the tent.

"I heard something about coffee."

He tipped his hat back with one finger in deference to the dimmer interior of the tent, and a lock of his blonde hair fell forward over his forehead. Tara's fingers itched to smooth it back. She clenched her hands to keep them at her sides.

"Tara said she's ready for a break," Maggie quickly chimed in. She gave Tara a sly smile and continued. "We were just talking about her walking around a bit, but she doesn't want to go by herself because of everything that's been going on. But you're here now, so it's perfect. You can take her."

Tara glared at her little sister. Oh, she was *so* going to pay for this.

She looked at Jace. "It's okay. Maggie can go fetch me a latte. I have things to do, anyway."

"Which can all wait," Maggie said. "You haven't been out of this tent all day. Go wander around." She made a shooing motion with her hands.

Jace grinned. "Maggie's right. You need to take a break." He took her hand and tugged her toward the exit. "Come on. I could use some coffee too. And you need to see Macy's outfit. It's a sight to behold."

Despite herself, Tara chuckled. "I bet it is." Macy had a flair for the dramatic. Knowing her, she'd turned her café into a saloon and was dressed like a saloon girl.

He pulled her out into the bright sunshine and the bustle of the festival. She smiled at all the activity. Children ran around, balloons tied to their wrists. Some of them wore fur hats and carried bow and arrows. Others had feed sack dolls clutched in their hands and sticky faces. Adults snacked on kettle corn out of paper bags and carried shopping bags as they perused the tents.

"I've never seen such a popular festival that doesn't have the traditional carnival games and rides. Not to mention the festival food."

"Yeah. The city council does a lot to market it as 'authentic.' We still have some modern conveniences, but we try to stick to the time period. This community has quite the history and is proud of it. It's a great way to honor it."

"Agreed."

She tugged against his hand, but he threaded his fingers through hers and held on. Not wanting to make a scene—and who was she kidding? It felt nice—she let him lead her through the throng to the main thoroughfare.

Not in any hurry, they meandered amongst the tents, stopping here and there to look closer. Tara's favorites were the demonstration tents. It was fun to watch the blacksmith craft a knife with a coal forge or see a stone carver make beautiful sculptures with just a chisel and a hammer.

In the leather worker's tent, Jace stopped to look at some hand-tooled belts, while Tara admired the bracelets the man had for sale. She loved leather jewelry.

Jace walked up behind her, a belt in his hand. He reached out to touch one of the bracelets. "Those are neat." He pointed at the board above the display. "You can get whatever you want on it." His eyes met hers. "You should get one with Lucy's name on it."

She dropped the bracelet she'd been looking at back onto the table. "And what do I say when one of my siblings asks me who Lucy is?"

"The truth."

She rolled her eyes. "That would go over well. 'She's my daughter, Thomas. The one I lost and decided not to tell you about, even though I was living at the ranch when I—'" She broke off and covered her mouth with the back of her hand as emotion clogged her throat and made tears well in her eyes.

Jace ran a hand down her arm. "Hey. I'm sorry. I didn't mean to upset you. I just think you need to bring her out into your life. She's part of it whether you hide her in the shadows or not, and if you ever want to move on in mourning her, you need to talk about her."

He reached around her and picked up two of the cuffs, one large and one smaller. "Tell you what. If you get one with Lucy's name, I'll get one with Haley's."

She looked up at him through her lashes, obstinance in her eyes. "How is that fair? You're not afraid to say her name."

"That's my point. You shouldn't be either."

Tara's mouth turned down in a frown as she weighed his words. Could she really tell everyone about her daughter after all this time? Would they understand and not hate her for keeping such an enormous secret?

She didn't know the answer to that, but she knew she was tired of hiding that precious life. Sean wouldn't have wanted her to keep their baby a secret.

"Okay, fine," she relented.

His smile was bright. "Good." He got the leather worker's attention and told him what they wanted.

The man took the cuffs and got to work, stamping their daughters' names in the leather. Each strike of the stamp to spell Lucy's name on the cuff cracked open the box in Tara's chest just a little further. Each strike made it just a little bit easier to breathe.

When the cuffs were done, Jace paid for them and his belt. He held up Tara's cuff with an expectant look. "Wrist, please."

She held up her left arm, and he snapped the dark brown leather around her wrist. Emotions in a blender, she fingered the engraved name, picturing her daughter's tiny face and her perfect little hands.

Sniffing hard, she looked up at Jace. He'd put on his own cuff and now stared down at her, tenderness and understanding shining from his deep blue eyes.

"Thank you," she whispered around the lump in her throat.

He brought a hand up and brushed away the tear on her cheek with his thumb. "You're welcome. Let's go get that latte now, shall we?"

She nodded, smiling through the tears. She sniffed again and took a deep breath, settling her emotions. "Please."

He offered her his hand again, and she took it without hesitation.

Back out in the sunshine, Tara lifted her face to its warmth and smiled. That box cracked open a little more.

Already close to Peppy Brewster, they soon reached the

café's door. Jace pulled it opened and Tara stepped inside. When her eyes adjusted to the darker interior, and she spotted her friend behind the counter, she couldn't stop the laugh that burst free.

Macy grinned at her and picked up a hand fan sitting next to the register and fluttered it near her face.

Tara laughed harder.

"I'd sing too, but no one wants to hear me do that," Macy said, stepping out from behind the counter to show off her full outfit.

She was indeed dressed as a saloon girl, but not just any saloon girl. She was a performer. Her dress was a rich green, contrasting beautifully with her auburn hair, which was curled and piled on top of her head and tied with a green velvet bow. A few tendrils hung loose around her face. Peacock feathers bobbed above her head with every move she made. The gown's bodice dipped low in front, almost indecently so. Black and gold laces crisscrossed the front, holding it together. The green taffeta skirt was ruched on either side of her hips, baring her legs to just above her knees in front and hanging low in the back. Dark stockings encased her long legs and black, lace-up boots completed her outfit.

"You look incredible. Where did you find that dress?"

"A costume shop in Denver. It was longer and more modest when I bought it. Rayna helped me alter it." She spun around, teetering on her high heels. "Isn't it great?"

Tara nodded. "It is. Please tell me you're wearing that to the dance tonight."

Macy's grin was wicked. "Of course I am. It'd be a waste, otherwise." She motioned to Tara's much more plain and modest lavender shirtwaist dress. "You've got something better than that to wear, right?" She waggled her eyebrows and grinned, her eyes flickering to Jace. "Something that shows off that bustier I know you're wearing under that boring dress?"

Tara's cheeks heated, and she glanced at Jace from the corner of her eye. His expression told her he was trying to imagine what her bustier looked like, and her blush deepened.

"I do have a party dress, yes," she told Macy.

"Can I come help you dress?" Macy's smile turned sly. "I'll bring my sewing kit to make sure you look your best."

Tara laughed, but shook a finger at her friend. "Oh, no. You can pull that off." She swirled her finger at Macy's gown. "But I'd just come off looking like a kid playing dress-up. I'd be messing with the bodice all night and praying nothing popped out when I bent over."

Jace coughed.

She looked over at him to see his cheeks were red.

He patted his chest and cleared his throat. "Sorry. Had a little tickle."

Macy laughed. "I'll just bet you did."

"Macy!"

"Oh, come on, Tara. It isn't like he hasn't already been imagining what you have under that dress." She turned and sauntered back behind the counter. Her dress swished as she walked and her heels clacked on the floor.

Tara shook her head. Macy should have been an actress.

"So, I'm guessing you want an iced latte." Macy leaned on the counter. "Or did you just come here to admire my outfit?" She patted her hair and grinned.

"Iced latte, madam." Tara curtsied. "If you please?"

"I do. What about you, Mr. Copper?"

Jace chuckled. "Just a black coffee."

Macy grimaced. "I should have been able to guess that."

She pulled a cup from the stack on the counter and filled it with the dark brew, then handed it to him. He walked to the sidebar where Macy kept lids and creamer to get a lid and a paper sleeve. Tara closed the distance to the counter and leaned on her elbows.

"Been busy?"

Macy nodded. "Very. It doesn't help that I have to keep stopping so people can take pictures."

Tara smiled. "You're the one who wore that. And you did a great job decorating this place." She looked around at the dining area. Macy had covered all the tables with indigo table cloths and replaced all her metal chairs with wooden ones. Wanted posters hung on the front of the counter and on the walls, along with some stuffed animal heads. She'd even lined up drinking glasses and empty liquor bottles on the display case.

"Where did you find all the chairs?"

"Some of them are my dining chairs. I took Declan's too. Rayna loaned me some they had out at the farm in storage. Brady brought me two from his place as well." She poured milk over ice in a plastic cup as espresso dripped into a stainless-steel pitcher.

Tara shook her head. "When did he find time to do that? He helped me all day yesterday on top of his ranch chores."

Macy dumped the coffee over the milk and put a lid on the cup. "It was pretty late when he brought them over." She handed Tara the cup. "Speaking of, have you seen him today? I thought he'd stop in—I offered him all the coffee he could drink today for bringing me those last chairs and some of the antlers—but he hasn't been in yet."

"No." She looked at Jace, who'd returned to her side. "Have you seen Brady today?"

He took a sip of his coffee and nodded. "I ran into him when I left the ranch this morning. He said he'd be in town later. There were things he needed to do first. He had Thomas with him, so they're probably doing some kind of vet check on the herd."

"Well, if you see him, make sure you send him my way. He

needs to see this." Macy primped her hair and adjusted her bodice.

Her brother didn't know it, but he was doomed. After everything that happened with London, Macy decided life was too short to pussy-foot around and set her sights on Brady. She'd had a crush on him for years, but he always treated her like one of his sisters. Tara doubted he'd think of her that way again after seeing her in that dress.

She dug in the pocket of her dress and pulled out a ten-dollar bill, handing it to her friend. "If he comes by, I'll make sure to tell him to stop in. Try not to give him a stroke, though, okay? We kind of need him around the ranch."

Macy laughed. "I make no promises."

"Poor Brady," Jace muttered.

Tara laughed. "He'll be fine. Come on. I should get back." She turned to Macy. "Thanks for the coffee."

"Yep. See you tonight."

Tara and Jace left the café and merged back into the throng of festival-goers. She sipped on her drink as they headed back toward the park at a much more brisk pace than when they'd left.

"So, when did that start between Macy and Brady?" Jace asked.

"It hasn't, really. Not yet, anyway. He's got no clue, but he's about to find out."

"He doesn't stand a chance, does he? She's a force to be reckoned with."

She giggled. "That's for sure. She's always liked him. But he got married to a hag a month after he graduated college. Peyton had him so bamboozled. She liked his money and turned on the charm. Somehow, she convinced him they should get married, even though we all warned him her designer boots and fancy purses meant she was a city girl." She shook her head. "It didn't last long. Once she got a taste of what it really meant to be the wife of a successful rancher, she balked. Started demanding he take her into Denver every weekend or to Aspen. When he was too busy, she went by herself."

"So, did they just decide it wasn't working and ended things?"

She shook her head. "No. She cheated on him. She'd jetted off to go skiing and came back Christmas Eve. It was their first Christmas together as husband and wife. I was upstairs getting ready for dinner when she got back, and she didn't know it. I heard her talking on the phone to her lover while she changed clothes. She told him she'd be back as soon as she could, and I quote, 'get out of this hellhole.'"

"Geez."

"Yeah."

"I take it you told Brady?"

She gave him a rueful smile. "Not exactly. I marched into the bedroom and told her I'd help her pack."

He laughed.

"She hung up real quick, then tried to tell me I heard it all wrong—that she was talking to one of her girlfriends. But you don't tell your *girl friend* you'll wear the Mrs. Claus costume and bring whipped cream for her to eat off your boobs unless she's your *girlfriend*, and Peyton most definitely didn't swing that way."

Jace choked on his coffee.

"Brady heard us arguing and came in to find out what was going on. It all kind of blew up then. He got her to confess, then kicked her out. She ran back to Aspen to her boy-toy."

"Wow. Good riddance."

"Yep. The best part was she tried to claim a piece of the ranch in the divorce. She thought he owned part of it, but it's in Mom and Dad's names. They put money into trusts for us, but we didn't get rights to the money until we turned thirty.

We were granted an allowance from it, which paid for housing and school. Brady was only twenty-four when they divorced, and because it wasn't legally his yet, she didn't get a penny."

"I bet that ticked her off."

She took another sip of her latte. "Big time. She appealed the ruling, but the trust is iron clad. She tried to smear Brady's name when she couldn't get what she wanted. I think Dad paid her off, because she just suddenly stopped. Brady's been pretty gun-shy about relationships since then."

"But he knows Macy. She wouldn't ever try something like that."

"Yeah, but she's wild and Brady's—well, Brady. He's quiet and introverted. He'd rather sit at home with a book than go to a party. Macy *is* the party."

They left the sidewalk and stepped into the grass, headed for the food tent.

"She'd be a better match for Thomas, but that will never happen."

"Rayna?"

She looked up at him, surprised. "How did you know?"

He shrugged. "I'm a detective, remember? I watch people. There's a history there."

"Long and complicated," she agreed.

They reached the tent, and she hesitated. As much as she hadn't wanted to go with him, now she didn't want him to leave. She fiddled with the cuff on her wrist, tracing the letters again.

"Jace—thank you for this." She tapped her bracelet. "It's silly, but I feel—lighter."

"It's not silly." He took her hands in his, rubbing the backs of them with his thumbs as he talked. "You've carried the burden of your grief alone for so long. It really does help to let others carry it too."

Feeling the press of tears again, Tara tamped a lid on her

emotions. She'd done enough crying in the last few days. "Well, I'm grateful you not only listened, but pushed me to share. I'm still terrified about telling the others, but even if they yell and stop talking to me for a while, I'll be okay. I know that now."

One corner of his mouth lifted. "I think you'll be surprised about how they react to your news, so don't be too nervous, okay?"

She nodded. She was glad he seemed so certain, because she sure wasn't. Maybe she could borrow a bit of his confidence.

"I need to get back to work." She tugged at her hands.

Instead of letting go, he pulled, and she landed against his chest with an oomph.

"I'll be back when the food tent closes to pick you up. Don't leave without me."

Her pulse picked up from the feel of his muscular torso under her hands, as well as the gleam in his eyes. She managed to nod, but anything she was going to say floated away into the ether when he leaned down and pressed a soft kiss to her lips.

He pulled away and stared at her for a moment before he took a deep breath and stepped back, letting go of her hands. "I'll see you later." He retreated several paces, then gave her a brief wave and turned, jogging back toward the vendor area.

Tara raised a hand to her lips as she watched him go. They still tingled from his touch. She was so confused. He was not the type of man she wanted, but every time she thought she'd built that wall back up against him, he did something else to take a chink out of it. And he'd just taken out a huge chink.

She twisted the cuff on her wrist and walked into the tent.

TWELVE

J ace let out a low whistle as Tara emerged from the hallway into the living room.

"Wow."

She did a little twirl for him and smiled. "I know it's not all that dramatic like Macy's dress, but I like it."

"No. It's—you look beautiful." His eyes roved over her tall frame in the deep blue, silk damask dress. It was short-sleeved in deference to the heat of summer, but it had a high neck. The bodice molded to her upper body and nipped in at the waist, showing off her generous curves before the dress flared out into a full skirt below a thick white sash. A row of pearl buttons ran up the back, stopping at the curve of her hips.

"How did you get that thing buttoned?" he asked. She'd have to be a contortionist to get to some of those pearls without help.

"It's got a hidden zipper."

Easy access.

Jace gave himself a mental smack. Thoughts like that would not make the evening a smooth one for him.

"You look nice too," she said, coming to a stop in front of him.

He flicked the black western tie at his neck. "I'm just glad Brady had a shirt I could borrow, or I wouldn't look anywhere near as fancy as you."

She smiled. "You stick around here and you'll need to get your own clothes for Pioneer Days."

He nodded. "I plan to."

"Where did you get that vest, though? I don't remember seeing my brothers wear it."

He ran a hand over the black leather. "It's mine. I wear it sometimes when I ride my motorcycle."

Her smile died and Jace couldn't help but wonder what he said to turn her mood.

She cleared her throat and stepped around him toward the door. "Well, I'm glad you look the part. Are you ready to go?"

Still perplexed, but not wanting to push her—he'd done enough of that with the Lucy bracelet earlier—he picked up his hat and followed her out the door to his truck. He helped her inside, making sure her skirts were out of the way of the door, then rounded the truck to get into the driver's seat.

"You know, to make this really authentic, we should all arrive in horse-drawn wagons."

Her frown smoothed out, and she smiled. "We actually did that one year. Dad said never again. None of us could sit without wincing for a few days. Buckboards provide very little in the way of padding or shocks."

He chuckled. "I suppose not."

They rode in silence for most of the drive until he passed London's B&B, The Lilac Inn.

"Have you found out any more about Doug and why he's been spying on me and breaking into my house?"

Jace's mood tanked, and his mouth flattened into a thin line. "No. We've put out a BOLO, but no one's seen him. His prints haven't matched anywhere else, either, but Katie's still running them through various databases. Seb made some calls too, to try to find out more about Sean's service record. I don't know if he'll get much, but it's worth a shot."

She nodded and stared out the window, brow furrowed.

He reached over and took her hand, noting she'd left on her bracelet. "We'll figure this out. And I'm not going anywhere until we do."

She looked at him. "I know. I'm just wondering how anything Sean did could lead to this. He was a good man. I just don't know what would be worth all this trouble."

He gave her fingers a squeeze. "Hopefully, Seb's inquiries will yield something. The break-in with you home adds some urgency to his request, but if the records are classified, we won't get much."

"No, the military is very tight-lipped about its missions. The best you can hope for is someone who is sympathetic and offers a kernel of something, but you won't get full reports or even summaries. I only got the redacted version of his last mission because his unit made a stink about it."

"Did you get anything from that file we found?"

Her brow furrowed. "Maybe. Something feels off about some of the missions."

He returned her frown. "How so?"

She shrugged. "It's hard to explain. Sean didn't give me details of his ops, but every once in a while he'd come back angry."

"About what?"

"Something one of his teammates did. I got the feeling they didn't always get along. But none of the mission details in the file reflect that. They were all sunshine and rainbows."

"So, you think there was strife between Sean and the other members of his team?"

"Maybe. Or just between other members, and it bothered

him. I'm not sure. He wouldn't ever talk about it. Any time I asked about why he was angry, he'd just say it was team dynamics, then do his best to push his anger aside so it didn't ruin the time we got to spend together."

Jace made a mental note to ask Seb to check out the other members of Sean's team. Maybe this wasn't about a mission, but about one of them.

"Did anything else about the file stick out?"

She shook her head. "Nope. Just that."

"Okay." He sighed, a little disappointed it hadn't yielded more. "Well, if anything else comes to mind, let me know."

She nodded and blew out a breath. "I will."

They cruised into town, and Jace headed for a parking lot near the park. He pulled into a space amidst all the other trucks and SUVs.

"Stay there. I'll come help you down," he said, turning off the vehicle.

He climbed out and went around to Tara's side. She'd opened the door and swung her legs out, so he grasped her waist and lifted her down. Her feet hit the ground, but he didn't let go. She was only inches away, and she smelled amazing. Like the sweetest and juiciest fruits of summer.

When she looked up, a similar thread of desire hummed in her eyes. Need made Jace sway closer and lean down. Their mouths brushed, but the sound of someone calling Tara's name made her jerk away.

He bit back the growl and turned to face the person who interrupted them. Rayna walked toward them in a royal purple dress, which made her violet eyes pop. Her raven hair was swirled into a bun on top of her head. A man in a dark brown vest, blue shirt, and dark jeans walked next to her.

"Nice outfits," she said when she reached them. "I love that dress. Did you two color-coordinate?" she asked, motioning to the dark blue shirt Jace borrowed from Brady.

"No, it just worked out that way," Tara said. She looked at the man. "Who's your friend?"

Jace wanted to know that too. Nearly as tall as himself, the newcomer had a hard edge to him. Scars marred the man's neck and face, and there was something about the way the stranger carried himself that set off Jace's radar.

"This is Derrick Thorpe." Rayna looked up at the man. "Derrick, this is my friend, Tara Miller, and our newest sheriff's deputy, Jace Travers."

The other man raised a hand in a wave and smiled. Only one side of his mouth moved. "Hello. It's nice to meet you both. Rayna's told me a lot about you, Tara."

Tara frowned, a perplexed look on her face. "Really? She's told me nothing about you." She pierced Rayna with a look.

The other woman had the good grace to look chagrined. "Sorry. We've been dating a couple months."

Tara raised a brow, but didn't ask any other questions. Jace could see them swirling in her eyes, though.

"You and I need to talk later," Tara said.

Rayna grinned, her eyes landing on Jace. "Yes, we do."

Tara's cheeks reddened.

Jace took her hand and tugged her toward the festival. He had questions too, but the parking lot was not the place for them. "Come on. We're missing the party."

She fell into step beside him, and he looped her arm through his. The other couple followed behind them.

"Thomas is going to freak," she whispered as they walked.

He agreed. "You really had no idea she was dating anyone?"

"No. She never mentioned him. I can't believe she brought him without warning us first. I could have at least prepared Thomas."

"Maybe that's the idea. Catching him off-guard."

She frowned up at him. "Why would she do that, though?

She and Thomas haven't been a thing for years. And she's dated other men since then."

"Has she ever brought one to an event like this where he would see them together?"

She thought for a moment. "No, I don't think so. But that doesn't explain why she wouldn't tell me, Macy, and London."

"I'm sure she has her reasons. You can grill her about them later. Right now, though, you're going to need to run interference." They'd reached the area of the park converted to a dance floor. He tipped his head to the far side where Thomas stood, talking with Brady and Seb.

"Dammit." Tara stared across the dance floor at her brothers. Why did he have to be right there? She needed a distraction. Just long enough so someone could prepare Thomas for Rayna's new beau.

She glanced at the couple who stood beside them. Rayna pointed out people to her date, an animated smile on her face. Tara's heart sank. It was going to kill Thomas to see her looking so happy with another man.

"If I entertain Rayna and Derrick for a few minutes, can you go over and break the news to Thomas?" she asked through a smile.

"Me?" he whispered, shocked. "Why can't you do it and I'll keep them occupied? He's your twin."

"And what will you do to keep them away? Virtually all the people you know are over there with him."

He huffed. "Fine."

She didn't wait for him to change his mind. Stepping away, she turned to her friend. "Hey, Rayna?"

Rayna stopped talking to Derrick and looked at Tara.

"How about we go find Macy and London? They're probably over at the refreshment table helping Mom. I think they'd love to meet your boyfriend."

"Oh, sure. That'd be great."

Tara smiled and turned, giving Jace's bicep a squeeze on her way past. She heard his sigh as she walked away, but tried not to glance back as he made his way over to her brothers.

Instead, she focused on the quiet man at Rayna's side.

"So, Derrick. Tell me about yourself since Rayna's been so secretive. Where are you from?"

"Montana originally. I live in Pueblo now."

"Oh? What do you do there?"

"I'm a contractor."

"He's building the new veteran's home there," Rayna said. She smiled up at him.

"That's nice. So, how did you two meet?"

"The farm market. He likes my tomatoes."

A ghost of a smile formed on the man's otherwise stoic face. A feeling of familiarity hit Tara. She felt like she'd seen him before, but couldn't place him.

"Highlight of my week when she comes to town."

Tara smiled. "She has that effect on people. Is this your first time to our city?"

He nodded. "It's quite the introduction." He motioned to the festivities around them.

"You came at a good time. Although, the next time you're in town, it will probably be rather boring."

They reached the refreshment tables, and Tara spotted London pouring punch into cups. Macy stood near the large coffee urns, checking that they were full.

London looked up and spotted her. She smiled and waved before her eyes went wide as she noticed the man next to Rayna.

Tara led them over to her and introduced the two.

London turned her surprised gaze on Rayna, then

narrowed her eyes at her friend. "Not cool keeping secrets." She looked up at Derrick, and her expression softened. "It's nice to meet you, though. I hope you know what you're getting into."

Tara did too. She hoped Thomas kept his cool. It was his own fault, though. If he wasn't such an idiot, he wouldn't have to put up with her dating other men.

Derrick frowned at London's comment, but before he could ask what she meant, Macy walked up. Tara saw his eyes widen as he took in the other woman's appearance. Macy had added some dramatic makeup and an emerald pendant that nestled in her cleavage, giving her maximum shock value.

Rayna laughed. "That dress turned out amazing! You look stunning."

Macy grinned. "Thanks. Now, who's the hunk you brought and why are we just now finding out he exists?" She stepped closer to him and held out a hand. "I'm Macy Briggs. It's nice to meet you."

He swallowed hard and took her hand. "Derrick Thorpe."

"Hmm." She arched a brow, then looked back at Rayna. "Explain."

Tara, too, looked at her expectantly. She wanted to know why Rayna kept the man a secret as well.

The band struck up their first chords, and Rayna seized the interruption. She grabbed Derrick's arm and pulled him toward the dance floor.

"We'll talk later. I want to dance."

Tara turned to stand next to her friends and watched the couple walk away. She studied Derrick, still getting the sense she'd met him. It was something about the way he carried himself. She didn't know where she'd seen him before, though. Those scars weren't something she would forget. They obscured his features to a great degree.

"Where did he come from?" Macy asked, interrupting her thoughts.

"No idea," Tara said. "She really didn't say anything to either of you?"

Both women shook their heads.

"We need to get her alone later," London said. "Pick her brain and find out why."

"Agreed," Macy said.

Tara looked at the two of them. "I'm going to go find Jace. I sent him to break the news to Thomas."

Both women winced.

"I don't know who I pity more," Macy said.

London shooed her away. "Go rescue your man. I'm sure Thomas is probably grilling him about Rayna's date. He doesn't have any more answers than we do."

Tara ignored the comment about Jace being hers. It wouldn't do her any good to argue. Her friends would think whatever they wanted.

She backed toward the dance floor. "Let me know when you want to corner her, and we'll get some answers."

They nodded, and Tara turned, skirting the edge of the floor now filled with dancers to where she'd seen her brothers. The men were easy to spot. All of them were well over six feet, and they towered over the people around them.

Even yards away, she could see the thunderclouds on Thomas' face. His brown eyes had blackened, and a deep frown marred his brow. Tension radiated from him, his shoulders stiff and back straight.

She twisted the cuff on her wrist as she tried to think of what to say to him. Blast Rayna, anyway. Why did she have to spring this on them all?

Jace saw her first. Relief crossed his face, and he stepped toward her, extending a hand. She took it, but instead of drawing her toward her brothers, he pushed her back toward the dance floor.

"There you are. Let's dance."

"What?" She tried to peer around him, but he spun her around, herding her away. "Jace?"

"Just keep walking," he muttered.

She frowned at him over her shoulder. "I need to talk to Thomas."

He shook his head. "No, you don't. I told him about Derrick. There's nothing you can say that will help. He's an adult. Let him figure things out on his own."

"But—"

He spun her into his arms and pulled her flush against his taller frame. "No buts. Thomas is a big boy."

She cast a worried glance toward her brothers as Jace whirled her around. Thomas had his arms crossed, and he glared in the direction she'd come from. Brady and Seb, who stood with him, both frowned, but their gazes were on Thomas, not Rayna.

"This is such a mess."

"Yep. But it's Thomas' mess."

Tara groaned and let her head rest against Jace's chest for a moment. "He's such an idiot."

His low chuckle rumbled through her. "Consider his angst payback for all the times he's teased you. I'm sure there were plenty."

She laughed and looked up. "Maybe a few."

He smiled. "Forget about him and Rayna for now. Let's just enjoy the dance."

Could she do that? Would it be such a bad thing to stop worrying about not only Thomas, but what was happening in her own life for a few hours?

The answer to that was easy. She let herself melt into Jace's strong body. "Okay."

His arm tightened around her, bringing her closer, and she got lost in his eyes as they spun around the dance floor to the music. Tara let go of the stress and her hang-ups about starting a relationship with him and just enjoyed the music and the company of a nice man. For the first time in a long time, she forgot about her past and the heartache that was her constant companion. She felt like herself again.

They circled the dance floor several times to the rhythm of the music, lost in their own world, until thirst made them stop. At the end of their fourth song, Jace led her to the refreshment table, where she gulped down a glass of punch.

Jace drank his own, then grabbed a second one. "It's too hot for this. Especially in these clothes."

She agreed, fanning herself with her hand. Sweat slicked her legs and trickled between her breasts under her bodice. The sun had just set, so the heat of the day had yet to ebb. What she wouldn't give for some air conditioning right now. Instead, she picked up another glass of punch. At least there was ice in it.

"Tara!"

She turned around to see Macy motioning her over from the edge of the dance floor. She had London with her. They pointed to their right, and Tara saw Rayna standing by herself, messing with her phone.

"I think now's our chance to find out more about Rayna's mystery man," she said, looking up at Jace. "Do you mind?"

He shook his head. "No. Go ahead. I'll go see if Thomas has calmed down any."

"Okay." She gave his arm a gentle squeeze, then hurried over to her friends.

"You two sure look cozy," Macy said when she reached them.

Tara waved a hand. "We're not talking about me and my love life. Let's go find out about Rayna's."

Macy frowned, but let it drop. "Fine." She spun on her heel and stalked toward their friend.

London and Tara shared a look and a smile, but followed her.

"Hey, girl," Macy said, as they got closer to Rayna.

The other woman looked up from her phone and smiled. "Hey."

"Where's Derrick?" London asked.

"He got a phone call he needed to take, so he went back to his truck, where it's quieter."

"Everything okay?" Tara asked.

Rayna shrugged. "He said it was about one of his buildings. They've been having problems keeping the site secure." She sighed. "I hope he doesn't have to leave. I've been looking forward to tonight for a while. It's the first time I've managed to get him to agree to meet you guys."

Tara frowned at that.

"Why wouldn't he want to meet us?" Macy asked, echoing Tara's thoughts.

"He's a little shy. You saw the scars on his face. They make him a little self-conscious. I told him you—like me—wouldn't care, but it still took a lot of sweet-talking for me to convince him to come."

"Is that why you've never mentioned him?" London asked.

"Sort of," Rayna hedged. "I wasn't sure things would go anywhere between us at first. It took a few dates before he really relaxed. Then, I didn't want to say anything until I could get him to meet you, because I knew you'd keep asking when you could. He wouldn't even let me take a picture to prove he was real."

"I guess I get that," Tara said. "If he's that self-conscious about his scars, he wouldn't want any photographs."

Rayna nodded. "So, that's why I sprang him on you. I'm

sorry I didn't mention him sooner. I just wasn't sure he'd show up tonight."

"Why are you dating him if he's so timid?" London asked. "That's not really your type."

"I know, but he's super sweet and nice when we're alone. He's funny and smart and kind. He just hates crowds." She gave the three of them pleading looks. "Am I forgiven?"

Tara, Macy, and London looked at each other, weighing what they'd been told, before looking back at her and nodding in unison.

"Good," Rayna said with a smile. She looked at Tara. "If we're done talking about my new man, let's talk about Tara's."

Tara groaned. "Let's not."

"Oh, let's," Macy said, grinning. "Things looked pretty intense out there on the dance floor. I don't think either of you noticed anyone else for a while."

She knew her cheeks were red, but she clamped her lips together and shrugged.

"Did you kiss him yet?" Rayna asked. "He looks like he'd be a good kisser."

Tara couldn't help but laugh. "Oh my God, you guys sound like high schoolers."

"Guys, she wants us to act like adults," Macy said. With a rather naughty grin, she looked at Tara. "Have you ripped his clothes off and come just looking at that chiseled body of his?"

Rayna and London giggled.

"Is that better?" Macy asked. "Is that adult enough for you?"

Tara covered her face—mostly to hide the grin wanting to break free. She should have known Macy would flip the script on her. "You're terrible," she said and dropped her hands.

Macy laughed. "It's why you love me. Now, answer the question."

The looks the others gave her told her there was no chance

she was getting away without answering short of a disaster drawing their attention.

She huffed and rolled her eyes. "I've seen him without a shirt."

Their eyes widened, and she rushed to cut them off.

"Because I needed his help when I thought someone had been in my house. He answered the door in just pajama bottoms."

Macy whistled. "Damn. I wish I'd been there. He's drool-worthy when he's fully clothed. What about the kissing part?"

Tara's cheeks turned red. She'd hoped to avoid that part of the question. "There have been a couple."

When she didn't elaborate, London cocked an eyebrow and rolled her hand. "And? How was it?"

"It was nice."

"Nice?" Rayna said. "That's all you've got?"

"What do you want me to say? He rocked my world, and now I'm ruined for any other man?"

They laughed.

"That's a start, yes," Rayna replied.

Tara moaned. "It was good. Really good. That's all you're going to get."

Macy opened her mouth to say more, but got distracted by Brady, who strolled past on his way to the punch bowl.

"Did you talk to him yet?" Tara asked.

Macy shook her head, still staring at him. "No. I was helping your mother, then mingled a bit with Declan and the mayor before we came over here."

London chuckled. "I bet the mayor loved your dress." Sarcasm dripped off her words.

Macy looked away from Brady to toss a saucy smile at London. "It was fun to watch him squirm when he had to introduce me to people. Teasing him makes my day. It's why I made sure to tag along with Deck when he said hello to the man."

"You need to run for the city council seat that'll be up for grabs in November," Rayna said. "Shake things up a bit."

"I'm not sure I could work with those fools after the way they treated Declan last month. They were ready to tar and feather him before the ink was even dry on the search warrant."

"They weren't the only ones who wanted to convict him with little evidence," London said. "Seb was ready to throttle the D.A. I really hope Maggie takes over his job one day."

So did Tara. Her little sister had high aspirations, but she was just starting her law career. She still had a long road before she'd be filling Daniel Kerr's shoes.

Brady turned just then and saw them. Tara waved and motioned him over.

"What are you doing?" Macy hissed.

She frowned at her friend. "I thought you wanted to talk to him? Show off your costume?"

"I do, but I was waiting until I figured out what I was going to say. I didn't want to come off looking like some floozy propositioning him."

"Too late," Rayna murmured. "Here he comes. You better think fast."

"You suck, Tara," Macy muttered.

Tara giggled. "Maybe this will teach you not to give me the third degree about Jace."

Macy rolled her eyes. "Not likely."

"At least you're honest."

"I can also honestly tell you, you're going to pay for this," she said before plastering a smile on her face as Brady reached them.

"Ladies. You all look very fetching." He looked at each of

them, but his eyes lingered on Macy and her audacious ensemble.

"Fetching?" Tara said. "Are you taking vocabulary lessons from Thomas?"

He glared at her. "I'm trying to be 'in character,'" he said, air quoting.

"Well, if you really want to do that, you should dance with Macy."

"Why?"

"What?" Macy spoke over Brady.

Tara held back the smile at her friend's expression, which promised severe retribution.

"She's the only one of us without a dance partner. A lady shouldn't have to suffer on the sidelines, watching everyone else dance just because she came alone."

"She's hardly dressed as a lady," Brady said. His eyes widened as he realized what he said. Redness crept up his neck, and he offered Macy a chagrined look. "No offense."

His comment seemed to be all Macy needed to break through her mental barrier. Her saucy grin reappeared. "At least I'm not a stick in the mud. Couldn't you have added a little color to that outfit? They had that in the eighteen-sixties, you know." She gestured to his clothes, which were varying shades of brown from head to toe.

A frown creased his forehead. "I'm sorry. I don't need to be the center of attention everywhere I go."

Macy put her balled fists on her hips. "Neither do I, but I do like to have fun, and this dress is fun. You should try it sometime."

"I do have fun. I just don't draw attention to myself to do it."

"Prove it."

"Excuse me?"

"You heard me. Prove it. Show me you know how to have

fun." Before he could reply, she took hold of his hand and pulled him toward the dance floor.

Tara chuckled and watched as her brother protested all the way to the floor, to no avail. When Macy wanted something, she was like a steamroller.

"Twenty bucks says we find them making out later," Rayna quipped.

London and Tara both laughed.

"I'm not taking that bet," London said.

"Me either."

Tara's phone came to life in her little drawstring-style purse, blasting out the theme to Mission Impossible, the ringtone she'd set for her editor. She groaned and fished it out, silencing it.

"Who was that?" London asked.

"My old editor. He keeps calling and texting me."

"What's he want?" Rayna asked.

"No idea. I refuse to answer or read his messages. I want nothing to do with photojournalism anymore."

"Why haven't you just blocked his number, then?" London said.

Tara shrugged. She almost had, but something kept her from pushing the button.

"I don't know. Professional courtesy, maybe." She put her phone away.

London raised a brow and shared a look with Rayna, but let the subject drop. "I'm going to find Seb and join them on the dance floor. He promised me dancing, and so far, all he's done is brood over Thomas and his bad attitude."

Rayna winced. "I'm sorry."

"You have nothing to be sorry for," Tara said. "If he wasn't such an idiot, he'd have no reason to brood. You are perfectly entitled to bring whoever you want to whatever you want. It's not like you two broke up recently. It's been years. He needs to either get over it or grovel at your feet and convince you to take him back."

Rayna giggled. "Watching Thomas grovel might be kind of funny. But it would be pointless. I've moved on. What we had was great, but we've both grown up and changed. I don't think we'd be a good fit anymore."

Tara just hummed a non-answer. She had her own opinions about Thomas and Rayna, but Jace was right. It wasn't her business. They were both adults who were fully capable of sorting out their own issues.

"I second the dancing thing," she said instead. "I've cooled down and gotten my second wind. Let's go find our dance partners, shall we?" She offered her arms to her friends.

Grinning, both women looped their hands around her elbows and the three of them set off together.

Thirteen

F eet aching, Tara sank into the cushy seats of Jace's truck. She couldn't remember the last time she'd danced so much. It had been fun, though, even if she was a sweaty mess.

Jace climbed in beside her and buckled up, then started the truck. Cool air blasted out of the vents onto her face.

"Oh, that feels so good." She reached behind her neck and lowered the zipper on her dress just a little to loosen the fabric and let some air in.

Jace whipped off his tie and unbuttoned the top two buttons of his shirt. He'd already removed his leather vest and tossed it in the backseat.

"I wish there was a pool on the ranch," he said, shifting the vehicle into gear and pulling out of the lot. "I'd dive in, clothes and all."

She readjusted one of the vents. "There's a two-track behind the horse pasture that leads to the river."

He groaned. "Don't tempt me."

Tara giggled and settled into her seat, more comfortable now that she'd cooled down some. "It probably wouldn't be the best idea. There's a lot of thistle near the river, and it's hard to see in the dark."

He sighed. "A shower it is."

"And the A/C cranked way up."

"Hell, yeah." He twisted the dials on the dash and more air blew out.

She propped her elbow on the window and leaned her head in her hand, watching the dark scenery go by as Jace drove them home. Fatigue pulled at her mind. It had been a long day.

"I had a good time tonight, thank you," she said quietly.

He glanced at her. Shadows danced over his face, high-lighting his firm jaw. The blonde stubble glinted in the light from the dashboard. She wanted to run her hand over it and feel its roughness.

"I'm glad. I did too."

She smiled at him, then looked out at the darkness again, letting her mind drift. She was nearly asleep when Jace turned into the ranch's long drive. The bump as they transitioned from pavement to stone made her eyes pop open. She yawned and sat up.

"Hey, do you mind if we stop at the restaurant for a minute?" she asked as the building came into view. "I want to make sure the staff has everything prepped for tomorrow."

"Sure."

He turned into Heartwood's parking lot and pulled around back, stopping near the staff entrance. Tara dug the key out of her little purse and opened her door to climb out.

"Stay there. I'll come help you down."

She opened her mouth to tell him that wasn't necessary, but then thought twice as her boot tangled in her skirt as she shifted to slide down. *Damn dress...* She couldn't wait to put on something else.

Jace's boots crunched on the gravel as he came around

the front of the truck. He reached out with those broad hands and wrapped them around her waist, lifting her down.

Once again, she found herself entirely too close to him. The musky smell of man reached her nose and fogged up her brain. Her eyes landed on the skin exposed on his neck by his open collar. Fine blonde hair peeked above the fabric. She wanted to sift her fingers through it and feel the rock-hard muscle beneath.

Her gaze wandered up the sinewy column of his neck, over his defined, stubble-covered jaw, to his deep blue eyes. He stared down at her with an intensity that sent a shiver down her spine.

One hand skated up her back to slide beneath the open neck of her bodice. His fingers tangled in the wispy hair at her nape. Tingles raced across her scalp, and she bit one corner of her mouth to hold back the moan in her throat.

The swiftness of her reaction sent panic hurtling through her. The desire threatened to consume her in ways it hadn't before. Alarmed with how fast he was worming his way past her defenses, she stepped out of his embrace.

"I should go check on things inside. It's late." Not waiting for a response, she walked around him to the back door.

He let out a growl of frustration. Stone crunched beneath his boots as he came toward her.

"Tara—"

She didn't let him finish. She thrust the key in the lock and, with a flick of her wrist, threw the door open and stepped inside. Reaching to her left, she felt for the light switches and flipped them on.

A gasp flew from her as light filled the room. Pots and pans littered the tables and the floor alongside utensils someone pulled from their drawers. The doors to both the walk-in refrigerator and freezer hung open, and she could see containers tipped over, some of them on the floor, their contents spilled all over the corrugated metal.

"What the hell?" Jace stepped in behind her.

Dazed, Tara wandered further into the kitchen. "Why? Why would someone do this?"

He walked up behind her and laid a hand on her arm. "Don't touch anything. We probably shouldn't go any further, either, until a crime scene unit clears the place."

Tears formed in her eyes, a few of them trickling over. She nodded and stepped back the way she'd come. It was probably for the best, anyway. She wasn't sure she could take seeing more.

Jace was already on his phone, calling for backup by the time they reached the door. She sagged against the doorframe, listening as he spoke first to dispatch, then her brother Seb.

"This was Doug, wasn't it?" she said when he hung up.

"Likely, yes."

"Why would he ransack my restaurant? There's nothing here that has anything to do with Sean."

Jace shrugged. "He wouldn't know that. Maybe he figured since he didn't find anything at your house or in any of the other buildings on the ranch, that you hid whatever he's looking for here."

"I didn't hide anything!" She flung her arms wide, then brought them back to cover her face as the tears started to fall in earnest.

He stepped forward and gathered her to his chest. "Hey, it's okay. I know you didn't."

She buried her face in his shirt and wrapped her arms around him. "What does he want?" she whispered.

His hand wrapped around her nape again, but this time it was comforting instead of arousing.

"I don't know, but we'll figure it out."

Tara sniffed and kept her face pressed against him. She

wanted to pretend none of this was happening. She'd had such a nice time tonight. It was a kick to the teeth to have it ruined like this.

"Come on. Let's go sit in the truck and wait on everyone to get here," he said, moving his hand to her shoulder.

She looked up at his words and got caught in his gaze. The sympathetic look on his face morphed into need, and his touch went from comforting to electrifying in a blink. With her emotions in a blender, she couldn't resist the pull this time. When he leaned down to press his lips to hers, she slid her arms around his neck and held on.

Jace knew he should stop—that he shouldn't have kissed her in the first place while she was upset—but his willpower was abysmal around Tara. Once his brain registered the desire in her eyes, his body took over, burning through his brain cells to leave nothing but pure need behind. It flooded his veins and made him cradle the back of her head to hold her in place so he could gain better access to her sweet mouth.

He swept his tongue over the seam of her lips, and she let him inside. The first taste of her honeyed sweetness sent a surge of heat through him, straight to his groin. He cupped her hips through her heavy skirts, pressing her closer as his body demanded release.

She gasped as his hard length came into contact with her belly. "Jace."

Set alight by the breathless moan of his name falling from her lips, he trailed hot kisses over her jaw and down her neck, nudging aside the loosened collar of her dress to find the hollow at the base of her throat. It pounded with every beat of her heart, releasing a heat that carried her intoxicating scent.

He breathed her in and bit down lightly on the soft skin over her collarbone.

A hoarse moan pushed past her lips, and she writhed in his arms. He swept his tongue over the spot, soothing it. The hands around his neck slid into his hair, and she tugged on the strands to pull him back to her mouth.

Their lips met again with more urgency as the desire built. Her hands drifted down his shoulders to his chest. He felt the breeze blow over his heated skin as she popped several buttons through their holes and moaned when her soft hands glided over his bare chest.

It was enough to send his need to another level. Wrapping his arms around her, he lifted her off her feet and walked the short distance to his truck, where he fumbled with the passenger side door handle.

The cab light flared to life as he yanked open the door. Backing into the passenger seat, he pulled her in on top of him. She straddled his thighs, and he reached for the switch to lower the back of the seat, never breaking their kiss.

She tugged on the bottom of his shirt and slid the last of the buttons free of their holes, then pushed the material aside to run her hands the length of his torso. Jace moaned and tore his mouth from hers. He sucked in a breath and buried his nose behind her ear, nipping at the sensitive skin. She rocked against him and raked her nails over his chest.

Jace growled and reached for the zipper on her dress, needing to feel her skin beneath his hands. The tick of the teeth sounded alongside their harsh breathing as he pulled the zipper down, parting the silky fabric. He splayed his hand over her back, eager to feel her bare skin, but his fingertips met the satin of the bustier she wore beneath.

"How do I get this thing off?" he demanded.

She sat back, her dress sliding down her arms, and she pulled her hands free, letting the bodice pool around her waist. A satisfied grin stretched over her face. "It ties at the bottom."

Jace's mouth went dry at the sight of her breasts spilling over the top of the bustier.

"Damn." He leaned forward to kiss the hills of creamy skin.

Her breath shuddered out, and she tunneled her hands back into his hair to hold him there. He found the tie on her bustier and tugged on it, feeling it loosen. Pulling on the laces, he slid them free of their holes, and the satiny garment fell open. He hooked a finger in the front and tore it free of her body.

Mesmerized by the sight of her full breasts, he looked his fill for a moment before reaching out to palm one perfect globe. He leaned forward and sucked the rosy tip of the other one into his mouth, then flicked it with his tongue. She rolled her hips. The friction made him groan.

She did it again, and he raised his head to spear her with a heated look.

"Are you trying to kill me?"

A saucy smile lifted one corner of her mouth. "If I am, we'll go together."

"Yeah? Well, any gentleman will make sure his woman goes first." He lowered his hands to the hem of her skirt and slid them under the heavy fabric. His fingers traced her soft, smooth legs to her thighs and around the curve of her hips to come to rest on her butt.

She closed her eyes and bit her lip, a flush climbing up her chest and over her face. He pressed his mouth to her neck and pushed one hand under the edge of her panties. Her loud moan filled the cab of the truck as he made contact with her wet core.

Stroking her with a gentle touch, he swirled his fingers over her swollen nub several times before dipping one long finger inside. She moaned once more, her fingers digging into his shoulders. Jace latched onto her breast, rolling the tip between his teeth while he continued to stroke and thrust with his hand. He flicked his thumb over that little bud, and she exploded, crying out as her climax ripped through her.

She rocked against his hand as she rode the wave of pleasure until it ebbed. Sated, she sagged against him, breathing hard. Jace withdrew his hand, letting it rest on the outside of her thigh under her skirt. A fierce need made him pulse behind the fly of his jeans, but the passenger seat of his truck was not the place he wanted to take her for the first time.

He willed away the ache in his pants and tried to concentrate on Tara.

"You okay?" he asked.

She sighed and nodded against his chest, then pushed up on her arms to look down at him with molten chocolate eyes. Some of her hair had slipped free of her braid, and a glow only produced by a good orgasm lit her skin in the light of the truck's interior.

A wicked look entered her eyes, and she slid back until she sat on his knees. "Your turn."

Before Jace could react, she snaked a hand out to run over the length of his erection. He ground his teeth together as a surge of pleasure smacked into him.

"Tara, no. I'd rather not have a wet spot on my pants when your brother gets here."

She paused for a moment, her fingers over his belt buckle, then a wide grin split her pretty face. She raised up a bit and fluffed out her skirt so it covered his lap. "Problem solved." Her hands dove under the fabric and made quick work of his belt and fly.

Jace sucked in a sharp breath as her hands burrowed beneath his boxers and made contact with his heated flesh. She freed him from the fabric, and he jerked in the seat as she squeezed. Tendons popped in his neck as his muscles coiled with the tension she created with every stroke.

"Oh, this won't take long," he groaned. His back arched, thrusting his hips up into her hand as he neared the edge. White dots danced in his vision.

She grinned, a satisfied gleam in her eyes, and picked up the pace.

With little warning, his climax hit, tearing a harsh shout from his chest. He sat up to grab what was left of her braid and press a searing kiss to her mouth as he rode the waves of pleasure. As the ripples faded, he pulled back, breathing hard.

He rested his forehead against hers. "I haven't done that in a car in probably fifteen years."

To his delight, she giggled. "Me either."

He savored their embrace for another moment before pulling back to look into her eyes, hoping he wouldn't see any regret. She gave him a soft smile, her expression content.

"We okay?" he asked, his voice low.

She sighed, some of the contentment leaving. "Hell if I know. But that happened and there's no going back."

He stared into her dark eyes. "I don't regret any of it."

She stared back. "I don't either. I may not be sure about us —that it's what's best—but I can't regret what you make me feel."

He looked down at her for another moment before pressing a hard kiss to her mouth, then pulling back. His eyes drifted down to her exposed chest, and he felt himself stir once again. With a groan, he leaned back and reached down to lift the back of the seat. "We should probably get dressed. Seb and the team will be here any time."

An amused smile lit her eyes. "I'm glad they didn't show up in the middle of that. Seb would probably kick your ass and then kick you out of his house." She shifted to climb off his lap, tugging the top of her dress up to cover herself as she got out of the truck.

Jace grinned back at her. "He could try." He fastened his pants and followed her out, handing her a handful of napkins from the glove compartment so she could clean her hands.

He gave her a heated look as he passed them to her. "I think I could find another place to sleep, though." His smile grew as she shivered.

She wasn't giving into him this time, though, and smacked his shoulder, a mock glare on her face. "Hand me my bustier, devil."

He laughed and leaned in to get the garment, trading her for the napkins, which he stuffed in his pocket.

"Um," she started, then broke off in a giggle. "I think you're going to have to help me put this back on." She held it up. It hung open, the tie dangling from only one hole.

He grinned. "I'd rather not."

Tara rolled her eyes, then let the top of her dress fall. Jace's smile vanished. She had the most perfect breasts. Full and soft with rosy tips.

His view was momentary, however, as she wrapped the bustier around herself, then turned to present him with her back.

With a sigh, he picked up the long tie and began threading it through the holes.

"Tell me if this is too tight," he said, tugging on the ends to snug it around her torso.

"It's good," she said as he tied it at the bottom.

Jace watched with unabashed appreciation as she adjusted herself so the bustier fit comfortably over her chest.

She glanced up and saw him staring. "You know, Seb will still know something happened if he pulls up and your shirt's open."

Her words dragged him out of his trance, and he

looked down at himself. A rueful smile spread over his face. "Yeah, I guess so." He started buttoning his shirt while Tara put her arms back in the bodice of her dress and pulled it up.

The sound of an engine coming up the drive reached their ears. They both turned to look toward the road. Two sets of headlights were headed up the driveway.

"Shit!" She spun around and pointed at her back. "Zip me up. Hurry!"

He abandoned the last couple buttons on his shirt and reached for the zipper. His hands slid off the tiny fob on the end as he tried to pull it over the curve of her waist. "Why do they have to make these things so fucking tiny?" He tried again, and it zipped up her spine in one smooth motion as he got a good grip.

Light bounced off the side of the restaurant as the cars grew closer.

"Tara, your hair." It was a mess, thanks to his hands.

Her eyes widened, and she patted her head. Fingers flying, she attacked the band holding it together, yanking it out. "Tuck in your shirt."

He stuffed the tails into his pants as she finger-combed her hair. Jace thanked his lucky stars his truck shielded them from view as they finished putting themselves back together.

"You good?" he asked.

She nodded. "Yeah."

They both stepped around the truck as Seb parked next to them, the CSI van right behind him.

Tara double checked her clothing as she rounded the front of Jace's truck to greet her brother. He was a keen observer and would notice something amiss.

Seb's tall frame emerged from his vehicle. His mouth was a thin line, and a crease sliced his brow. "How bad is it?"

Her mood nose-dived at her brother's simple question. Tears formed in her eyes as she pictured the destruction inside.

He cursed. "That bad, huh?"

She crossed her arms and nodded.

Jace curled a hand over her shoulder in comfort. "He didn't bother to hide his search this time."

The doors on the CSI van slammed shut. Katie walked up to them along with one of the other techs, a young woman named Emma.

"Did you touch anything?" Katie asked.

"Just the door and the light switches," Tara said. "We didn't discover the break-in until we turned the lights on."

"Why didn't your alarm go off?" Seb asked.

"I don't know," Tara said, frowning. It should have, she realized. "I didn't even think to check."

Seb looked at Jace for an answer, and it hit Tara that he should have checked the alarm system. Before she could think of an excuse, he jumped in.

"I haven't looked at it. We turned around and came back outside, then I stayed with her. With the level of escalation, I didn't want to leave her alone."

Seb exhaled a long breath and rubbed his forehead. "Okay. Well, let's go check now." He turned to Katie. "You ready to do your thing?"

She held up her camera and the silver case she carried. "Sure am, boss man."

He tipped his head toward the building. "We'll be right behind you."

With a nod, she and Emma stepped past them and entered the restaurant.

Tara stared after them, her mind already going to all she needed to do to clean the place up.

"You okay?" Seb asked.

She looked away from the door and gave Seb a brief nod. "Yeah. I was really upset. Now, I'm just pissed. This is getting ridiculous."

"Agreed," Jace said. "We need to do a deeper dive on Brown. Have you found out anything more about who he really is?"

"Not yet, no. I asked an analyst I know to look into his records. He said on first glance they're legit, but once he dug deeper, he noticed some inconsistencies. He's trying to peel off the layer of false information, but it's taking time. Whoever created his fake identity is really good."

"Have you had any luck getting more info about Sean's service record?"

Seb scoffed. "It's classified out the wazoo. I got a, 'we'll look into it and call you back.'" He rolled his eyes. "They're not going to call me back."

Jace touched Tara's arm. She looked up at him. "I think we need to sit down and go through your memories. See what names you can remember. Faces. Anything that seemed out of the ordinary. You were a reporter, so I'm betting it's in that mind of yours somewhere."

She nodded. It sounded daunting—and she'd rather not think about those years—but if it helped stop this craziness, she was willing to try. "I might still have some of my old notes, too. When I left San Diego, I just threw all that in a couple boxes. They're in the spare bedroom closet."

"Brown didn't get to them, did he?" Seb asked.

She shrugged. "I don't know. I forgot all about them until now."

"Go home and check while we wait for Katie to give the all-clear."

Urgency propelled her toward Jace's truck. The answer to

what this was all about could be within reach. If Doug hadn't already found it.

She let Jace help her into the seat. He ran around front and climbed in beside her, starting the engine. Her mind whirled as she tried to remember what was in those boxes. She never threw her notes away after she finished a story because she never knew if the next one would be connected or not. She remembered every article she ever wrote, but she'd taken copious notes and wasn't sure she would notice a few pages missing.

The truck came to a halt in her driveway, and Jace was around the vehicle to help her out by the time she had her seatbelt off. She dug in her purse for the key, locating it right away. Inserting it into the lock, she pushed the door open and turned on the light. More chaos greeted her.

"Fuck," Jace's whispered exclamation echoed her thoughts.

This time, though, there were no tears. Anger burned white-hot in her chest. Not caring if she disturbed evidence, she stomped across the floor to the hallway, headed for the spare room.

"Tara, wait."

"No. I'm at least going to see if the boxes are gone." She rounded the corner to the bedroom-turned-office and flipped the light switch. The files on her desk were scattered all over its surface and on the floor. Her filing cabinet stood open, manila folders sticking up every which way.

She ignored it all and stepped over to the walk-in closet, which stood open. The inside looked much the same as the rest of the room. If it had been on a shelf or a hanger, it was now on the floor. Her eyes darted around the mess. She moved further into the mess, tossing items aside as she went.

"We really should leave this stuff alone until Katie processes the room."

Tara glanced at him as she bent over to lift a suitcase out of her way. "I'm not waiting to look for answers, Jace. I've had enough of this shit." She kicked at a pile of clothes. "But I guess I have to, because he took the fucking boxes!"

Jace came to stand next to her, wrapping a gentle hand around her bicep. "Hey, it's okay. We'll find answers another way." He tugged lightly on her arm. "Come on."

She huffed out a harsh breath and shook her arm free of his grip, stomping past him. Pissed didn't begin to describe the anger she felt.

They exited the house, making sure to lock it behind them. Without a word, they climbed into the vehicle and he drove them back to the restaurant.

Tara fumed silently on the short ride. She was done. Whoever was behind all this had terrorized her long enough. She was going to find whatever it was they wanted and stop them.

Once at Heartwood, they walked in the back door and joined Seb where he stood near a table, watching Katie and her assistant work.

Seb glanced over, then did a double-take at the look on Tara's face. "Shit. Don't tell me. They were gone?"

"Yep."

He groaned. "This was the perfect night for this. We were all gone. I hope those trail cameras Dad and Brady set up caught *something*."

"What about the security system here?" Jace asked. "Did you look at it?"

Seb nodded. "The line was bypassed, so it never rang to the police station or the alarm company. I haven't checked the video feed yet. I'm waiting on Katie to process the office. I doubt there will be anything on the cameras, though, if they took the time to disable the alarm system. Our best bet is the trail cameras. No one knows about those."

Tara took her phone from her purse.

"What are you doing?" Seb asked.

"Calling Brady. You said he and Dad set them up. While we're dealing with this mess, he can go get the memory cards out of them. I want answers, Sebastian."

She didn't wait for his reply. Thumbing open the device, she found Brady's name in her contact list.

"Hey, Tara," Brady said when he picked up. "Did I forget something at the festival? I thought I grabbed everything I was supposed to."

"It's not that. Someone broke into the restaurant and my house and ransacked both."

He muttered an oath.

"Seb said you put up some trail cameras. Can you come remove the memory cards so we can look at the footage?"

"Yep. Give me a bit. There are several. Where are you?"

"At the restaurant. Forensics is here processing the place."

"Okay. I'll be there in a bit." He hung up.

She put her phone away. "He's pulling the cards."

"Good," Jace said. "Hopefully, there will be something to tell us who's behind this."

Tara prayed that was the case. She was done being a victim.

FOURTEEN

A cup of coffee landed in front of Jace's face as he sat in front of his laptop at one of the tables in the restaurant's dining area. He looked up to see Seb pulling out the chair opposite him, a mug of his own in his hand.

"Find anything yet?"

Jace sighed and sat back, picking up the steaming coffee. "Maybe." He blew over the rim of the cup and took a sip before spinning the computer around for Seb to see. "I haven't been through all the cards yet, but one near the restaurant caught someone moving in the shadows alongside the building. I'm hoping the ones set up near the houses will have caught more."

Seb clicked through the pictures on the camera. "Let's hope so. This image isn't very clear. It looks like a man, but that's about as much as you can tell. I'm not sure we'll get much more from the other cameras. If the guy went through the back door of her house again, we may not see much of anything. There are no trees or fence posts close to Tara's back door, so Dad and Brady didn't put any up back there. They put two on the light post where the drive splits—one aimed at Mom and Dad's and the other at all our houses—and one on the power pole closest to Tara's with a view of her front door. But that's it."

"That's what I'm afraid of," Jace said.

He turned the laptop around and ejected the memory card, then inserted another. Seb scooted his chair around so he could see the screen.

"Which one is this?"

"The one with the view of Tara's door."

The card loaded, and Jace opened the file. There were only a handful of images, and none of them were of the intruder. Once he and Tara left that evening for the dance, the next image the camera recorded was of them returning to look for the boxes of Tara's notes.

"Dammit." Jace punched the button to eject the card, then tossed in on the table with the two he'd already looked at. He picked up the last card and shoved it into the slot. "This one will probably be more of the same. It's the one aimed at your parents' place."

He clicked on the folder. None of the images were of anyone who wasn't supposed to be there.

Jace fought the urge to slam the laptop closed. Instead, he ran his hands over his face and sighed. "I knew the cameras were a longshot, but I'm still disappointed."

"Me too."

Jace dropped his hands, sighing. "We should probably go help in the kitchen. Tara's in disaster management mode right now, trying to salvage what she can of the food for tomorrow."

"I know. She's got the entire family in there helping her set things back to rights."

Jace pushed away from the table. "Hopefully, with all of

us working, it won't take too long. It's already after midnight."

Seb groaned as he stood. "Don't remind me. We're all going to be dead on our feet tomorrow."

"At least you get to go straight to bed when you get home. Tara's house is still a mess."

"Why don't you two come home with us? Abigail's at her friend's house. Tara can have her room and you can bunk in the living room. London has a bigger couch now, so you won't have to sleep on the floor like I did." His mouth quirked as they walked toward the kitchen.

"That's okay. I think we'll just stay at your house. She can have the bed, and I'll sack out in the recliner." Jace pushed through the swinging doors.

"You sure?"

He nodded. "Yeah. We'd just have to drive back out here in the morning, anyway."

"Okay. Well, if you change your mind, let me know."

"I will." He looked away from Seb to the controlled chaos around him.

The Archers had spread out. Some were tackling the task of washing all the dishes, others were combining containers of food, while the rest cleaned up the spilled food and wiped down tables.

Tara saw them and pointed to the supply room. "You two can grab the broom and mop and start on the floors."

The two men shared a look before Seb went to get a broom, and Jace walked toward her.

She glanced up from making notes on a piece of paper when he stopped beside her.

"Seb and I were talking. We should sleep at his house tonight and tackle your place tomorrow."

She hesitated only a moment before nodding. "Okay.

That'll leave me more time to make sure the restaurant is cleaned up properly."

Jace laid a hand over hers. "No. It'll leave you more time to sleep."

"But I—"

He cut her off. "All you need is to assess the food for the festival. The rest can be done tomorrow by your staff."

Her worried eyes scanned the room. Jace laid a finger on her jaw and turned her head to look at him.

"We *all* need to rest, Tara. If you stay, do you really think the rest of your family will go home?"

She sagged against the table. "Dammit. Why do you have to be so logical?"

He grinned. "It's my superpower. Now, where are you with figuring out the food damage?"

A long sigh pushed through her lips. "So far, most of it seems to be confined to the sides and produce. The meat is in large tubs that don't appear to have been messed with. It was more the stuff in boxes or crowded together on a shelf. I think he looked anywhere you could hide something small."

He looked around and noticed she was right. Drawers and shelves were in disarray, but not all their contents were on the floor. It looked like whoever did this moved stuff around but didn't dump everything. Whatever they were looking for was small, but not so tiny it would get lost in amongst a bunch of other things.

That made sense, though. Jace had a feeling they were searching for information, which could be on a flash drive. It would be easy to hide, but hard to find.

"Okay, so what do you need done to fix the food situation?"

She looked down at her list. "I need to make another large batch of baked beans, which means frying up several pounds of bacon. I also need another three batches of custard, more fruit cut up—which I'm going to have to get from the grocery —and more fish fry batter."

"Do you have everything to make all that?"

"Except for the fruit and the custard, yes. I need more eggs for the custard."

He gave her a quick nod before looking up and letting out a sharp whistle. All movement in the kitchen ceased as everyone turned to look at him.

"Tara has a plan to get the festival food back on track, but we need you all to help." He looked down at her and motioned for her to continue.

Eyes wide at the sudden change of course, she quickly gathered herself and squared her shoulders. Standing straighter, she clutched her notebook in her hands.

"We've got enough of the kitchen cleaned we can get started cooking." She laid out what items needed to be replaced. "This is doable. The custard is going to take the longest and will be on me mostly, since it's rather temperamental."

"What do you want us to do?" Maggie asked.

"Go around to everyone's house and bring me all the eggs you can find. I need six dozen. Check the chicken coop if you have to."

Maggie nodded.

"I'll check the coop," Thomas said.

Tara turned to her mother. "Mom, can you start frying bacon?"

"Yep. This is for the beans, right?"

"Yes."

"Do you have enough beans?"

Tara nodded. "I'll just have to use what I have on hand for the restaurant. There's a case in the supply room."

"I'll get those opened and on the stove," Lee said.

"What kind of fruit do you need?" Brady asked. "We all

have some and could pool what we have, so we aren't scrambling in the morning."

"Peaches, strawberries, raspberries, blueberries, melons—your basic summer fruit."

"Okay. I'll go with Maggie and Thomas and see what I can come up with."

"That leaves the fish fry," London said. "Seb and I can handle that. Jace can help you with the custard once you have the eggs."

Jace clapped his hands. "Looks like we have a plan. Let's get busy."

The group broke into motion, each person beginning their assigned task. He looked down at Tara.

"How about you and I go grab some clothes and take them over to Seb's while we have a few minutes, so we don't have to do it later?"

"Yeah. I guess that would be a good idea." She set her notes back on the table. "I'd like to get out of this dress too. It's not the best thing to make custard in."

He put a hand on her back and guided her toward the door.

"We're going to go change and find her some clothes for tomorrow," Jace said to Seb.

"Take your time. It'll be a bit before the others get back with the rest of the supplies. We've got the rest of this under control."

"Thanks, Seb," Tara said.

"It's what family's for, T."

She offered him a tremulous smile. Jace took her hand and tugged her outside, helping her inside his truck. She sagged into the seat they had so much fun in only a couple hours ago and closed her eyes.

"You okay?" he asked, climbing in beside her.

She looked over at him, her eyelids heavy. "Yeah. Just tired. It's been a long week."

"And you've been running on adrenaline. You have to crash sometime."

She made a face at him. "I hate that word."

"What word? Crash?"

"No. Adrenaline."

He frowned at her as he turned out of the restaurant parking lot. "What's wrong with the word adrenaline?"

"It's not the word so much as the havoc it wreaks."

She didn't elaborate, leaving him wondering what she meant by that. It wasn't until they were nearly at the house that she spoke again.

"Sean was an adrenaline-junkie. It's one reason he joined the teams." She sighed, looking out the window. "I can't help but wonder if he'd still be alive if he hadn't."

That explained a lot. Some of her comments about his motorcycle and choice of free time floated through his mind. It wasn't *him* she didn't like. It was what he represented.

So, how the hell do I compete with a dead man?

He turned into her drive and parked behind the CSU van, his thoughts heavy. It was more than just the memory of her husband he had to overcome. It was the illusion of safety she thought she could get from someone who had a less dangerous job and hobbies.

"Are we going to be able to go inside to get what we want?"

Jace nodded. "They should be close to finished."

He came around and lifted her down, taking her hand to lead her inside.

The chaos inside was no less jarring than the first time, though Katie and Emma had righted some of the furniture as they processed the house.

"Katie?" Jace called. "It's Jace and Tara."

"We're in the bedroom," she called back. "You can come through."

They walked down the hall to the master bedroom. Tara sucked in a breath at the sight, and Jace's eyes widened. The mattress and box springs were both off the bed. The nightstands were pulled away from the wall, and their drawers hung open. All the dresser drawers were open and what clothing was left in them hung out. He could see into the closet to see that it looked much like the spare bedroom one did. The shelves were bare, hangers stripped of their clothing. The intruder had even taken the pictures off the bedroom walls, though thankfully, he'd set them down to lean against the wall rather than toss them.

Katie rose from dusting the front of the dresser, her camera slung around her neck. "We're about done."

"Take your time," Jace said. "We're going to stay next door tonight. We just stopped so she could grab some clothes."

The CSI looked over her shoulder at the open closet door. "Hey, Emma?"

"Yeah?"

"You about done?"

"Yep." The younger woman appeared in the doorway. "I just took the last of the pictures." She stepped out of the closet toward her boss.

Katie turned back to Jace and Tara. "I just need to finish the dresser and the nightstands and we're done. You can go get what you need from the closet."

Tara lifted her skirts and stepped over the mess. Jace stayed back and propped his hands on his hips, looking at the mess.

"Did you find anything?" he asked once Tara disappeared.

Her mouth drew into a thin line, and she adjusted her glasses with the back of her hand. "Some prints, but they're probably Tara's or yours. Otherwise, it's just a bunch of destruction. We photographed it all in case anything is missing."

Jace sighed. "I didn't really expect anything else." He ran his hands through his hair. "Okay. I'm going to go gather a few of my things." He gave the closet another quick look where he could hear Tara rummaging through her belongings, then spun around to go find his toothbrush.

FIFTEEN

Sunlight peeked through the blinds, landing on Tara's face. She stirred, squinting against the brightness. Blinking, she looked around the room, disoriented until she realized where she was. With a groan, she let her head fall back to the mattress and pulled the pillow over her head. She didn't want to get up. The list of things she needed to do today was overwhelming.

But she couldn't hide out in bed forever. All her problems would still be waiting for her. She'd learned that lesson a long time ago.

She rolled over and turned off the alarm on her phone that had yet to ring. Sitting up, she realized she smelled coffee.

A yawn stole over her, and she stretched before standing and going to the bag she packed to take out a t-shirt and shorts. A quick shower later, she was dressed and walking into the main living area.

Jace sat at the table, staring at his phone. He looked up when she entered and smiled.

"Hey. Did you get any sleep?"

Tara walked over to the coffeepot. "Some. Not enough."

She poured herself a mug of coffee and turned around. "I will need copious amounts of this stuff today."

He stood and walked into the kitchen, stopping in front of her. One corner of his mouth lifted. "Laced with a little whiskey?" He refreshed his cup.

Her lips took on a sardonic tilt. "When we put my house back together later, there will be wine involved, I can promise you that."

"I'll order us a pizza, and we'll tackle it after we eat."

She took a sip of her coffee, wincing as the hot liquid scorched her mouth. "I don't know how you drink this stuff straight out of the pot."

"Comes with the job. You either build callouses on your tongue or fall asleep at your desk." He took a drink. "So, do I have to wear that outfit again today?"

She grinned. "Yes. And what are you complaining about? Your clothes aren't much different from what you normally wear." She gestured to his jeans and gray t-shirt with the word "Army" emblazoned over his chest. "I'm stuck in that damn lavender shirtwaist dress."

Heat flashed in his eyes and Tara's body responded in kind.

"Can I help you put the bustier on again?"

She laughed. "No. I don't think we'd make it out of the house."

He set his mug on the counter and leaned forward, one arm snaking around her waist to pull her against him. Tara's brain short-circuited.

Jace took the coffee cup from her hand and set it next to his.

"I don't want coffee spilled down my back."

Any quip she was going to make got obliterated as he pressed his mouth to hers. She looped her arms around his neck and kissed him back. The fire they lit last night roared back to life. Tara forgot all about her to-do list.

She knew this wasn't wise—not if she wanted to guard her heart—but her body had fully taken over her brain at this point. It wanted more of what he'd done to it in the truck, so when his hands skated up her ribcage under her shirt, she returned the favor. Her hands met warm skin over sinew and bone as she slid them beneath his t-shirt.

His fingers closed around her breast, sending bolts of light through her body to her core. She even heard bells.

Through the fog of desire, she realized the ringing wasn't in her head about the same time he broke the kiss with a groan.

"What is that?"

"My phone." He released her to take it from his back pocket, then looked at the screen. "It's Seb." He swiped his thumb over the screen. "Travers."

Tara stood there, listening to the low rumble of her brother's voice. She couldn't make out anything he said, but by the ever-increasing frown on Jace's face, something had happened.

"Okay. I'm on my way." He hung up. His jaw muscles worked as he digested the phone call.

"What? What's wrong?"

"There's been an accident on the highway. A car went over the side of the ravine and into the river. The deputy who responded called for the coroner. Seb's on his way and wants me there to help investigate. I need to go."

"Of course." She turned to the cabinets and opened the one that held the coffee cups, pulling out one of Seb's travel mugs. "Take this with you." She filled it and popped the lid on, holding it out.

"Thanks," he said, his fingers closing around the metal. They brushed hers, sending a current up her arm. His eyes darkened, and she knew he felt it too.

He cleared his throat. "Seb said he called your parents. They're on their way over to help you load up the food and go with you into town."

"That's fine," she said as he backed out of the kitchen and into the living room, where he sat down on the couch to put on his boots. His t-shirt rode up his arms as he tied the laces, revealing his tattoos and reminding her he needed a uniform shirt. She spun around and went into the bedroom where several new, short-sleeve, khaki button-up shirts with the department's logo hung in the almost empty closet. Tara took the nearest one off the hanger and headed back to the living room.

"Here." She held the shirt out to him.

"Thanks." He took it and put it on, fingers flying over the buttons. "There was a hat on the shelf in the closet with the department's logo on it. Can you grab it for me?"

She nodded and ran back to get it. When she returned to the living room, he was double-checking the gun belt he'd fastened around his waist.

Tara handed him the hat, a little sad to see him cover up all that gorgeous blonde hair.

"I'll stop in at the festival when I can. Don't go anywhere alone."

"I won't. Be careful." She followed him toward the door.

He scooped his truck keys off the entryway table. "I will. I'll see you later." He leaned down to press a quick kiss to her lips, then was out the door.

Tara stood in the doorway as he climbed in his truck, waving as he backed out of the drive and sped away. When she shut the door, it hit her just how domestic they'd been.

She ran her hands through her hair and sighed. They needed to find whoever was terrorizing her so she could have her own space again before she lost all rationality when it came to Jace Travers.

Flashing lights clued Jace in to the accident scene as he drove down the highway leading out of town. He pulled around the cruiser blocking the road and parked behind Seb's truck, then climbed out. A large tow truck with a boom arm sat at the edge of the roadway, its operator standing outside, staring below, as he worked several levers on the side of the truck. A winch motor whined as it reeled the cable back in.

Jace walked toward the man and the scene of all the action. When he reached the truck, he looked down over the edge. Several firefighters, including Declan Briggs, stood staggered on the mountainside, guiding wires attached to a basket that held a body bag. The medical examiner, Dr. Alex Randall, walked with the basket.

At the bottom of the ravine, he saw Seb's tall figure standing near the car. Jace walked over to the firefighter supervising the body extraction, and asked to use his radio.

He pressed the talk button. "Sheriff, it's Travers. Where do you want me?"

The radio crackled to life. "Come down here. You need to see this."

Curious, Jace radioed an affirmative and handed the fireman back his radio, then headed for the edge of the road and started the long, sideways walk to the river at the bottom of the ravine.

Dirt slid beneath his shoes, making his step falter more than once. Jace was thankful for the small trees and saplings that dotted the ground. He used several to slow his descent.

"What've you got?" he called once he was close.

Seb stood on a boulder at the edge of the river, peering into the car, which was on its roof. He looked up at Jace's question, a concerned look on his face.

"Recognize the car?"

Jace came to a halt at the river's edge and frowned at his boss before looking at the car. It was a black, late-model Mercedes SUV. No one he knew drove that kind of car.

"No. Should I?"

Seb hopped off the boulder. "Probably not. The only reason I do is because it was parked outside the inn every night. It's Doug Brown's car."

Jace's eyes widened.

"That's him they're hauling up the mountain." Seb gestured to the rescue basket, now almost at the road.

"Holy shit."

"Yep."

"How long's he been down here?"

"Randall's best guess right now is two days."

Dread churned Jace's gut. "Fuck. That means it wasn't Brown who trashed the restaurant and Tara's house."

"Nope. I think whoever hired him has run out of patience. The danger level just got a whole lot higher."

Jace scrubbed a hand over his face and stared at the mangled SUV. "So, was this really an accident and the person we're looking for got desperate and decided to do his own search, or did he run out of patience with Brown and decided to take matters into his own hands?"

"That's the same damn question I've been asking myself since I saw who was in the car. My gut says the latter, but we won't know for sure until we get the vehicle out of the water and Katie gets her hands on it."

"This is a nightmare," Jace muttered, readjusting his hat. Terror crept in around the edges of his mind as it sunk in that the threat to Tara had grown. He wasn't sure he could live through losing her too.

~

Laughter surrounded her, but Tara's thoughts were far from happy as she sliced and plated cornbread for the church crowd about to descend on them. London had been by earlier to tell her it was Doug Brown who was involved in the crash on the highway.

She didn't know what to think, knowing he was dead. Did it mean all the weird shit was going to stop? Or would it now come from someone else? Someone they had no idea to look out for? She hoped Seb and Jace found some kind of clue in his car to point them toward who hired him.

"Tara."

Preoccupied with her thoughts, she failed to recognize the voice calling her name before she turned around. When she did, the knife slipped from her hand, falling to the ground with a soft thud, as her brain registered the identity of the man standing inside the tent flap.

"Rob?"

Her editor smiled, showing his slightly crooked teeth and a set of crow's feet around his eyes that were deeper since she saw him last. Silver streaked his dark hair, giving him a distinguished look.

"Hi."

Anger boiled up, overriding the shock at seeing him and pulling her out of her stupor. "What the hell are you doing here? Didn't you get the hint that I don't want to come back when I didn't answer or return any of your calls or texts?"

His eyes widened a bit. "I'm not here to convince you to come back to work for me. Did you not listen to my messages or read anything I sent you?"

She shook her head. "No. I'm done with that chapter of my life."

He closed his eyes for a moment, muttering to himself in Spanish. When he looked back at her, concern shone from their dark depths. "I wish you had. Is there some place we can talk?"

Perplexed, but still not convinced he wouldn't try to get her to come back to her old job, she picked up the tray of cornbread and moved around him. "I can't talk right now. We're going to get slammed any minute."

He stepped in front of her, halting her progress. "Please, Tara. It's about Sean."

The tray wobbled in her hands. She took a breath to steady herself before she dumped cornbread all over the ground. "What?"

Ray's eyes shifted around the tent, his expression serious. "Someone contacted me and told me some things you should know. Is there somewhere quiet we can go?"

Heart thumping, her mind whirled. What the hell was going on? First, they found the folder on Sean's last tour; now, her editor showed up out of the blue with information about him.

"Let me take this tray up front. We can sit at one of the tables. I'm not leaving the tent."

He looked like he wanted to protest, but she walked away before he could voice it. She stepped past the partition separating the prep area from the diners and made her way to the tables they'd set up as a counter. Hands shaking, she set the tray on the table behind the register.

Jenny looked up from where she stood stuffing napkin dispensers. The smile on her face died when she saw Tara's expression. "Honey, what's the matter?"

"Rob's here."

"Rob?" Her brow furrowed, then her eyes widened as she made the connection. "As in your old editor, Rob?"

Tara nodded.

"What does he want?"

"He says he has some information about Sean."

Shock crossed Jenny's face. "What is going on? What was your husband involved in over there?"

Tara shrugged. "I have no idea. I'm going to see what he has to say. We'll be at a table if you need me."

"We'll be fine. You go. Get some answers." She laid a hand on Tara's arm.

"Or more questions. We'll see." She drew in a deep breath and walked away.

Rob stood at the edge of the partition. She motioned him forward and led him to an empty table away from the other diners. They sat across from one another, and Tara folded her hands in her lap to hide the nervous tremor running through them.

"It's been a long time," Rob said. "How're you doing?"

"I'm good. Or at least I was until someone started harassing me and breaking into my house and business."

His eyes widened before he closed them and hung his head. He opened them again with a sigh. "I knew I should have come here sooner."

"Why are you here at all? What do you have to tell me about Sean?"

He leaned forward, his voice low. "A few months ago, I got a phone call from a guy asking to meet me. When I asked what he wanted to talk about, he said 'Sean Miller,' then refused to say more on the phone. Didn't even tell me his name. Just gave me a time and a place, and that he'd find me when I got there. You'll never guess who turned up."

"I'm not in the mood for games, Rob. Just tell me."

He frowned at her. "Boy, you've turned into a sourpuss since you left California."

She glared at him.

He held up his hands. "All right, all right. It was Evan Shephard."

The breath left Tara's lungs. That was a name she

hadn't heard in a long time. She swallowed a couple times before she sucked in some air and managed to talk. "Why did one of Sean's teammates want to talk to you about him?"

"Seems he'd been diagnosed with terminal cancer and wanted to clear his conscience before he met his maker."

"Clear his conscience about what?"

Rob shrugged. "Don't know. All he told me was he had information about Sean's death, and that it was somewhere safe."

She sat back and stared at him for a few moments. "His death? What about it? Al-Aziz killed him. And why wouldn't he bring the information with him to the meeting, or at least tell you what it was?"

"He said he wanted to make sure I wasn't followed. Told me I would receive a package in the next few days that explained everything, then he left. I never got the package."

Tara frowned. "He didn't mail it?"

Rob shook his head. "He never got the chance. He was killed when his house exploded that night."

Her eyes grew wide.

"Whatever he knew, someone didn't want it to see the light of day."

She covered her face with her hands. "That explains why all this is happening now instead of right after he died. But what I don't understand is why they're coming after me. I don't know anything about his death other than what I was told."

"Maybe it's not what you know, but what you don't know you have."

"Huh?"

"My guess is Sean had something incriminating on someone and hid it. It might still be in your possession and whoever it implicates wants to make sure it's destroyed."

"Why wouldn't they just blow up my house like they did Evan's, then?"

"Because you live on your family's ranch. It could be anywhere there, and blowing up all the buildings would bring a lot of attention. Do you still have anything of Sean's?"

She nodded. "Some. Mostly pictures and mementos. I gave away all his clothes and other stuff. His parents took some things." Her eyes widened. "Oh my God. Jim and Kathy. Are they okay?" She hadn't even thought to check on them after Seb and Jace uncovered Sean's involvement.

"As far as I know, they're fine. I haven't checked in on them, but I did an internet search on Sean's name after I talked to Evan and nothing recent came up involving them."

She breathed a little easier, but still vowed to have Seb or Jace search police reports to see if anything had happened.

"Maybe you should go through his things—your things—and see what you can find. And I don't just mean take a quick peek. I mean, take things apart. Shake stuff that shouldn't rattle. Sean was a SEAL and a damn smart man. He wouldn't put it—whatever *it* is—in plain sight."

A rueful laugh passed her lips. "I guess it's a good thing my house is already trashed. I can go through everything when I put it all away."

He reached across the table and covered her hand with his. "I'm sorry. I know this is bringing up a lot of bad memories."

"Actually, it's been a bit cathartic. Don't get me wrong, I'm ready for all this to stop, but it's forced me to confront some emotions I never really dealt with."

"I'm glad. I worried about you when you left. I wish you'd kept in touch."

She sighed. "I know I should have, but I had to make a clean break. Any reminder of the Middle East was too much."

"Tara?"

She looked toward the tent entrance at the deep voice

saying her name. Jace's tall frame wove through the picnic tables.

"Hi." She turned and smiled up at him when he reached her table. "How's the investigation going?"

The brief look he gave her said they would talk later. He looked at Rob and held out a hand. "Hi. Jace Travers. I work with her brother, Seb."

Rob gave her a quizzical look. "Seb's a local cop? I thought he was FBI."

"He's the sheriff now. He left the FBI about two years ago.

Rob nodded. "Got it." He held out a hand to Jace. "Rob Maldonado. Tara's editor."

"Editor?" A deep frown marred Jace's face as he shook Rob's hand. He turned to her. "Are you going back into journalism?"

She waved her hands. "No. God, no." She slid over on the picnic bench and patted the wood. "Sit down. You need to hear this."

He lifted one long leg over the bench and sat, facing her. His knee pressed into her thigh, spreading a warmth through her body that had nothing to do with the summer temperatures.

She forced her mind back on topic. "So, Rob's been calling and messaging me for a while now. I haven't answered or even read any of his texts, because photojournalism is the last thing I want to get back into. But he wasn't trying to talk me into coming back. One of Sean's teammates came to him a few months ago with information about Sean's death, but before he could give it to Rob, the guy died when his house exploded."

Jace's eyebrows shot up, and he looked at Rob. "And you don't know what he wanted to tell you?"

"No, but the timing of the explosion worried me enough I started trying to contact her to tell her to keep an eye out."

"Did the fire inspector release a cause for the explosion?" Jace asked.

Rob nodded, mouth in a grim line. "Gas leak." He scoffed. "Like I believe that."

Tara didn't either.

"Evan got me thinking, though. About why he was so paranoid. The only answer I can come up with is someone on the team was involved in Sean's death."

Jace sat a little straighter and leveled a look on her. "I told you the details of his last mission seemed weird."

She blew out a breath. It was looking like there was a great deal more to Sean's death than a regional war lord taking out the enemy.

"I'd say you're probably right. I think Sean was set up." Rob said.

Tara sucked in a quick breath, tears forming. Why would his own teammates—his friends—do such a thing? Anger simmered in her gut for the nameless person responsible for her husband's death.

Jace laid a hand on her back, rubbing soothing circles, and looked at Rob. "Have you talked to any other members of his team?"

"No. I think the only reason I'm not dead is because Evan never got the chance to tell me much. I'm not poking that can of worms without some solid proof already in hand."

A contemplative expression crossed Jace's face.

"What are you thinking?" Tara asked him.

"Seb put in inquiries with the Navy about Sean's SEAL team, but I think we might be able to find out more by doing a more basic search. Background checks, news stories—from both here and the Middle East—even conspiracy blogs. It might give us a place to start in figuring out what Shephard wanted to expose."

"I can start on the news stories," Rob said. "I have access

to all the archives. I can even point you toward some of the nut-job conspiracy bloggers."

"Good. If one of you gets me a list of Sean's teammates, I'll start the background checks." His phone beeped, and he pulled it out of his pants pocket to read the text. He sighed. "After I go sit in on Brown's autopsy. Dr. Randall's ready to start." He sent a quick reply, then put the phone away.

"Do you want some lunch before you leave?" Tara asked. "The roasted chicken would keep if you didn't want to eat it right away."

"No, that's okay. I'll come back when I'm done and get something then. I'm going to be ready for a break at that point." He leaned forward and pressed a kiss to her mouth before standing.

He held out a hand to Rob. "Mr. Maldonado, it was nice to meet you. Thank you for the information."

Rob stood and took Jace's hand. "Call me Rob, and it was no problem. I just wanted to make sure Tara was safe."

"That's my goal too. Again, it was nice meeting you." He tipped his hat to Rob, then looked down at Tara. "I'll see you in a few hours."

She nodded, and he turned and loped away.

Rob sat back down, a smirk on his face. "Works with your brother, huh? Seems like he would have been better off introducing himself as your boyfriend."

Tara blushed. "Yes, well, we haven't really talked about what we are."

"You might want to do that sooner rather than later, because the look he gave me when he walked up and saw us holding hands indicated that he very much considers you his."

Her blush deepened. "It's complicated, Rob."

"Only if you make it that way." He rapped his knuckles on the table. "Now, how about some of that roasted chicken you mentioned? That sounds fantastic. I'm starving."

Tara laughed and stood. "I see your bottomless pit of a stomach hasn't changed."

He grinned. "Nope."

She motioned him toward the register. "Come on. Let's get you some food."

Sixteen

Jace tugged the ear loops of his mask over his ears and inhaled the sharp bite of peppermint essential oil. He walked over to the autopsy table where Dr. Randall was busy setting out his tools.

"What can you tell me so far, Doc?"

Randall looked up. "He's really beat up. And I'd say it's from more than just the crash. I found bruising inconsistent with an accident."

"Such as?"

"His knuckles, for one," Alex said, pointing to Brown's hands.

Jace looked at the man's hand closest to him. Bruises marred the knuckles. He glanced back up at the M.E. "Yeah, those look like they came from a fight."

"That's what I thought. I already scraped and clipped his nails and sent those to the lab. He's got some inconsistent bruises on his torso, too. They look like they might be from blows from a fist." He motioned to several round discolorations. "The other thing that struck me is the lack of a seatbelt bruise."

"What do you mean?"

"He was buckled into the car, went down a steep ravine, and crashed into the river. There should be a mark from the seatbelt, but there isn't. Even if he died from the crash, there would still be something, but there's nothing. I think he was dead before the car went off the road."

Jace's eyes widened above his mask. "Okay. So what killed him, then?"

Alex picked up a scalpel. "That's a good question. Let's find out." He touched the knife to Brown's chest and made a Y-incision.

"I'm going to call Seb quick and tell him what you think."

Alex nodded, focused on his task.

Jace slipped out of the room and pulled out his phone. Finding Seb's name in his contacts, he placed the call. His boss picked up on the third ring.

"So, Randall thinks Brown was dead before the car went off the road," he said without preamble.

"Goddammit. I knew it was too easy to think he'd just had an accident. I swear, someone put up a 'Murderers Welcome' sign outside of town and forgot to tell me." Seb expelled a heavy sigh. "So, why does he think Brown was already dead?"

"Weird bruising. There are signs he was in a fight, and he's lacking injuries he should have had in a wreck like that. Randall just started, so I don't know cause of death yet, but it's not going to be from the accident."

"Which begs the question, how did he and his car get down in the ravine if he was already dead?"

"Yep." Jace glanced through the windows set into the double doors of the morgue. Alex had removed the ribcage and was examining the inside of Brown's chest.

"I'll have the deputies canvas up the road from the accident site and see if there's any evidence of another person. Let me know what else he finds."

"Will do." Jace hung up and stepped back into the morgue. He grabbed a stool from under the counter and rolled it over to sit by the empty table next to where Alex worked.

Leaning an elbow on the table, he closed his eyes and rubbed at his temple, pushing on the point above his left eyebrow where an ache pulsed.

"You okay?"

He looked at the M.E. who watched him through his visor.

"Yeah, I'm good. Just tired, and it's given me a bit of a headache. It's certainly been an interesting first week on the job."

Alex chuckled. "Trial by fire."

"That's the truth."

"How's Tara holding up?"

"She's doing okay. I think she's going to need a vacation, though, when this is all over just to recharge a bit."

A knowing grin split Alex's face. "So, where are you taking her?"

Jace laughed. "To be determined." He sobered a bit. "I have to get her to agree to date me first."

Alex arched a brow as surprise rolled over his features. "You're not already dating?"

Jace shook his head.

"Hmm. You two sure looked cozy strolling through town yesterday."

And last night, Jace couldn't help but think. "I'm growing on her, but she still has some things she needs to work through. Ironically, the stalking and break-ins have helped with that."

"Well, I hope she comes around. She's nice, but she seems a little sad. It'd be great to see her really happy."

"Agreed." Jace sighed. "I just need to find out who's terrorizing her so she can concentrate on herself."

"I have faith," Alex replied, moving down to Brown's abdominal contents. "Seb's good at his job. He wouldn't have hired you if you weren't too."

Jace knew he was right, but with this case, he wondered if his skills were enough. He'd met nothing but roadblock after roadblock at every turn. He needed something to break—just one little piece to fall out to show him which way to look.

His eyes traveled over the body on the table. He hoped Alex found something to give them a lead.

"So, tell me about yourself, Doc," he said, changing the subject. He needed a distraction. "You from here?"

Alex shook his head. "No. Oregon. I grew up on the coast near the California border. Went to med school at UCLA and did my residency in Phoenix, then my forensic fellowship in Salt Lake City. I worked in the M.E.'s office there as an assistant medical examiner until the position opened up here. I've been in Silver Gap almost four years."

"What made you decide to come here? I mean, this place is tiny compared to the places you've lived."

Alex dictated a few notes into the microphone hanging over the table before answering Jace's question. "I grew up in a small town, and city life was wearing on me. That, and I wanted to run my own lab."

"You know what I don't understand? How a county this small has its own M.E. We're close enough to both Denver and Colorado Springs that you'd think the job would be farmed out to one of them."

"It was for a while, but the hospital here is fantastic." He picked up his scalpel again and began cutting organs free. "You can thank the Archers for that. A few years ago, they donated a substantial sum for the creation of a forensic science and pathology center." He grinned. "I think they were trying to entice Seb to come home, but they also saw a need here. Before the center opened, all unexplained deaths were sent to one of the bigger cities, where it could be weeks before they released the body to relatives for burial. It weighs on families to have to wait so long for closure."

Jace understood that all too well. His family had been sent to North Platte, and it took several weeks before he'd been able to bury them.

He clasped his hands in his lap, his thumb rubbing the edge of the leather bracelet on his right wrist. "Do you get enough work to justify a full-time M.E.? I mean, you must or you wouldn't be here. I just can't imagine it, though."

"I'm technically the center's director. This is only a part of my job. We have enough unexpected, unexplained deaths in the county, though, that I do several autopsies a month. Although they've been a little more exciting in the last few weeks, I have to admit."

"No kidding." Jace smiled at the doctor.

Alex started to smile back, but a deep frown overtook it as he lifted the heart free of the chest.

"What?" Jace rose to step closer.

"I think Mr. Brown has just offered you his first clue." Alex laid the heart on the portable table set up to his right and used his scalpel to cut into it.

"What do you mean?"

Alex made a few more quick cuts, then lifted out a piece of plastic. "This. It's a mechanical aortic valve. And it's got a serial number."

Hope surged in Jace's chest. "We can trace that and find out who he really is."

"Exactly."

~

Beads of sweat rolled down Tara's face as she stowed the last load of things that needed to go back to the restaurant in the bed of Thomas' truck. She closed the tailgate and leaned against it, wiping away the moisture on the sleeve of her dress.

"Is that it?" he asked, coming out of the tent.

She nodded. "Yep. Thanks for coming to help me clean up." Jace had called earlier to ask if she could get one of her brothers to help her clean up and take her back to the ranch. His fatal accident had turned into a homicide.

He came to stand next to her and shrugged. "Not a problem. You saved me from a night of working on the books for my clinic."

"Well, you're welcome." She sighed and fanned herself with her hand, roasting in her dress. She should have brought a change of clothes with her to clean up in.

One corner of his mouth lifted as he looked down at her. He looped an arm around her shoulders and pulled her into a side hug. "You're welcome."

She brought her hand up and patted his chest, hugging him back. He covered it with his own, and his fingers bumped the bracelet on her wrist. She stiffened and started to pull away, but he looked down at the cuff before she could.

A frown turned down his mouth as he saw the name. "Jace said she's buried on the ranch at the lake. I'd like to see where sometime."

Tara snatched her hand back and straightened, staring at her twin, wide-eyed. "What?" The word came out less than a whisper, because there wasn't any air in her lungs.

But then, what he said fully registered, and she sucked in a breath as the anger hit, sharp and hot.

"He told you about her?" Red bloomed on her cheeks, and her eyes narrowed.

Thomas waved his hands. "No. Well, yes. He did. Sort of." He winced and ran a hand through his hair. "I already knew about the baby. I just didn't know you had a girl or her name, or even that she was buried on the ranch. He only filled in the blanks on Friday after I saw him talking to Mom while we were setting up. She hugged him hard and had this shocked, but happy, look on her face and tears in her eyes. When I asked him about it, all he said was they were talking about something you told him the night before. I put two and two together, and he told me the rest."

He took her hands in his as she retreated to shocked silence.

"Why didn't you tell us? We would have been there for you." Anguish colored his deep voice.

Guilt punched her in the gut. She bit her lip and looked away. "I know, but I couldn't. It hurt so much—losing Sean, then losing Lucy—I could barely breathe, let alone talk about her."

She looked back up at him. "And I didn't want any more pitying looks. I'd had enough of those from people expressing their sympathy over my husband's death. By the time I felt like I could handle it all, months had passed and then it felt weird to just come out and say, 'Hey, guys. Remember when I was in the hospital and had surgery? It wasn't for my appendix. It was to deliver my daughter, who I miscarried at nineteen weeks, and to keep me from bleeding to death.'" Her voice broke.

Tears formed in Thomas' eyes and he hauled her into his chest, wrapping his arms around her in a tight hug.

"I wish you had, anyway," he whispered into her hair. "I'm so sorry, T."

She swallowed back the tears and looked up at him. "I'm sorry too. I should have told you—all of you." Now that she had, she realized what a burden the secret was. She'd had no idea how freeing it would feel to talk about Lucy with her family.

He released her and wiped off the wetness on his face. "It's okay. I'm just glad you finally seem to be healing. Jace has been good for you."

She rolled her eyes and wiped at her own face. "Yeah, I suppose." *Like yanking out stitches without cutting them first was good for you.*

Thomas stared at her for a few seconds. "I know you think he's like Sean. That he'll go off and do something dangerous and get killed. But you can't let fear control your life. You could miss out on the best thing to ever happen to you if you do. Trust me, I know."

Tara frowned, her emotions jumbled. "Thomas—"

He held up his hands and backed away, cutting her off. "I'm just saying. Don't discount what you could have with him because you're afraid." He turned on his heel and headed for the truck cab.

She stared after him for a moment, his words echoing through her mind. It wasn't a stretch for her to realize he was right—about both things—but she wasn't sure she could push past the paralyzing fear to give Jace a chance.

The rumble of the truck's engine turning over shook her from her thoughts. She headed for the passenger seat and climbed inside.

"Why didn't you ever ask me about what happened? And how long have you known?" she asked, buckling her seatbelt.

He glanced over at her. "I knew the minute I hugged you the first time. You tried to make us all think you'd just gained weight, but baby belly and fat belly don't feel remotely the same," he said with a grin.

She laughed. "I didn't think I was showing enough for anyone to tell."

He pulled the truck away from the curb and pointed it toward home. "If it helps, I don't think anyone but the family figured it out."

"Wait. You *all* knew?" Her eyes bulged as she digested that fact.

"Mmm-hmm. When you went into the hospital, Mom spun some yarn about appendicitis. We could tell she was lying, so we had a family meeting without Mom and Dad. We'd all figured it out, but didn't want to say anything for fear we were wrong. Once we discovered that we all knew, we decided to respect your privacy, figuring you'd come clean when you were ready. Only you never did."

She sat back and stared out the windshield, unable to believe she'd kept a secret that wasn't a secret all these years.

"One thing I don't understand, though, is why you didn't tell us before you miscarried."

She sighed. "We wanted to surprise everyone with an ultrasound and a gender when we came home to visit, which is why I didn't say anything when I first found out. That, and I didn't want Mom to worry while I was still overseas. Once Sean was killed, I couldn't bring myself to say something and have people tell me how lucky I was to still have a piece of him. I didn't want a piece. I wanted *him*. It was more a tactic to keep me from hurting someone else than self-preservation."

He chuckled. "Okay, that makes sense. Your temper and impulsiveness got you into more than your share of trouble when we were young."

She smiled back at him. "It still does." Her gaze went back to the scenery, but she didn't see it. "I was so angry. At the war lord for killing him. The military for sending him on the mission. Sean's team for not doing more to protect him or to keep him alive. God, for allowing it to happen. Hell, even Sean himself, for dying and leaving me. I barely made it through the funeral. All I wanted to do was scream. Then, it was just shock as it sank in that he was really gone. I still don't remember driving home from California."

Thomas reached over and patted her leg. "Well, you don't

have to carry the grief alone anymore. We'll all be here for you."

She gave him a tremulous smile. "I know. Thank you."

"Anytime, T."

Feeling lighter than she had in years, Tara relaxed. The knowledge that her family mourned with her was like a balm to her wounded soul. She smiled and watched the trees fly by as Thomas drove them home, feeling like she was finally on the path to regaining herself.

SEVENTEEN

The front door to the main house opened, letting in a wave of hot, dry air as Jace stepped through the doorway. Tara looked up from her seat on her parents' couch as he strode inside to come stand next to her.

She beamed up at him. "Hi."

A smile tugged at his lips. "Hi." He glanced around at her family, who sat with her. Photo albums laid spread across the coffee table and in her mother's and London's laps. "What's going on?"

She rose to stand in front of him. "Something that should have happened a long time ago." She glanced over her shoulder at the others, smiling. They smiled back at her. "But I think I'm ready to go home now."

He squinted, looking down at her in curiosity, before his expression cleared and understanding dawned in his eyes. "You told them."

A bright smile spread over her face. "I did."

Jace smiled, and Tara's heart did a little flip-flop in her chest as it turned his already handsome face into breathtaking.

"Good." He motioned to the photo albums. "So, what's all this?"

"We were just reminiscing. We also planned a family picnic for the holiday tomorrow. At the lake."

"You're invited," Brady said from his chair.

Tara nodded, stepping closer. "Yes. This wouldn't have happened if you hadn't pushed me to bring her back into my life. Into their lives."

He swallowed hard, Adam's apple bobbing. "I'd be honored to come with you."

"Good, because I wasn't going to let you say no," she said.

He chuckled. "Of course you weren't." He reached out and stroked a finger down the side of her cheek. "Are you sure you don't want to stay a little longer?"

She glanced at the others. Her mother made a little shooing motion with her hand.

Turning back to Jace, she nodded. "I'm sure. Let's go."

He held out a hand, and she took it.

"We'll see you guys tomorrow," she said to the others.

They nodded and said goodbye. Jace gave them all a smile and a nod, then led her toward the door.

"You know, they're all going to start talking about us the minute the door closes, right?" she murmured as they walked away.

His grin was naughty. "I can guarantee it'll be tamer than what's going through my mind right now."

She blushed and slapped at his arm playfully. "Devil."

He pushed open the door, leading her to his truck. "Maybe a bit."

They reached the vehicle, but before she could open her door, he sandwiched her between the truck and his muscular frame. Her breath left her on a whoosh as he pressed against her. Those deep blue eyes of his stared down at her, a tenderness giving them a soft edge.

"I'm proud of you. That couldn't have been easy."

She put her hands on his chest and stared at his collar, toying with it. "It helped that they already knew." She glanced up. "Thomas saw my bracelet and admitted he knew about her. That they all did. When we got back, I called everyone over to Mom and Dad's and told them about her. Once it was all out, it was like the heavy air you get after a rainstorm just suddenly cleared. I didn't know how much my secret weighed us all down."

"Yeah?" He curled a lock of her hair around his finger as he listened to her talk.

She smiled at him, appreciating how he listened to her. "Yeah. We had a nice talk in there. I wish I'd confided in him back then." She sniffed, remembering the hurt in her siblings' eyes when she came clean about Lucy. She was so very sorry for all the pain she caused them and vowed to never keep secrets from her family again.

"I'm glad you told them everything. It can only get better from here now."

She nodded. "I know."

He leaned down and pecked her on the lips. "Let's go back to your house. I bought pizza on my way out of town. I know it's a bit late, but we can eat and then at least get started on the cleanup."

"Sounds good. I'm starving." She climbed into his truck, heart lighter than it had been in years. Even the prospect of cleaning up her ransacked house couldn't dampen her spirit tonight.

EIGHTEEN

Light-hearted laughter echoed off the mountain as Tara and her family rode through the pass to the small lake on their property. Even though she knew where they were going and why, she wasn't anxious or sad. Lucy would always be part of her life, but she was gone. It was long past time Tara realized that and moved forward instead of staying stagnant in her grief.

Tara glanced around at her family, thankful for them more than ever. They had accepted her reasons for not telling them about the baby and forgiven her. Their understanding was more than she deserved. Lucy hadn't been hers to grieve alone. She'd been a granddaughter and a niece, and Tara was sorry she'd deprived them of loving her for so long.

"You ready for this?" Jace asked from beside her as the lake came into view.

She looked up at him astride Pike's younger brother, Elbert. The horse had Pike's silver coloring, but not his temperament. He liked to run and wasn't always happy to be reined in, which could make him a bit difficult. If Tara hadn't seen Jace ride, she would have never let him on the horse. Elbert seemed to like him, though. He was behaving.

"Yeah, I'm good. I'm not even nervous. I should have done this a long time ago. Thank you for helping me realize that."

"Glad I could help."

"Hey, you two!"

Tara turned her attention to Maggie, who'd come to a halt ahead of them. A devil-may-care smile covered her pretty face.

"Wanna race?" She waggled her eyebrows.

Tara looked at Jace, a bit of a thrill going through her. It had been a while since she'd raced her siblings.

He grinned down at her. "I'm game."

She turned back to her sister and kicked Brandywine into a trot. "You're on." She looked at her brothers. "How about you guys?"

"Hell, yeah," Thomas said, sidling up next to her on his black mare, Raven.

"You know you're going to lose, right?" Brady said to him, lining up on Thomas's other side. His horse, Titan, tossed his chestnut-colored head and let out a snort.

Thomas scoffed. "In your dreams."

"You're both going to lose," Seb said, coming up on the outside. Pike danced beneath him, anticipating the race.

"Oh, whatever," Maggie replied, rolling her eyes. "Beatrice is going to kick all your asses." She patted her horse's flaxen neck. "Ain't that right, Bea?"

"I think you're all wrong," Tara said.

"Oh, please," Thomas said. "You think Brandywine's going to beat us, especially Seb on Pike?"

She grinned at her twin. "I didn't say I was going to win. I think Jace and Elbert are going to leave you in the dust." She looked over at Jace and winked.

He grinned down at her. Elbert snorted and pawed at the ground, ready to run.

Yeah, her brothers didn't stand a chance.

"Well, let's find out, shall we?" Lee said. He and Jenny sat perpendicular to them, London and Abigail on either side.

"You going to join us, London?" Tara called.

She laughed. "That's a hard no. Delilah's a fine horse, but she's in no hurry." She patted the black and white piebald on the neck. The horse had her nose on the ground, nibbling at the weeds beneath her feet.

"Everybody line up," Jenny said. "Maggie, scooch back. You might have gotten a head start at ten, but you don't now."

Maggie rolled her eyes and gave Jenny a rueful smile. Elbert danced forward as she pulled Beatrice back with the others. Jace reined him in, but the horse stomped, bobbing his head as he stood in line.

"You better hang on," Tara said.

"No shit. I think you're right about who's going to win. Whether he takes me with him or not, Elbert's going to be the first over the line." He pulled on the reins again as Elbert shuffled forward.

"Okay. First to pass the gnarled oak wins," Lee said, pointing several hundred yards away at a lone tree a hundred feet from the lakeshore.

Tara leaned forward, ready to nudge Brandywine into action.

"Ready. Set. Go!" Lee's voice boomed over the plain.

The line of horses shot forward, riders hunched over their backs. Wind whipped past Tara's face as Brandywine galloped across the ground, doing her best to keep up with the bigger, faster horses.

After a hundred yards, it was apparent neither she nor Maggie were going to win the race. Even Thomas—whose mare was the biggest of the three—fell behind the others. Pike and Elbert ran neck and neck, Titan only half a length back.

Tara didn't slow down, though. She wanted an up-close view of the finish.

With a hundred yards to go, Brady fell further back as the two silver geldings kicked it into another gear. In moments, they were several lengths ahead of the chestnut horse and light years ahead of everyone else.

Tara watched with glee as Elbert pulled past Pike and shot past the tree by nearly a full length.

She whooped, standing in her saddle and cheering as Jace slowed and turned his horse back toward them.

"Where did you learn to ride like that?" Seb asked, coming back as well.

Jace grinned, readjusting his ball cap. "I grew up on a farm. I rode nearly every day."

"Well, it shows," Brady said. "You floated in that saddle. I'm not sure Elbert knew you were on his back."

"He's an incredible horse. I thought Pike was fast, but Elbert's something else."

Lee, Jenny, London, and Abigail trotted up, joining the group under the shade of the large oak.

"Baby, I lost," Seb said, pouting to his fiancée.

She grinned. "You certainly did."

"You can make it better later." He waggled his eyebrows at her.

Abigail made a retching sound. "Grandma Jenny, make them stop."

The group laughed.

"Now, children," Jenny started, the stern warning belied by the twinkle in her eyes.

Abigail rolled her eyes while Seb grinned at her.

"Come on. Let's go give these horses a drink." Seb turned Pike toward the lake, the others following behind.

Once the animals drank their fill, they tied them to the tree and a hitching post they'd put in years earlier.

By unspoken agreement, Tara led them along the shoreline, past the oak, to Lucy's grave. Jace took her hand, offering silent support. She squeezed it, thankful for his presence. She wasn't nervous about showing the site to her family, but it still hurt to know her baby was gone.

Near a group of boulders, she stopped and bent down to push aside some tall grass. Nestled against the rocks was a small granite marker.

She ran a hand over the smooth stone, tracing her daughter's name, before looking up at her family, who'd formed a half circle around her. Tears shimmered in her mother's eyes.

"Meet Lucy."

Nineteen

Jace leaned back on his elbows, legs crossed at the ankle as he watched Tara, Thomas, and Maggie skip stones across the lake's glassy surface. A fierce pride burned in his chest for the woman who'd stolen his heart. When she'd kneeled down to reveal Lucy's gravestone, then looked up at them with her heart in her eyes, he'd fallen in love with her right there. He couldn't believe it happened so fast, but he couldn't deny how he felt.

Seb sat down next to him, two plastic containers full of apple pie in his hands. Jace sat up as he handed him one, along with a fork.

"Thanks." He pulled off the lid and speared a chunk of gooey apple.

"Yep." Seb opened his own container and took a bite.

"So, I heard from Sean's commander."

Jace looked over in surprise. "Yeah? What did he have to say?"

"Not much. He indicated he couldn't talk over the phone. Said he'd be here day after tomorrow."

"Hmm." Jace took another bite and stared out at the

water. "Did he seem scared, or just unwilling to talk about classified stuff on an unsecured line?"

Seb paused. "Worried. He seemed worried."

"You think he knows something?"

"Maybe. He at least suspects something."

"You hear anything on the DNA from under Brown's nails or about the heart valve Dr. Randall found?"

"Not yet. I didn't really expect to, though, with the holiday. I'm just glad Alex agreed to do the autopsy yesterday instead of waiting until tomorrow."

"That's one perk of being a small county."

"And of having your own M.E. I can't help but think how long this case could draw out if we had to send the body to Denver or Colorado Springs. Of how long my sister would have to live in fear. It's been long enough already."

Jace's eyes traveled to Tara, who laughed at something Thomas said. At least up here, she didn't have to worry about someone coming after her.

"I owe you a debt of thanks," Seb said, his voice soft.

Jace looked over to see he also watched his siblings near the water.

Seb turned to him. "If it weren't for you, I'm not sure she ever would have told us about Lucy. So, thank you for that. You've allowed my family to mourn out in the open and together, and you've helped my sister heal."

He shifted and stared down at his hands, poking at the last bits of pie in the container. "She reminded me so much of myself. Stuck in denial and anger. I'm just glad she didn't push me away when I pushed her to open up."

"Thomas told me about your family. I'm sorry. I can't imagine what it's been like." He laid a hand on Jace's shoulder. "But just know, you aren't alone anymore. We're your family now." He let his arm drop. "Not to replace what you lost, but to add to it."

Emotion made Jace's chest tight. "Thanks, Seb." He huffed, an ironic smile tugging one corner of his mouth. "Who'd have thought a serial killer would change my life for the better?"

Seb chuckled. "I guess it's true that there's always good in any situation."

The sound of horses galloping drew their attention to their left. Lee and Brady rode low over the backs of their mounts as they returned from the ride they'd taken over the ridge to check on a few stragglers from their herd.

Jace grinned. "I guess your dad didn't want to be left out of the racing."

Seb smiled back, but it quickly faded as he watched them get closer.

"What?"

"Something's wrong. They're not smiling." He stood, concern on his face.

Jace rose and followed him away from the lake to meet the men as they came to a halt in a cloud of dust.

"We need to go," Brady said. "There's a fire to the west. We could see it from the ridge. It's only saving grace is it's headed away from town."

"Shit. There's no cell reception up here, and I forgot the satellite radio. Unless either of you grabbed it?" Seb said.

They both shook their heads.

He swiped a hand over his face. "Okay, let's get packed up. Hopefully, someone else will see it and report it, but we can't bank on that."

"It was still small. Maybe a hundred acres. But with as dry as it's been, it won't take it long to grow," Brady said.

The others, seeing the commotion, came over to find out what was going on. Lee filled them in.

"You and Jace go ahead. Your horses are the fastest," Jenny

said. "We'll get everything cleaned up and meet you at the ranch later."

Jace was moving even as Jenny spoke, knowing how fast a wildfire could grow out of control. It could burn thousands of acres before the firefighters even arrived.

He took Tara's hand for a moment and met her concerned eyes. "Stay with your family until I come back."

She nodded. "I will. Be careful."

He gave her a quick kiss and released her hand. "Yep." Turning, he sprinted toward Elbert, Seb right beside him.

Jace reached the gelding, hands flying as he untied the silver horse. Tossing the reins over the animal's head, he put his foot in the stirrup and mounted up. "Is there a faster way down the mountain?" he asked, backing the horse away from the tree.

"If we go west, we'll get into cell range faster. It'll take us longer to get home, though."

"They can come get us with a trailer. We need to call Declan." Jace turned his horse the way Lee and Brady had come.

"Agreed. Let's go."

Jace gave Elbert a nudge to his flank and tapped the reins against his neck. The big horse, sensing his rider's urgency, leaped forward and galloped away from the others.

They rode full bore across the plain until it started to rise as they climbed the ridge. Both horses slowed as they ascended, but kept a steady pace.

When they crested the top, Seb's sharp intake of air echoed Jace's shock. They jerked their horses to a stop to take in the scene before them. Fire whipped through the trees several miles to their west, consuming timber as it made its way north.

"Lord, have mercy," Seb muttered. "That's not good."

"That's more than a hundred acres." *A lot* more. "We need

to get reception. Fast." He nudged Elbert back into action and they took off down the ridge as quick as they dared.

Both horses proved to be as nimble-footed as they were fast, agilely picking their way over rocks and then branches as they passed the timberline.

"Whatever horses you bred to get these two, you need to do it again," Jace said as he settled back into the saddle after Elbert jumped a fallen tree at a fast canter and never broke stride.

A corner of Seb's mouth quirked. "I'm wishing we hadn't castrated either of them."

So was Jace. He'd never ridden a horse like Elbert. He had a smooth, rolling gait and an awareness of himself in his environment unlike any he'd ever seen. It was like riding a cloud.

The forest opened before them to the river, which up here wasn't much more than a stream. They led both horses into the shallow water, splashing across in moments.

"We're getting close," Seb said, as they dove back into the woods. "The road's about a mile from here."

"Good. I can smell smoke now."

"Me too." Seb's voice was grim.

The flatter ground this side of the river allowed them to push the horses faster, and they emerged from the trees a few minutes later. Horse shoes clattered on the pavement in an uneven staccato as Elbert and Pike protested the sudden change of pace to a walk.

Elbert tossed his head and took several quick steps to the side, still eager to run.

"Whoa, slow down, boy. Sheesh, you just never quit." The horse calmed at the sound of his voice, snorting a breath as his hour-long dash came to an end.

"Check your phone," Seb called.

Jace stood in the saddle and stuffed his hand in his front pocket to fish out his cell. He punched the home button, and it lit up. "I've got a bar." He looked back at Seb. "Is yours any better?"

"No. Hopefully, a call will go through." He scrolled through his contacts and touched one of them, then brought the phone to his ear.

Jace prayed it connected. They could try texting, but it would be easier to give all the details through a call.

"Deck! Thank God. It's Seb. There's a fire southeast of town. It's expanding rapidly and moving south."

Letting out a breath of relief, Jace let his shoulders relax as he listened to the rest of Seb's call. He hoped Declan could mobilize the hotshot crew before the fire grew much larger.

Seb ended the call and expelled a sigh. "He got a call from the Nyderts a few minutes ago. They spotted it and called it in." He looked up at the sky, then back at Jace. "Jesus, what a day."

"I'll second that."

"Come on." Seb tipped his head to his left. "Let's head toward town. It's closer than the ranch, and I need to help with emergency management."

As Jace swung Elbert around to follow, uneasiness settled in his gut. Something else was coming. He could feel it.

Twenty

The sound of boots on the front porch pulled Tara from her nap on her parents' couch. She sat up and stretched, then rose to answer the soft knock. She padded over to the door in her bare feet and flipped on the outside light.

Jace waved at her. Even through the beveled glass, she could see the fatigue pinching his face. Unlocking the door, she pulled it open.

"Hi." She stepped back and motioned him inside.

"Hey. Sorry I'm so late." His voice was low in deference to the hour.

"It's okay. We haven't been home all that long. After we got back, the others helped me clean my house, then Mom and I went to the restaurant to check on things there. Cassie and the rest of the staff did a great job righting everything. We're ready for business tomorrow. How're the firefighting efforts going?"

Jace sighed and rubbed at his tired eyes. "They've gotten a start. It's only about five percent contained, and it's grown to three thousand acres. They're hoping the wind doesn't shift. If it does, it could blow back toward town or even out here."

"Yeah, that's what Dad and Brady are worried about. They rode back out on fresh horses right after they picked up Pike and Elbert. They want to herd some of the cattle closer to home and away from the fire. They took camping supplies with them and several of the ranch hands."

"Can they get that many head out of here if the fire swings this way?"

"They won't transport them, but leave gates open so they can get away from the fire. Parts of the pastures closest to the ranch buildings are bare of vegetation as a firebreak."

A yawn cracked his jaw as he nodded. "Sorry. Are you ready to go?"

"Yep." She slid her feet into her shoes and picked up her purse.

He led her back to the door, and she locked it behind them.

"I'm glad your dad thought to have your brothers drive my truck and Seb's into town when they came to get the horses. I didn't really think about how I'd get back out here when we rode into town."

She hopped up into the truck and smiled. "I bet it was a sight to see you two riding in."

He smiled back, his teeth flashing white in the dark interior, and backed the vehicle out of the driveway, heading for her house. "We did get quite a few looks. That might have been because we weren't exactly walking. I have learned that Elbert, while he knows that speed, detests it."

She laughed. "Yeah, he's a bundle of energy, that's for sure."

He shook his head, disbelief clear in his voice. "And this was *after* our mad dash down the mountain."

She giggled. "Do you have a crush?"

A low laugh rumbled from his chest. "Maybe a little."

He pulled into her drive and shut off the vehicle. They got

out and walked up to the front door. She unlocked it and let them in, turning on the lights.

"Wow. You guys did a lot of work this evening." He shut and locked the door behind them. "Did you find anything?"

"No." Disgust laced her voice. "I still have the bedroom closet left to do, but after that, I don't know where else to look." She kicked her shoes off and tossed her purse onto the table by the door.

Jace set his keys next to her bag and toed off his boots. "Maybe he really didn't have anything and this guy just thought he did. If whatever Sean knew was as damning as I think it is, whoever is behind all this would do whatever it took to make sure there was nothing to implicate him. Even if he's chasing nothing."

She sighed. "Well, whatever it is, I don't want to think about it anymore tonight. It's been a roller coaster of a day, and all I want is to take a bath and go to bed."

His eyes darkened, and Tara could tell he was thinking about her in the tub. Her body warmed as she imagined him in there with her.

"Tara, don't look at me like that. Not if you want to sleep."

His low voice rolled over her, making her shiver. She studied his handsome face, taking in the strong, square, stubbled jaw; those firm lips; and his deep, ocean blue eyes, which held a depth of emotions she knew were showing in her own.

She took a shaky breath. "Maybe I don't want to sleep."

He was inches away in one long stride.

"Are you sure?"

In answer, she looped her arms around his neck and pressed a kiss to his lips.

He speared his fingers into her hair, wrecking the braid she'd put it in that morning, and angled her head to deepen the kiss. She was on fire and he'd barely touched her. Her feet left the floor as he lifted her and began walking toward the bedrooms.

They reached her room, stumbling over the threshold in the dark. He headed for the bed, banging his shin on the post.

Tara giggled as he cursed into her mouth.

He pulled back. "You think that's funny, do you?" His hands wrapped around her waist and he peeled her free of his body to toss her onto the bed.

She squealed as she went airborne, then bounced into the mountain of pillows. "I'll kiss it and make it better," she said on a laugh.

In the glow of the moonlight coming through the window, she could just make out the predatory grin on his face.

"Not until I've kissed all of you first."

A shiver went through her. He needed to join her on the bed. Now.

She sat up and grabbed a fistful of his shirt and yanked him forward. He toppled onto her, making them both laugh. Her giggles died in her throat, though, when he pressed his mouth to her collarbone and nipped. She wove her fingers into his golden hair, clutching the strands as he fanned the fire raging in her body with just his mouth.

He moved down to her chest, trailing his lips over her sensitized skin. Tara let out a frustrated groan as the fabric of her top and bra dampened the feel. She pushed him back so she could sit up and pull the tank over her head.

"Slow down, there, killer," he said as she reached for the clasp on her bra. "There's no rush."

Defiance snapped in her eyes. She didn't want slow. Slow could come later.

Holding his gaze, she continued to reach for the clasp, undoing it with a quick turn of her wrists. The garment fell away, exposing her to his eyes and touch.

"Minx." He pulled her to him, closing his mouth over the tip of one breast.

Much better...

She threw her head back, awash in sensation. He drove her higher with his teeth and tongue until the urge to take off the rest of her clothing and his overwhelmed her. She tugged on his hair, raising his face.

"Get naked."

He grinned, a playful tilt to his head. "But I'm having fun."

She returned his smile, her expression coquettish. "You'll have more fun if you take off your clothes." She trailed her hands down his shoulders and over his chest. A fine tremor ran through his muscles at her touch.

He backed away, shucking his t-shirt as he moved. Tara bit the corner of her bottom lip as he exposed his muscled torso to the moonlight. His tattoos stood out in stark relief on his skin in the dark.

The rasp of his zipper drew her eyes down over his washboard abs to his waist. The fabric of his jeans parted, freeing his engorged manhood. She reached out to hook her fingers in the waistband of his boxers, tugging them down as he removed his pants. He kicked them free of his feet, and she extended one hand to trace a finger down his length, eliciting a hiss.

Loving the feel of silk over steel, she did it again. Before she could reach the tip, he grabbed her wrist, halting her progress.

"Your turn," he growled.

Pushing her back, she fell into the pillows again. He kneeled on the bed, straddling her knees, and unfastened her shorts. Tara lifted her hips to help him slide them and her panties down her legs. Once free of her body, he threw them over the side of the bed to join his clothes.

She sat up and locked her hands around his neck, pulling

him down to her for a mind-numbing kiss. He shifted his weight to rest between her legs.

A moan followed by a rough whimper escaped her as she felt his hard length rest against her heated flesh. "I need you. So bad."

She felt him smile against her breast. He trailed a hand down the outside of her thigh, then over her knee and up the inside of her leg. Every inch closer he moved to her center, raised the temperature in the room until Tara felt like she would burst into flames. At the first touch of his fingers through her folds, she jerked at the spike in intensity. Never had it felt this good.

"Jace, please."

In answer, he dipped a finger into her channel, gently stroking.

"Not yet. I haven't kissed you everywhere."

He leaned down, feathering kisses over her breasts and abdomen, all while continuing to stroke her with his hand. Tara's need built, stoking the fire that wanted to engulf her. He scooted back a bit, his lips moving to her hipbones, then her legs. When he pulled his hand away so he could reach her ankles and feet, she cried out her displeasure, cursing him.

His low laugh was barely audible. "Patience, my dear."

Screw patience...

Tara vaulted forward, pushing him back as she rose until he was on his back, lying diagonally across the bed. She straddled his hips, his erection teasing her entrance.

"I told you you'd have more fun without your clothes." Raising up, she lowered herself onto him.

They both moaned at the exquisite friction. Her skin flushed, heat suffusing her entire body, while Jace's muscles coiled. Veins stood out in his neck and arms as he held himself still, letting her body adjust.

Once she was comfortable, she leaned forward to rest her

palms on his chest and lifted her hips. She was wound so tight already, it would only take a few strokes for her to find her release.

When it hit, she was unprepared for the magnitude. It obliterated all rational thought from her head, set her body on fire faster than a flashover, and left her breathing like she'd just climbed Pike's Peak at a run.

While she was still coming down off her high, Jace rolled them over without breaking their connection, taking control. As her first orgasm faded, he built a second. This time, when she went over the edge, he went with her.

Tara opened her eyes to darkness, a heavy weight over her middle. She tensed, her nightmare still fresh in her mind, before she remembered where she was and who she was with. Jace's slow, even breathing didn't change as she lifted his arm and got out of bed. She found her underwear and picked up his t-shirt from the floor, slipping both items on, then retreated to the kitchen.

Her hands shook as she took a glass from the cabinet and filled it with water. Despite her relaxed, happy state when she'd fallen asleep, nightmares still plagued her. She knew it was probably from the trauma of the last week and her brain trying to process all the changes in her life, but it didn't make the dreams less frightening.

This time, she'd dreamed of a nameless, faceless man who broke in to carry her away, killing Jace as he tried to save her. It highlighted not only her fear about the person wreaking havoc on her life but also her feelings for the man sleeping in her bed. The latter, more than anything, was what made her hands shake; the depth of pain and grief she experienced in the dream when the intruder shot Jace. Was on par with, or stronger, than how she felt when Sean died, and that scared the life out of her.

She gulped down her water and stared out the kitchen window at the moonlit landscape. There were still a couple hours to morning, but she would never be able to go back to sleep now. Finishing her water, she set the glass in the sink and turned around. She needed something to do to keep her occupied.

On quiet feet, she went back to the bedroom. Jace had rolled onto his stomach and the covers had slipped down to his waist, baring his muscular back and the raven inked on his skin. She itched to crawl back into bed and trace the bird, but she didn't dare. Last night had left her reeling. The intensity of their actions scared her. She needed to process everything, and climbing back into bed would not accomplish that.

Instead, she walked across the room without a sound to the closet and shut herself inside. She would finish the last of the clean-up since she was wide awake.

"This is such a mess," she whispered with a sigh. She bent down and started sorting things into piles—clothes, hangers, shoes, and the stuff that was on the shelves. It didn't take her long to get it all separated. Once she had her piles, she started hanging up the clothes, thankful her stalker hadn't trashed her clothing. It was just rumpled. Nothing an iron couldn't fix.

Humming softly to herself, she worked, finding a rhythm and getting lost in her task. She stretched to put a photo album on the shelf when the door flew open.

"Freeze!"

Tara shrieked and jumped back. Her foot hit the pile of shoes on the floor and she stumbled. Reaching out, she grabbed the clothes she'd just hung, halting her fall but undoing some of her work.

"Jesus, Tara." Exasperation and relief colored Jace's voice.

She regained her balance and looked up in time to see him

lower his weapon and thumb the safety on. He stood in the doorway clad only in his boxer briefs. His sleep-tousled hair fell over his forehead, softening the annoyed look on his face.

"What the hell are you doing in here? It's five-thirty."

Annoyed herself at her reaction to his near-naked state, she yanked the now empty hangers off the rod and started stuffing them into the sweaters she'd pulled off. "I couldn't sleep. This seemed like the most productive way to spend the time. Why are you barging in here with your gun drawn?"

"I woke up, and you weren't in bed, so I checked the bathroom and the living area. When I didn't find you there, I came back in here looking for signs of where you went. That's when I noticed the light under the door."

"And you assumed it was our mystery intruder?"

"I didn't know what to think. After everything that's happened, I certainly wasn't going to discount the idea." He huffed a breath and laid his pistol on a shelf before stepping further inside. "The next time you can't sleep, tell me so I don't think the worst, please."

She looked at him through her lashes and nodded. Turning away, she hung up the sweater in her hands and picked up another. He needed to go back to bed. Like, now. The sight of all his tanned skin and dark tattoos was waking up her lady parts. As good as it had been between them, she wasn't keen on a repeat. Enough of her emotions were already involved. And she was still raw from her nightmare.

But he didn't leave. He walked over to the pile of clothes and started folding her jeans.

"You don't have to help. I can do this by myself."

He looked at her mid-fold. She tried to keep her expression neutral, but when he narrowed his eyes, she knew she'd failed. He set the pants on a shelf, then took a long stride to stand in front of her, a frown drawing down his brows.

"Okay. What's wrong?"

"Nothing." She bent and picked up the shoe box that served as her memory box. It was something she'd started as a teenager, and she hadn't been able to break the habit as an adult. Like everything else, it was knocked off the shelf, its contents all over the closet floor. Instead of looking at Jace, she searched the pile of miscellaneous items she'd gathered for the things that went in the box.

"It's not nothing. You're snappy. Why are you pissed?"

She shoved a handful of pictures into the box. "I'm not pissed. I just want to get this done."

"Then you should want my help."

A growl of frustration pushed its way through her throat. She reached for more pictures and kept her mouth shut. She was afraid of what would come out if she didn't.

"This will never work if you won't talk to me, Tara." He picked up her ring box and held it out.

Seeing the box in his hand—the symbol of the love she'd had and lost—set loose the emotions jumbled up inside her.

"I don't even know what *this* is! You've come barreling into my life and found all the little cracks in my walls and shoved your way through, leaving a bigger hole than you found. I honestly don't know whether to love you or hate you right now." She snatched the box from his hand while he sat there with a stunned expression. She started to toss it into the shoe box, but a rattle inside it stopped her.

Tears welled in her eyes. That bastard better not have damaged her rings when he tore her house apart. She lifted the lid to see the bands still nestled securely in the velvet padding. She shook the box again, and it rattled once more.

"Is it supposed to do that?"

"No." She pulled on the tab at the back to lift the padding, but there was nothing under it. "Where's it coming from?" She gave it another shake. Now that the box was empty, she could feel something in the bottom hit the sides.

"I think it's got a false bottom." She laid her rings on the closet floor and turned the box over in her hands, scrutinizing it.

Jace scooted closer to look too. "Run your fingers over the edges. You might be able to feel what you can't see."

She touched the seam, letting her finger glide over the smooth black leather. Two-thirds of the way around, she felt a rough edge.

"There's something…" Her voice trailed off as she stuck her thumbnail into the seam and pushed. It slid between the bottom and the side of the box. She curled it under the edge and pulled up. The bottom of the ring box popped open.

"Holy shit," she breathed.

She reached in and lifted out a small USB drive and looked at Jace. His eyes were as wide as hers.

"How did you not know that was there?"

She showed him the bottom of the box. There was a piece of tape hanging loose. "It must have come free when the guy tossed the house."

Jace plucked it from her fingers, a smile of triumph turning up one side of his mouth. "Let's go see what's on it, shall we?"

They rose and left the closet, Jace leading the way to the spare bedroom and her laptop. He pulled out the desk chair and spun it, motioning for her to sit down. She took a seat and lifted the lid on the computer. The screen lit up, asking for her password. Her fingers flew as she typed it in.

When the screen changed, she held out her hand for the drive. Jace put it in her palm. Tara slid it into one of the USB ports and tapped her foot on the floor while she waited for the computer to read the files.

Come on, Sean. You better have left me something to work with…

The box that popped up, though, was not a list of files on the drive. She read the message in disbelief.

"He encrypted it? Fuck!" Tara let her head fall with a thunk onto the desk.

Jace cursed, and she heard him pace away.

She sat up. "If he wasn't already dead, I'd kill him." With a hard sigh, she leaned back in the chair and spun around to look at Jace. "What now?"

He ran a hand through his hair. The blonde strands becoming more tousled than they were before. She covered her eyes, rubbing at her face to disguise the move. He was killing her with the fresh from bed after a bout of mind-blowing sex vibe.

"Maybe Seb knows someone who can crack it," he said.

She chanced a look at him, keeping her eyes on his face.

"Do you have any idea what kind of encryption he would have used?"

"No. But it may be something extremely complicated. Sean handled communications for the team. Decrypting messages was part of his job description." She moaned. "I shouldn't be surprised he'd do something like this. Especially if what's on that drive is worth killing over."

Jace walked up to her and leaned down. Every cell in her body went on alert at the proximity of his near-naked body in her space. He didn't kiss her, though. Instead, he leaned around her to eject the USB stick from the computer.

He straightened and held out a hand. "Come on."

She frowned, but took his hand. He pulled her out of the chair.

"Where are we going?"

"To get dressed. By the time we shower and eat, it won't be that much earlier than when I normally leave for work."

She tensed when they entered her bedroom and he led her to the master bath. As much as she admired all the masculinity on display, she was not in the right frame of mind to have a repeat of last night. She was beginning to feel like bees were buzzing through her brain. Emotions came at her from every direction, none of them lingering long enough for her to process them. She needed some space, so she could think.

But he didn't try to join her. He left her standing in the doorway, with a kiss to her forehead and a lingering look that showed understanding, but also some sadness.

That last bit killed her. She stared at the now closed door, frustration making tears gather in her eyes.

"Dammit."

The last thing she wanted to do was upset him. He'd been nothing but patient and kind with her. Why couldn't she get her act together and be the kind of woman he deserved?

Twenty-One

J ace stared at his computer screen, not really seeing the list of emails he scrolled through. His mind was on Tara and her reaction to their lovemaking. Last night had been something else. It was like touching the sun and living to tell about it. Exhilarating and unbelievable. He thought she'd felt the same way. She certainly hadn't complained before they fell asleep.

But something changed between then and when she woke up. He just wished he knew what and how to fix it.

The computer dinged, drawing Jace out of his thoughts. He focused on the screen, seeing he had a new message. His heart kicked up a notch as he realized it was from the rep at the company that made the valve Dr. Randall found implanted in Brown's chest.

He clicked on the email and skimmed the contents. Triumph surged, pushing away thoughts of his relationship with Tara. Finally, they had a solid lead.

Switching screens, he typed Brown's actual name into the database, along with a few other parameters to narrow the search. Several names popped up. He clicked on the first one and tried not to shout his feeling of victory when Brown's face stared back at him. Jace scrolled through the file, noting the man's occupation and city of residence.

He pushed away from his desk and headed next door to Seb's office. The door was a jar, so he rapped his knuckles on it, then stepped inside.

Seb looked up from his computer.

"Matthew Douglas Claybaugh."

The other man frowned. "Who's that?"

"Doug Brown."

His eyes widened. "You got a hit on the implant?"

"Yep. And I already ran his name. He's a PI from Colorado Springs."

"What the hell? Who would hire a PI from there to come here and spy on my sister?" Seb sighed. "Go to Colorado Springs. Find his office and house. I'll get you a warrant for both, then I'll call their police department to get you some backup. I'd go with you, but I've got a bunch of meetings this morning."

"Let me take Gentry. He's a quick study and a good cop."

Seb nodded and waved a hand, shooing him out the door. "Go."

Jace whirled, his heart pounding. It was time to bring Tara's nightmare to an end.

~

The heavenly scent of fresh coffee and pastries assailed Tara's nose as she stepped through the door of Peppy Brewster. She needed a latte fix. And some girl talk.

Macy waved from behind the counter, then pointed toward the back corner of the café. "Have a seat with the others and I'll bring your coffee over in a minute."

Tara nodded and left her to finish ringing up the customer

at the counter. She walked over to her friends and pulled out a chair, sinking into it with a sigh.

"I'm so glad you suggested this," she said, looking at London.

London smiled. "I figured you had some explaining to do. Wine would probably be better, but it's ten a.m."

Tara leaned forward on her elbows, scrubbing her hands over her face. She'd been dreading this conversation. "Can we wait for Macy, so I only have to say this once?"

"Sure," Rayna said. "You can tell us what has you frowning while we wait."

"Having to explain why I kept my baby a secret isn't enough of a reason?"

She just shook her head.

Tara huffed. "Fine. It's Jace."

"What about him?" London asked.

"All my reasons for not wanting a relationship with him still stand, but I'll be damned if I can stay away."

"Then don't," London said. "Take it from someone who waited far too long to act on her feelings. Seb and I wasted a lot of years. I'll always regret the time we could have had and didn't. Don't be like us."

"What scares you?" Rayna asked, ever insightful.

"He's so much like Sean—always ready to rush into danger. I'm not sure I can handle losing someone else I love."

"Will it matter if you're together or not if he dies?" Rayna's question was soft.

"If who dies?" Macy said, walking up to the table, two coffee cups in her hand. She handed one to Tara, then sat down.

"Jace," London said. "Tara's still opposed to a relationship because she's worried he's going to die on the job."

"Or riding his motorcycle, or riding Elbert at breakneck

speeds, or for a myriad of other adrenaline-inducing reasons," Tara said.

"You know, you used to do the adrenaline-inducing stuff too," Macy pointed out. She took a sip of her drink, then continued. "I have pictures if you've forgotten."

"No, I haven't forgotten. That's just not me anymore."

"Oh, that's bullshit," Rayna said. "No one who breaks into the principal's house to take pictures of him sleeping in his easy chair in his boxers with chip crumbs all over his chest suddenly decides she no longer enjoys being an adrenaline junkie. You can't sit there and tell me you don't want Jace to take you out on his motorcycle and take the mountain roads just a little too fast."

Tara bit her lip, but said nothing. She couldn't. She *had* thought about that. More than once.

"You've let fear rule your life since Sean died. Now, the real you wants out, and it's challenging you big time. The question is, who are you going to let win? 'Real' you or 'scared' you?" Rayna said.

"I think she'll let the real her win," Macy said.

Tara looked at them, bemused, as they talked about her like she wasn't sitting there.

"Scared her wouldn't jump Jace's bones. She'd keep him at arm's length. But there isn't a straight, unattached woman on the planet who wouldn't let that man have his way with her."

A blush lit Tara's face. She lifted her coffee cup to hide it, but it did little good.

London sat forward and pointed at her. "You slept with him!"

"Say it louder for the people across the street," Tara said in a loud whisper. "I don't think they heard you."

She had the good grace to look chagrined. "Sorry. But you did. I know you did!"

Tara looked off to the side. "That might be true, yes."

Macy squealed. "Do tell." Her face turned serious, and she leaned forward. "It didn't suck, did it?

Tara laughed. "No. It most definitely did not suck."

"So, if you slept with him, does that mean scared Tara's on the run?" Macy asked.

Tara groaned. "I don't know. Maybe. I just don't know if I'm ready, you know?"

"Why?" Rayna asked. "Sean's been gone three years. Are you still in love with him?"

"A part of me is, yes. I will always love Sean. I'm just not sure I can get past the pain of losing him to let myself love again."

"I think you already do love him," London said. "He got more out of you in a week than your entire family did in years. There's obviously something there."

"Yeah, but he understands because he's been there."

"True, but do you really think you would have shared what you did with just any man?" Rayna said.

Tara pursed her lips as she considered that. "I'm not sure. Probably not." She sighed. "I just need to think. To process what's happening. With everything else going on, my feelings have taken a backseat."

"Well, we're here for you if you need to sort things out more," Macy said.

Tara nodded. "I appreciate it. I don't deserve friends like you. I feel like I let everyone down by keeping Lucy a secret."

Rayna covered Tara's hand. "Honey, the only person you let down was yourself. You dealt with her death and Sean's all alone out of fear of the pain, failing to understand that you have to push through it to heal. More than anything, I think that's what Jace has made you see. Am I right?"

Tara nodded again. She *was* right. He'd pushed her to confront her feelings instead of continuing to bury them. Because of him, she was beginning to feel like her old self.

She sighed and sat back, taking a sip of her latte and staring thoughtfully around the café. This thing with the stalker needed to end so she could concentrate on how she felt and what she really wanted moving forward.

The voice in the back of her head, shouting Jace's name, was getting louder.

~

"So, this is Claybaugh's office?" Aaron Gentry looked through the windshield at the three-story brownstone in downtown Colorado Springs.

Jace leaned forward over the steering wheel to look at the building. "This is the address listed on his PI's license." He shut the truck off and reached for the door handle. "Come on. Let's go see what we can find."

They climbed out and walked up the sidewalk. A detective from the Colorado Springs police department met them at the door.

Jace held out a hand. "Chief Deputy Jace Travers." He motioned to Aaron. "This is Deputy Aaron Gentry."

The detective took his hand and shook it. "Detective Charlie Gibson. Your boss called and filled me in. I have to say, I'm not surprised Claybaugh was in on something dirty." He turned toward the building's front door.

"Really? Why do you say that?"

"He's always been shady. Can't exactly say his methods were on the up and up."

Gibson motioned to the door. "You got a key for this?"

"No." Jace pulled a lock picking kit from the cargo pocket on his pants. He kneeled in front of the door and inserted two of the long, thin rods into the lock, manipulating them until he heard the snick of the tumblers turning. Withdrawing the picks, he stood and turned the knob. The door swung inward.

"I think I understand why the sheriff hired you," Aaron said, walking into Claybaugh's office behind him. "You two are a lot alike."

"Your sheriff picks locks?" Gibson asked. He turned on the lights and shut the door behind them.

"If necessary," Jace replied. "Seb was FBI. I was Army. We both bring a little color to the job."

Gibson grinned. "I think I might need to visit sometime." He clapped his hands together and looked around the room. "So, what are we looking for?"

"Anything that might tell us who hired him to surveil Tara Miller."

The three of them split up and spent the next several hours searching Claybaugh's office, finding nothing about their case, but enough about others to know he was blackmailing several people.

Jace laid the last file in the box Gibson was taking back to his precinct and glanced at Gentry. "I think we need to look at some of these others as suspects in Claybaugh's death."

The young deputy lifted a brow. "You really think one of them is responsible?"

He shrugged. "It's possible. I still like our unknown ringleader for it, but I'm not writing off anyone at this point." He looked at Gibson. "You know if there's any video surveillance around this place?"

"I'll check with the businesses around here, but this place doesn't have any."

He had a feeling this whole site would be a bust. It was doubtful Claybaugh's client would want to be seen in such a public place where he could be connected to the PI.

"Let's head over to his house. It'll probably yield about as much as this place, but maybe we'll get lucky."

Gibson picked up his box and led the way outside. They

split up, going to their respective vehicles. Jace plugged Claybaugh's home address into his GPS and started his truck.

The drive through town was quick. He turned into an affluent neighborhood and wound his way up the tree-lined street as they climbed the hill. He pulled up to a terracotta-colored, rambling two-story house.

Gentry let out a low whistle at the sight of the house. "I think we're in the wrong line of work."

Jace put the truck in park and unfastened his seatbelt. "Yeah, well, I'm willing to bet he got most of this through his blackmail schemes." He opened his door and climbed out.

Gibson pulled up behind them.

Not waiting on the detective, Jace headed for the front door. He used his lock picks again to open it. An alarm blared as the door swung inward.

"I'll get that silenced," Gibson said, pulling out his phone.

Jace nodded and started wandering.

"This is like a showplace," Gentry said. "It doesn't even look like anyone lives here."

He agreed. But Claybaugh was out of town for several months, so there wouldn't be much to keep tidy. "Start upstairs. I'll check down here."

Gentry gave him a nod and took off up the staircase. Jace wandered through the living room, peering in the massive entertainment cabinet and finding nothing but some expensive equipment.

The alarm cut out, the silence almost as deafening as the noise. He heard Gibson walk across the tile floor.

"I've got the kitchen," the other man said.

Jace headed down the hallway, turning into a den. He sighed and scratched the back of his head as he stared at the book-lined shelves. This was going to take a while.

∼

"The upstairs is clean," Gentry said, walking into the den a couple hours later.

Jace looked up from where he crouched in front of the bookshelf on the far end of the room. He put the last book back on the shelf, wincing as his knees popped when he stood. "I should have let you search down here."

Gentry flashed a quick, amused grin. "Did you find anything?"

"No." Frustration bit Jace's gut. Couldn't the guy have at least had a hidey-hole somewhere with a clue as to who hired him?

Gibson walked in. "Rest of the downstairs is clear. No papers pertaining to anything outside the house. I found a couple thumb drives, but it was tax statements and pictures."

Anger at the lack of leads had Jace clenching his fists as he strode from the room. He'd wasted an entire day, and all he had to show for it was a gnawing hunger because he skipped lunch. His boots echoed in the entryway. He pushed through the front door, stopping at the end of the sidewalk. Hands braced on his hips, he tipped his face to the sky, biting back the urge to yell out his frustrations.

"You know. I didn't notice any cameras as part of Claybaugh's security, but I'm willing to bet the neighbors across the street have one of those video doorbells."

Jace looked at Gentry, curious. "What makes you think that?"

"One, their car. It's got all the latest tech. Two, they have children." He pointed to the basketball hoop and bicycles in the driveway. "And three, while I was upstairs, I noticed they got a package delivery. The woman who answered the door looked like she was on a first name basis with the driver. With the rise in package thefts—"

"They'd want a camera system to monitor their porch." Jace cut him off. "I knew there was a reason I brought you."

Gentry grinned, and the two of them jogged across the street to knock on the neighbor's door. Gibson ran up behind them.

"What are we doing?"

Jace pointed at the camera doorbell Aaron had rightly presumed they had. "Checking video feed."

The front door swung open to reveal a middle-aged woman in leggings and a tank top, her blonde hair caught up in a high ponytail.

"May I help you?"

All three men held up their badges.

"Ma'am, we're here investigating the death of your neighbor, Matthew Claybaugh," Jace said.

She gasped, a hand going to her throat. "Oh my God! What happened?"

"That's what we're trying to figure out. Would you be willing to share the footage from your doorbell camera with us? It may have caught an image of the man we're looking for."

She cleared her throat and stepped back, holding the door wide. "Yes, of course. Please, come in."

They stepped inside, and she led them through the foyer and down a long hallway to an office.

"All the video feed is stored on our cloud." She sat down at the desk and opened the laptop sitting there, logging in. "What day are you looking for?"

"We're not really sure. Could you go back a few weeks and fast-forward? We want activity at his house."

She gave them a skeptical look. "Are you sure you want to go back that far? Even on fast-forward, that will take a while for you to go through."

Jace nodded. "We're sure."

She stared at him another moment before looking down at the computer. "Okay." She pulled up the video feed and selected the date. "Here you go. I'll let you sit here and look through it, since you know what it is you're trying to find. Would you like anything to drink?" she asked, rising from the chair.

"No, thank you, ma'am."

She smiled. "You're welcome. I'll be in the kitchen if you need me."

"Thank you. We appreciate it."

"You're welcome. I hope you find what you're looking for. Mr. Claybaugh was nice. Quiet, but nice."

She walked away, and Jace sat down in her now vacant seat. Aaron and Gibson came around to stand behind him.

"Are you really going to go through weeks of footage?" Aaron asked. "Wouldn't it be better for us to take the file back to the station and go over it there instead of tying up her computer?"

"I want to have a quick look first before we do that. I'm betting our killer paid Claybaugh a visit sometime after London overheard that conversation during the serial killer investigation. He left the inn for over a week after Marsters died."

"And you think he came back here," Aaron concluded.

"Yep."

Jace cued up the footage for the day Claybaugh left Silver Gap and hit fast-forward. They saw him turn into his driveway late that night. Two days later, they saw a dark blue truck pull into the drive in the middle of the night. Jace stopped the replay and started it up at normal speed.

"It's too far away to see the license plate," Gibson remarked.

"Maybe. The video is actually great quality. Our crime lab might be able to enhance it. Gentry, go get the homeowner. We need her permission to make a copy of this."

As the younger man ran off to do as asked, Jace hit fast-forward again. The truck left about an hour later. He sped up the feed further, but the only other vehicle to go in and out of Claybaugh's drive was his Mercedes SUV.

Aaron walked back in with the woman in tow.

"You found something?" she asked.

"Possibly. We just need your permission for a section of video." He pulled up the date and time he was interested in.

"Take whatever you need."

"Could you email the footage?"

"Of course."

Jace stood and motioned for her to sit. "I've got it queued up. From where it starts to an hour afterward is what we need."

"Okay." She made a copy of the video he requested and sent it to the email address Jace gave her for the forensics lab.

"There you go, gentlemen." She smiled up at them.

"Thank you, ma'am," Jace said. "You've been a great help."

"You're welcome. If you need to look at our security tapes again, please let me know."

"I'll do that." He handed her a business card, then motioned to the others. "We'll see ourselves out."

Gentry and Gibson followed him through the house and outside. Jace itched to get on the road. Not just to get back to Tara, but to look at that footage. He hoped Katie could work her magic on it while they drove back.

He turned to Detective Gibson. "Charlie, thanks for your assistance today."

The other man shook his hand. "Anytime. You may have solved several cases for me just with what we found at Claybaugh's office. You need anything else, don't hesitate to call."

"I will keep that in mind." He thanked the detective again, and they went their separate ways.

"Do you really think Katie can get anything from that footage?" Gentry asked, as they pulled away from the house.

"God, I hope so. There's a really clear shot of the rear of the truck as he pulls into the drive. It's just a matter of whether he was too far away."

"She's going to love you. First the encrypted thumb drive and now the security footage."

"I'll recommend her for a raise. Especially if she can crack that encryption."

Edginess made Jace press harder on the accelerator. Everything they needed was in those two things. He just hoped they could access the information before the mastermind behind all this found out what they had.

Tara looked up as the front door of London's B&B opened. Jace's tall form entered, sending her heart rate skyrocketing. After being around him so much the last week, a full day without him was torture. She wanted to turn him around and take him back to her house, where they could be alone. Instead, there were things they needed to catch him up on. Like the identity of the man sitting across from her.

Jace walked into the room and sat down next to her on the loveseat. He smiled at her, his eyes conveying he'd missed her, before turning to the stranger in their midst.

"Jace, this is Commander Tim Jacobsen," Seb said. "He was Sean's CO. Commander, this is my chief deputy, Jace Travers."

The older man smiled, revealing a nest of crow's feet around his eyes. "Pleasure to meet you, Deputy."

"Likewise," Jace said.

"The commander's been filling us in on Sean's final mission. Why don't you tell him what you told us? The cliffnotes version, anyway," Seb said.

"So, after Seb contacted me, I reviewed the mission report,

and I noticed something. Some of the statements the men gave seem too consistent. They each wrote their own statement of the incident, but they all read as though one person wrote them all."

"Did they?"

Jacobsen shook his head. "No. They were separated and debriefed, then told to write their mission reports."

"Why wasn't this flagged before?"

"I wasn't the one to review their reports, so I don't know."

"Why not?"

"It was a death investigation on a rather high-profile mission, so it went to the base commander, Colonel Paul Mazur. I was left making arrangements to transport Sean's body home and evaluate the mental status of the rest of his team."

"And what was your take on the latter?"

"I talked to each of them individually, and they all seemed distraught at his death, some more than others. Shephard took it particularly hard."

Tara seethed as she listened to the commander's tale. She'd be willing to bet the reason Evan was so upset was because of guilt. But whatever he knew, he'd taken to his grave. She hoped the thumb drive they found had enough evidence to put whoever was behind all this in prison for a very long time.

"They were also evaluated by a Navy psychologist and approved for duty after a short period of leave."

"We know what happened to Shephard, but what about the rest of the team?" Seb asked.

"Petty Officer Liam Dotson is still in the Navy. He's been promoted to Chief Petty Officer and is still part of the SEAL teams. Lieutenant Commander Jared Fetter was severely injured a little over a year ago in an IED attack and medically discharged."

"Were there any other SEAL teams stationed on Bagram at the same time?"

Jacobsen nodded. "One. It was a six-man team."

"Do you know what happened to them?" Seb asked.

"No. I can find out, but I doubt they had anything to do with that mission. They were on one of their own, rescuing an Afghani informant and his family."

"What did you find in Colorado Springs?" Seb asked, turning to Jace.

Tara wanted to know that too. She'd only received a text saying he was headed home.

"Not much. An image of a truck going to Claybaugh's house in the middle of the night from a neighbor's doorbell camera during the week he left the inn. I sent it to Katie. I'm hoping she can zoom in on the license plate and get us a name. Whatever documents he had—if any at all—about who hired him were either taken by whoever killed him or they washed away in the river."

"I'm going to have to get that poor woman a raise after this," Seb muttered. "Okay. I think it's time to call it a day for now. Until Katie can get us something, and the background searches I ran on the rest of Sean's team come back, we're at an impasse. London's been cooking up a storm, so how about we all eat and try to relax?"

"I like that idea," Jace said. "I skipped lunch and only downed a protein bar on the way home."

As they rose to go to the dining room, an uneasiness hit Tara. She tried to shrug it off as she followed the others out of the room, sure it was just a reaction to the waiting game they had to play. But a small part of her brain kept insisting that wasn't it, and she'd be damned if she could shut it up.

Twenty-Two

The ring of his cell brought Jace out of a deep sleep. Tara groaned beside him as he slapped at the nightstand, trying to find the phone.

"Make it stop," she muttered, pulling her pillow over her head.

"I'm trying." Exasperation colored his tone. He finally found it, but not before knocking it on the floor.

Cursing whoever was calling him at such an hour, he sat up, flipping back the covers. He bent over, snatching the offending item off the rug. Unease skittered down his spine as he saw Seb's name on the screen.

He answered, leaning over to shake Tara awake, knowing whatever the sheriff was calling about would require them to get up. "Yeah, Seb?"

"The crime lab exploded."

All the air whooshed out of Jace's lungs.

Their evidence...

For a moment, he sat on the edge of the bed, too stunned to move. Then reality rushed back. He sucked in a harsh breath, his mind spinning.

"What happened? Was anyone hurt?"

"Don't know yet. There were people inside, but I've got reports that the fire alarm went off about a minute before it blew."

"Gas leak?"

"Maybe. Just get down here. Bring Tara, so she isn't alone. She can hang with Macy. She came in with Declan."

"On our way." He hung up.

Soft light lit up the bedroom as Tara turned on the lamp next to the bed.

"What's going on?"

He turned to look at her. She sat up in bed, the sheet tucked under her arms.

"The crime lab blew up."

Her eyes widened. "Oh my God! Is everyone okay? And what about the evidence Katie was working on?"

"Seb didn't have any answers yet. Come on. We need to go."

She frowned. "I have to go too?"

"I'm not leaving you alone. Seb said Macy's there. You can stay with her."

She groaned, but got out of bed. "Fine."

They dressed quickly, grabbed jackets to combat the cool night air, and were out the door.

He drove the ten miles to town in record time, pulling up to the police complex amid mass chaos. Flames still licked at the crime lab, the fire department spraying water on the building, trying to knock back the fire. Police cars lined the street on both ends, keeping back curious onlookers.

Jace parked at the end of the line, and they got out, jogging toward the melee. He nodded at Reeves, who stood at the perimeter, then ducked under the crime scene tape, Tara's hand tucked firmly into his.

"This is crazy," Tara said.

He agreed. He was also pretty sure whatever caused the explosion wasn't an accident. It was too much of a coincidence.

Seb waved at them from near one of the fire trucks. Declan stood next to him, barking orders into a radio. They hurried over.

"Any news?" Jace asked.

"There's two missing. A tech and the janitor," Seb replied.

"I'm guessing there's no information on what caused the explosion yet?"

"Actually, I think it was a bomb," Declan said.

Tara gasped. "What?"

"None of the people who evacuated reported smelling gas or had symptoms of exposure—light-headedness, headache, nausea. All they've said is that the fire alarm went off, and the place blew up about a minute later. Several of them barely cleared the door before it blew; they have shrapnel and percussive injuries. We had to fly the night shift supervisor to Denver for treatment."

"Oh my God," Tara breathed. She swayed into Jace.

He squeezed her hand. "We're back to square one now on this case, aren't we?"

Seb's expression was grim. "Unless Katie can get a license plate from that video, yes. Whatever was on that thumb drive of Sean's is long gone."

"That's what we're going to let the bad guy think."

They all spun around at the sound of Katie Mitchum's voice. She stood there, a pensive expression on her face as she looked at her burning lab.

Seb narrowed his eyes. "What do you mean?"

She focused on them and stepped closer, lowering her voice. "I mean, I took the drive home with me today to work on it. It's right here." She patted her pants pocket.

"Oh my God, Katie, I could kiss you!" Tara cried.

She held out a hand. "Don't kiss me yet. I still haven't cracked the encryption. I think I'm close, though. I've got it narrowed down to two different cyphers, but they're both complex algorithms that take time to run."

Jace could see the wheels turn in Seb's mind.

"Okay. Katie, you are officially in protective custody."

"What? Oh, *man!*" She stamped her foot. "Is that really necessary?"

"Yes," Seb and Jace said together.

"If the person who did this finds out they didn't destroy the drive, and they figure out you have it, you could be in a lot of danger," Seb continued. "We need you to crack the encryption, so I'm afraid you're stuck with me or one of my deputies until we discover what's on that thing."

He turned to Jace. "Take her and Tara over to Peppy Brewster. Macy's there making coffee for all the first responders. Once things die down, I'll take Katie back to the inn with me. She can stay with us tonight until we can make other arrangements."

"Wait, I don't have any clothes or anything," she protested.

"I'm sure London has some pajamas you can wear. I'll have a deputy escort you home in the morning so you can change and pack a bag."

She groaned, smoothing her hands over her dark ponytail. "This sucks."

Tara hooked an arm through the other woman's. "I know how you feel."

"Hey!" Jace said.

She turned to look at him, and he held out his arms. "I thought we were good."

Her grin was quick. "Well, we are now."

He rolled his eyes. "Let's get you two over to the café." He glanced at his boss. "I'll be right back."

They started through the crowd, ducking under the

barrier, and walked down the sidewalk toward Macy's coffee shop. When they stepped inside the café, the scent of fresh coffee hit them. Macy stood behind the counter, pouring coffee into paper cups. She had a line of drink carriers full of coffee ready to go. She turned around at their entrance, pausing in her task.

"Hey. What are you guys doing in here?"

"I need to go back and help Seb with the investigation," Jace said. "Tara can't be alone, and now, neither can Ms. Mitchum."

Macy frowned. "Why?"

"Because she's saved all our asses," Tara said, moving toward the counter. She walked around to stand beside her friend and picked up a carafe to fill cups. "She took the flash drive I found home with her. No one but us and Seb know that as of right now. We're aiming to keep it that way."

"Oh, that's great! Okay. So, the blast wasn't an accident?"

"Doesn't look that way," Jace said. "I need to get back. You three good?"

They all nodded. Jace walked forward and leaned over the counter, motioning Tara closer with the crook of a finger. She leaned in and he placed a quick kiss on her lips. "Stay put, okay? I'll have a deputy swing by here every so often and check on you."

"Okay. Be careful."

"I will." He bit his tongue to keep the other words he wanted to say from coming out. As much as their relationship had progressed, she wasn't ready to hear him say he loved her yet. Spinning on his heel, he headed back to the lab.

TWENTY-THREE

"Ha!"

Jace looked up from his desk at the exclamation coming from the squad room. Standing, he walked out of his office to see Katie doing a little jig at the desk where they'd set her up.

Seb came out of his office, and they shared an amused look, before walking toward the woman.

"You find something?" Seb asked.

She looked up with a smile that could light the sun. "You bet your ass I did, Sheriff. A buddy of mine has some experimental photo enhancement software, so I sent him the picture of that truck. He got a license plate number, and I ran it. It belongs to Derrick Thorpe, a contractor out of Pueblo."

Both men sucked in a breath and looked at each other. Alarm bells clanged in Jace's brain.

"Rayna," Seb whispered, eyes wide.

Jace looked down at Katie. "Do you have addresses for Thorpe? Home and business?"

Her smile fell as she took in their expressions. "Um, yeah. I take it we know who this is?"

A grim nod from them both was her only answer.

Jace wished he didn't. He hated the thought of how devastated Rayna would be.

Katie turned back to her computer monitor, clicking through screens, then writing down the information on a notepad. She tore off the sheet of paper and held it out to him.

He took it and glanced at Seb. "I'll get a warrant, then call Pueblo PD and see if they can pick him up."

Seb nodded. "I'll go find Rayna and talk to her. See what she might know. I doubt it's much, but she might be able to give us his location if he isn't already in the wind."

Jace's feet were already moving. "Sounds good. Thanks, Katie!" he tossed over his shoulder.

Adrenaline surged. It was time to nab this guy.

Tara glanced up as the door to Rayna's greenhouse opened. She smiled at Seb as he walked in, but it soon died as she took in the grim set to his features.

He saw her, and his frown deepened. "What are you doing here?"

She pointed to the crates of produce at her feet. "Rayna had a surplus and offered it to me. And don't worry. I didn't drive here myself. She came and got me. And yes, I texted Jace."

He waved away her explanation. "You're fine. That's not why I'm here. I need to talk to Rayna." His eyes traveled to the raven-haired woman standing three rows away, where she picked tomatoes.

"Me?" Rayna pointed at herself. "About what?"

Seb hesitated, looking at Tara briefly before his gaze returned to Rayna.

Tara put down the clippers she was using to pick fresh

basil. "Seb? What is it?" It wasn't like him to hesitate. Something was wrong.

He took off his hat and ran a hand through his dark hair, sighing. "It's about your boyfriend, Ray," he said, using the nickname Thomas coined for her when they were children.

Rayna swallowed hard, her eyes round. "Derrick? What about him?"

"He—" Seb paused and started again. "Rayna, he was seen going to Claybaugh's—Doug Brown's—house the same week Claybaugh left Silver Gap."

Tara's eyes widened. She turned to look at her friend, who wore an equally flabbergasted expression.

"What? No. You must have the wrong person. Whoever saw him must be mistaken."

"It's on video." Seb's voice was soft.

"Oh my God," Tara breathed.

Rayna backed away from the row of plants, bumping into the raised bed behind her. Her hands flew out to steady herself, but she kept moving, rounding the row to come stand next to Tara. "No. No, it's not him."

"The license plate on the truck matches. I'm sorry."

She snapped her fingers and pointed at him. "There! Maybe someone drove his truck. He works with a lot of people."

"How likely is he to loan out his vehicle?"

Rayna frowned, her shoulder slumping. "Not very. He doesn't really have many friends."

"When was the last time you spoke to him?"

"Yesterday. We were supposed to go to dinner, but he called and canceled. Said something came up on his project."

"Do you know the address of that project?"

She shook her head. "No. He never took me there. I just know it's on the northeast side of Pueblo."

"Okay. What can you tell me about his past?"

"Not too much. He said he was from Montana. Near Billings. And he was military. It's how he got the scars."

Seb stiffened. "When did he get injured?"

Rayna shrugged. "A year ago, maybe. He got caught in an IED explosion."

"Shit."

"What?" Tara asked.

"Did he look familiar to you?" Seb fired back.

Tara frowned. "Maybe a little. It was more the way he carried himself than his face. Why?"

"I think Derrick Thorpe is actually Jared Fetter."

She stared at him, dumbstruck. "What?" She knew she sounded like a broken record, but she couldn't help it.

"Commander Jacobsen said Fetter was injured in an IED explosion a little over a year ago and medically discharged, remember? If this is about Sean, it makes sense that Thorpe is Fetter."

"He's been lying to me? All this time?" Rayna said, her voice quivering. "He used me?" She trailed off to a whisper as the tears fell.

Seb's phone buzzed, and he pulled it from his pocket to check it, giving Tara and Rayna a moment to absorb what he just told them. Tara reached out to her friend, running a comforting hand over Rayna's shoulder.

The other woman looked up at her through watery eyes. "I'm so sorry. I didn't know, I swear."

"Shhh. I know you didn't."

"Rayna."

They both looked at Seb as he spoke.

"Do you know anywhere Thorpe might go? That was Jace. Pueblo PD didn't find him at home or his office."

She wiped her eyes. "Just that project site, but like I said, I'm not sure where it is."

"You said it's a veteran's facility?"

She nodded. "It's supposed to be apartments for disabled vets and a community center open to anyone who's served."

"That should be easy enough to find. Is there anywhere else he frequents?"

"Um, just a diner near his office. Marie's."

"Okay." His phone buzzed again. He read the message and uttered an oath.

"Now what?" Tara stared at her brother, exasperation making her tone sharp.

"The wildfire turned. One of the tankers spotted it when they flew over our lake to get water. It's headed toward the ranch now."

"How much time do we have?"

"A few hours at most. I need to go."

"Yep. I'm coming with you."

He nodded. "Let's go."

Tara turned to say goodbye to Rayna. "I'll call you later. Go tell your parents about the fire. If you guys need help, let me know and I'll have Brady send some of the hands over."

Rayna nodded. "We should be good. But I'll call if we need anything."

"Tara, come on," Seb urged from the door.

She waved at Rayna again and ran after her brother. They got into his SUV, and he pulled away with the lights flashing.

"Call Brady. Let him know what's going on. We need to get the pasture gates open closest to the house and get the cattle down off the mountain before we load the horses."

She did as he asked while he drove them the three miles to the ranch. After she hung up, she made a list in her head of what she needed to get from both the restaurant and her house. She hoped the firefighters could get ahead of it so it didn't damage much of the ranch, but they were going to be prepared for the worst.

Gravel tinked against the undercarriage of the SUV as Seb turned onto the main drive.

"Where do you want me to take you?"

"The restaurant. I'll help Cassie get it shut down and get everyone out."

"Sounds good."

Moments later, he pulled into the Heartwood's parking lot and around to the back door.

"Head to Mom and Dad's when you're done. We'll all meet there later."

She tugged on the door handle. "Yep." She hopped out and shut the door, hurrying toward the building. Using her key, she unlocked the kitchen door, waving to Seb, who waited to see she was safely inside. He tapped the horn and pulled away.

"Hey, boss lady," Cassie said.

Tara turned to see her assistant smiling at her.

"Did you get the produce from Rayna?"

"No. We need to shut everything down and get the customers out of here. The wildfire turned and is headed this way."

The younger woman's eyes grew large. She put down the knife she was using to chop onions and wiped her hands on the towel tucked into her waist apron. "Oh, geez. Okay. What do you want me to do?"

"Shut the kitchen down. I'll go out and talk to the wait staff and have them get everyone checked out and on their way. Thankfully, it's mid-afternoon, so there aren't too many people here."

Cassie jumped into action, clapping her hands to gain everyone's attention. Tara slipped out the door to the dining area, grabbing the first server she saw and filling her in.

She cruised through the dining room, pulling each of her servers aside to tell them what was happening and what she wanted them to do. Once that was done, she helped them fetch to-go boxes and cash out their tables. Within thirty minutes, they had the dining room clear.

After sending the wait staff home and clearing out the cash register, she went back to the kitchen to see Cassie had everything under control. Tara went to her office to gather the files she needed and the restaurant's computer, as well as the petty cash box. She set it all on the end of one of the tables, then jumped into the fray to help finish with the kitchen clean-up.

Once the food was put away and the stoves and grills shut down, she sent the staff home.

"Can you drop me off at my house before you leave?" she asked Cassie. "Seb dropped me off, and my car is in my garage."

"Sure."

Tara picked up the computer and the cash box while Cassie held the door open and then locked it behind them. They climbed into the younger woman's dark green SUV and drove the short distance to Tara's house.

"Thanks for the ride." She dug her house key from her purse, then opened her door, juggling her load.

"Anytime. Let me know if you need anything."

"I will. I'll call you tonight or tomorrow. We should know how things shape up by then."

"Sounds good. Be careful."

"Yep, you too." Tara kicked the car door shut with her foot and loped toward her porch. She would pack a bag, grab her important documents and a few family photos, then head over to her parents' to see where she could be of use in the evacuation.

Pushing inside, she bumped the door shut with her hip and walked to her kitchen, where she set down the things from the restaurant. She walked down the hall to her bedroom and into her closet, taking out her suitcase and laying it on her bed. The next time she came out of the closet, she had an armful of clothes, which she dumped into the open case.

She heard the front door open, then the heavy thud of boots on the floor.

"I'm back here," she called, assuming it was Jace or one of her brothers coming to check on her. She hoped it was Jace. What happened with Rayna earlier left her thinking how lucky she was to have found a man who didn't lie or tell half-truths. To know he cared about her for *her* and not for what she could do for him. It was getting harder to deny to herself that she was in love with him. In fact, she didn't want to deny it anymore.

Humming to herself, she retreated to her closet to get more clothes.

"I was just packing up a few things before I head over to Mom and Dad's." She came out of the closet with another armload. "Have you heard any more about how close—"

The words died in her throat. It wasn't Jace or one of her brothers standing in the doorway.

"Derrick." She decided to play dumb and find out what he wanted. After pausing a step, she continued toward the bed—and closer to the weapon Jace placed in her nightstand the other day. "What are you doing here? Rayna's at the Double Moon, helping her parents prep for evacuation. Shouldn't you be there too?"

He stepped further into the room. "You know, for such a skilled journalist, you're a terrible liar."

She dumped her load of clothes into the suitcase and edged toward the nightstand. "I don't know what you're talking about. Rayna really is at home."

He smiled, his half-frozen face adding to the scary look in his hazel eyes. She shifted her feet, making sure it put her closer to the table.

"Oh, come on, Tara. You don't remember me? I know I look a little different, but the change isn't *that* dramatic. Surely, you remember kicking my ass at poker. Or did you only have eyes for Sean and can't remember any of the members of his team?"

Anger surged at the mention of her husband. She narrowed her eyes at him. "I remember all of you," she hissed.

"Good." The smile left his face. "Now, how about you tell me where the rest of what Sean took is hidden?"

She frowned. "What are you talking about?"

"Don't play dumb with me. I know you found a flash drive with evidence he compiled about what we did, but where's the artifact?"

Artifact?

"I have no idea."

He lunged forward and grabbed her arm, squeezing hard enough to bruise. She gritted her teeth to keep from crying out.

"Where is it?" he growled. "That thing is my ticket to freedom." He shook her. "Tell me where you hid it!"

A wildness entered his hazel eyes, scaring her more than anything he or Brown had done to her in the last few weeks. She took another step backwardbackward, tugging against his hold. Her mind whirled as she tried to come up with a plan.

"Fine," she bit out. "I buried it. In a lockbox out back."

"Let's go." He pulled her toward the door, but she dug in her heels.

"I need to get the key for the box."

"I don't need a key. The locks on those things are flimsy." He tugged on her arm again.

"Not this one. It's one of those fire safes. The key is in the nightstand."

He arched a brow and scoffed. "Yeah, right."

"Seriously, it is. You can get it yourself." She pointed at the table and held her breath. She had an idea, but he needed to let her go if this was going to work.

Frowning, he stared at her a moment, before releasing her arm and walking toward the head of the bed.

As soon as his fingers left her skin and he bent toward the drawer, she dove for the closet.

"Hey!"

Surprise only gave her an extra second, but it was enough for her to reach the shotgun propped in the corner opposite the door. She grabbed it as she entered, turning and racking it at the same time.

He came to a halt as she leveled the gun on him, holding up his hands.

"You won't shoot me." A cocky, self-assured grin quirked the side of his face not paralyzed, giving him an evil look.

Tara glared. "Try me. I'm not the same woman you remember, Jared."

He shrugged. "Maybe not, but I still don't think you have what it takes to kill a person."

"Who said anything about killing you?"

The grin disappeared and a hard, dangerous glint entered his eyes. "You want to get past me, you'll have to."

His hands lowered a fraction, giving Tara a moment of warning before he moved. As he stepped forward to disarm her, she fired. Buckshot peppered the right side of his chest and shoulder. The impact knocked him sideways, spinning him into the racks of clothing. She dashed past him and out of the bedroom.

"That was the wrong thing to do, Tara." His voice carried down the hallway. She heard his boots on the floor as he came after her. "You should have learned from your husband not to mess with me."

Horror filled her as she realized Al-Aziz didn't kill Sean. Jared did.

As she entered the living room, she glanced over her shoulder to see him emerge from the bedroom. Blood soaked the right side of his shirt. Anger turned his eyes to steel.

He stalked toward her.

She turned and raised the shotgun, racking another round. She was done running and hiding.

"You killed Sean? Why?"

He paused, leaning against the wall and staring at her. "He caught on to our scheme. Started gathering evidence to take us down. We couldn't let that happen. I thought the whole thing died with him, but imagine my surprise when Evan called to tell me he was dying and couldn't take the secret of what really happened to his grave. When he contacted your old editor, I knew it was only a matter of time until you started digging and found the flash drive and the artifact Sean stole from me."

"I still don't know what artifact you're talking about. That part wasn't a lie."

A laugh started low in his chest, but quickly got hung up as he winced in pain from the movement. A grimacing smile came over his face. "It's probably been staring you in the face. It was a gold hair comb with lapis lazuli inlay. I just don't know what you did with it. Claybaugh searched the ranch from top to bottom."

Tara's eyes widened as she realized what he was talking about. He never found the comb because it wasn't on the ranch. She'd let Macy borrow it months ago and forgotten. She'd no idea it wasn't something Sean bought for her as a present. It had been at the bottom of his bugout bag, wrapped in one of his shirts.

"So, you *do* know what I'm talking about." He took another step toward her as he rightly read her expression, the look on his face menacing. "Where is it?"

"Not here. And I'm not telling you where it is, either.

You're going to sit down on the ground and wait for Seb or Jace to get here and take you into custody."

He took another step closer. "Not likely."

Tara tucked the shotgun in tighter to her shoulder. "Jared, don't. You know I'll shoot you."

"Before I shoot you first?"

As his words registered, he brought a pistol up—her pistol —from the back of his waistband.

Tara pulled the trigger.

This time, the buckshot hit him square in the upper chest and neck. His shot went wild as he fell, gurgling as blood filled his airway.

She racked the shotgun again, the tip following him to the floor. She kept the gun trained on him until he was no longer moving and his breathing changed from a gurgling to a choking noise before it stopped altogether.

She let her arms relax, her shoulders slumping. Blowing out a breath, she pushed the hair off her forehead, her hand shaking as her adrenaline wore off and reality filtered in. There was a dead man in her living room—whom she killed—but it was finally over.

Twenty-Four

J ace's phone rang as he opened the door to his truck to drive back to the ranch. Pueblo PD was still looking for Fetter. Until they found him, there wasn't much to do, so he was headed to the ranch to help the Archers evacuate. He hoped the firefighters could stop the fire before it reached the ranch buildings or threatened the herd.

He took his phone from his pocket as he stepped up into the truck and saw the police department's number on it. Curious what could have come up in the thirty seconds since he left the building, he answered the call.

"Travers."

"Jace, it's Katie. I just cracked the encryption on the thumb drive. I tried calling the sheriff, but he's not answering. You need to read this stuff. Lieutenant Miller had evidence Fetter was smuggling artifacts out of the Middle East to sell on the black market, and he wasn't working alone. There are four other people named in the documents."

That certainly explained Fetter's desire to get the drive back. He'd be facing some extensive prison time if that information saw the light of day. So would the others listed.

"Wait." The number of people involved registered in his mind. There were only four men on Sean's SEAL team, *including* him.

He gripped the phone so hard it was a wonder it didn't break. "Did you say *four* others?"

"Mmm-hmm."

He heard her fingers clack across the keys. "Oh, wait, there's five. He found the broker too." She rattled off the names.

Jace felt his blood run cold. They'd been looking in the wrong place.

"Okay, thanks, Katie. Keep trying to get a hold of the sheriff."

"You got it. Bye."

She hung up, and he dialed Tara.

"Come on, come on. Pick up the phone, babe," he muttered, listening to it ring.

When it rolled to voicemail, he cursed and started the truck, a bad feeling settling in his stomach. He just hoped he didn't get there too late.

Tara set the shotgun against the wall, her entire body trembling from shock and adrenaline. She needed a stiff drink and to call Jace. In that order. She stepped toward the kitchen.

The sound of the back door opening brought her to a halt. Her eyes widened as Commander Jacobsen strolled through, clapping.

She stared at him, not quite sure what was happening. He stopped a few feet away, his eyes straying to Fetter's body, then back to her.

"I owe you a debt of thanks," he said, one side of his mouth tilting up in a smile.

"What?" She couldn't keep the bewildered note out of her voice even as a sense of horror creeped back in.

He pointed to Fetter. "You've eliminated one headache for me. Dotson met an—unfortunate—accident a few days ago. With Fetter out of the picture, you're all that's left before I can hop on a plane to the Middle East. I plan to live out my days sipping Turkish coffee and fine Italian wine on my private beach."

The horror bloomed, filling her chest and stealing her breath. "It was you? You were behind all this?"

"Not initially. Fetter started it, but they cut me in once I discovered what they were up to. It's been a lucrative side business. I get rid of you, and I'll never have to work again." He withdrew a pistol from his waistband. "Especially since all the evidence blew up in the lab." His smile was cold. "Did you like that? I tried to be the good guy and let the lab employees get out. I'm not a monster, after all. I think I missed a few, though."

She narrowed her eyes at him as she thought about the two people in the ICU in Denver, as well as the lab tech and janitor Declan's team found in the rubble early this morning. He sure didn't sound very sorry for what happened to them.

He lifted the gun and pointed it at her chest. "No hard feelings, Tara. It's just business, and you're standing in my way."

"Wait!" She held her hands out in front of her. "What about the artifact?"

Jacobsen frowned, but the gun didn't waver. "What artifact?"

Tara arched a brow in surprise. "You don't know?"

"Know what?"

"Sean took a comb from Fetter before Fetter killed him. I found it years ago, but thought it was a gift he never got to give me."

The muscles in his jaw twitched. She could see him weighing her words.

"You're lying."

"I'm not. That's why Jared was here. He wanted to get it back, so there wasn't anything else to tie him to Sean's death."

His eyes flicked to Fetter's body again. He readjusted his grip on the gun. "Where is it?"

"I buried it outback after we figured out what it was."

"You buried it?" He scoffed. "You really expect me to believe that?"

She shrugged, praying all those years playing poker paid off. "I don't care whether you do or not. It's the truth." She needed him to believe her. The plan forming in her head required her to get close to him.

"Fine. Show me." He stepped to the side so she could pass, but kept his weapon trained on her.

Tara forced her muscles to stay relaxed as she walked toward him. As she drew even with him, she spun to her left, her hands smacking into his wrist and the gun. It skittered into the living room and under the couch.

Before he could react to losing his weapon, she swung a leg low and swept his feet out from under him. As she turned to run, his hand caught her ankle and she fell to the floor, banging her knees on the wood.

Thankful for the adrenaline rush that dulled the pain, she rolled to her back and kicked out with her other foot, connecting with his face. She felt his nose crunch beneath her shoe, and blood spurted from his nostrils as he grunted.

Yanking her leg free of his grip, she scrambled backward and got to her feet. Jacobsen stood too, blood dripping in a thick ribbon down his chin.

"I was just going to shoot you. Make it quick and painless. Now, it's going to fucking hurt."

Her eyes flicked to her shotgun. It was too far out of reach, but thankfully, she was between him and the gun, so he couldn't use it against her. She was going to have to find a different way to stop him.

"You have to get a hold of me first," she taunted. Slowly, she backed away, an image of the other side of the half wall flashing through her head. Being a neat-freak had its advantages. Like knowing exactly how many steps it was around the wall and how many inches her knife set was from the edge of the counter.

"You know you can't outrun me, right?" He advanced toward her.

Tara kept backing away. Four more steps and she would be at the doorway.

"You might be tall, but you're still a woman."

She fought the urge to roll her eyes as she continued her backward walk. This guy had so many people fooled. He played the cultured, nice guy role very well, but he was nothing more than a chauvinistic, greedy asshole.

Her foot cleared the doorway to the kitchen. Heart pounding, she snapped her left hand out and snagged a paring knife from the block. Whirling, she transferred the knife to her dominant hand and let it fly as she faced Jacobsen again. Her throwing skills were a little rusty, but she still managed to hit his thigh. He bellowed and dropped to one knee.

Tara didn't wait around to see if he pulled it out. She turned and ran out the back door. Her eyes scanned the area for anyone, but it seemed as though everyone was still out herding cattle off the mountain. She knew her parents were at home, packing up important family documents, but there was no way she was going to lure that sadistic bastard anywhere near them.

Her gaze landed on Brandywine, grazing in the pasture on the backside of the horse barn.

The blast of her shotgun startled Tara, and she stumbled.

She managed to stay upright and looked over her shoulder to see Jacobsen hobbling toward her, her shotgun in his hands. He racked it again and raised it, but it was out of shells. She thanked her lucky stars he missed the first time.

He tossed it to the ground with a growl and started running toward her, his gait slower thanks to the knife wound.

Shit! Even wounded, he was quick. Legs pumping, she ran for the corral. She didn't slow as she came up to the fence. Her foot hit the bottom rail, and she vaulted over the top. She let out a sharp whistle, drawing the horses to her, Brandywine at the front.

"Time to go for a ride, girl." Tara grasped a handful of the mare's mane and hopped onto her back. Squeezing tight with her thighs, she turned the horse toward the mountains and away from her family.

She glanced back to see Jacobsen scramble over the fence and walk up to one of the other horses—a docile mare named Winnie. To her utter disbelief, he swung up onto her back and began to ride after her.

Tara faced forward, her mind spinning as an idea formed. She knew these hills better than anyone. There was a high probability she could lose him—or deliberately get him lost.

She gave Brandywine another squeeze, urging her to go faster. This had to work. She had a man to get back to, so she could tell him she loved him.

Jace made it to the ranch turnoff in record time, barely slowing as he drove up the stone drive. A quick glance at the restaurant revealed a deserted parking lot, so he continued toward her house, screeching to a halt in the driveway.

Uneasiness crept up his spine. Nothing seemed amiss, but he couldn't shake the feeling something was wrong.

He walked up to the front door and gave the knob a twist. It spun, and he pushed the door inward, stepping over the threshold, his hand on the butt of his gun.

His eyes landed on the body sprawled at the mouth of the hallway. He hurried forward on light feet.

Shit. It was Fetter.

He bent down to check for a pulse, finding none. Rising, he stepped around the body and drew his weapon, moving into the hall to check the bedrooms. Both were empty, but he saw signs of a struggle in the master bedroom.

Jace retraced his steps, seeing more blood in the kitchen. He checked the garage, and when he found no sign of Tara, he backtracked and went through the back door. Blood peppered the brown grass just past the edge of the house and led in a trail toward the horse barn.

"Goddamn, son-of-a-bitch!" He took out his phone and dialed Seb. It went to voicemail, and he cursed again. He scrolled through his contacts until he found Brady's number. After the fifth ring, Jace was ready to give up and drive over to the main house to find *anyone*, when Brady picked up.

"Hello?"

"Brady! Is Seb with you? Or Tara?"

"Seb's here. I haven't seen Tara."

"Put Seb on the phone."

He heard rustling as Brady passed the phone to his brother.

"What's up?"

"Katie and I have been trying to reach you. She cracked the encryption on the thumb drive. And I just found Fetter dead inside Tara's house. He's been shot. There's no sign of Tara, though. Just a blood trail leading away from the back of the house toward the horse barn."

Seb muttered several oaths, and Jace heard some rustling. "Dammit. I put my phone on vibrate somehow. Brady and I are out opening pasture gates. I'm not sure anyone is near the ranch buildings. Only the horses are there and we're not ready to load them up and move them off the property yet."

Jace turned and broke into a jog to go back to his truck. "I'm headed there now. Check your email." He hung up, sprinting the last few yards to his vehicle.

He climbed inside and cranked the engine, throwing the truck into reverse and backing up onto the road, then slamming it into drive and gunning it for the barn.

In seconds, he was parked haphazardly in front of the large structure. Gun drawn, he ran inside. His heartbeat thundered in his ears as he searched each stall and the workrooms. There was no sign of anyone. He ran out into the pasture, hoping he wouldn't find Tara injured—or worse—on the ground.

His mind noted something else, though. Brandywine was missing. He started counting animals, running back into the barn to see how many horses were still in their stalls, and came up short one more.

A soft whicker drew his attention. He turned to see Elbert standing at the entrance to the pasture, watching him.

Jace walked up to the horse, who tossed his head and nudged his shoulder.

"Hey, boy."

Elbert pawed at the ground and nudged him again.

He frowned. "Do you know where Tara is?"

Another nudge and a snort.

This is crazy. A horse can't tell me where she is.

But as he looked into Elbert's dark eyes, he couldn't shake the feeling the horse knew exactly where she was.

Jace blew out a breath. "Fine." He took a lead rope off the wall and attached it to Elbert's halter, leading him to the tack room. He tied the animal to a peg on the wall and went inside the room to grab what he needed.

As quick as he'd ever saddled a horse, he had Elbert ready to go in minutes. Before he left, he called Seb.

"Hey. I think she's headed up into the mountains with Jacobsen on her tail. Brandywine and another horse are missing. I'm taking Elbert and going after them.

Seb cursed. "Take one of the satellite radios in the office. Use channel three. I'll let Dad know so he can monitor it. Be careful, Jace. I just heard from Declan. The fire's still coming, and it's getting closer."

Trepidation made his muscles tense. "I will." He hung up and jogged across the aisle to the barn office. The door was locked. He didn't know where the key was and didn't have time to search for it, so he stepped back and delivered a swift kick to the wood near the lock. The door swung inward. He walked inside and grabbed a radio, then ran back to his horse and stowed it in a saddlebag before untying the reins and stepping into the saddle.

"All right, Elbert. Show me where she went." He snapped the reins and squeezed the horse's sides.

Elbert gave a loud whinny and lunged forward, racing across the pasture to the gate. He thundered over the ground, faster than he ever had.

The fence loomed before them. Jace sat up to rein him in, so he could open the gate, but Elbert refused to slow.

"Shit!" He bent low and prayed as Elbert lengthened his gait. Within feet of the fence, he felt the horse's muscles coil, then release in a mighty push as he vaulted over the top rail to land smoothly on the other side, never breaking stride.

God, he loved this horse.

He gave Elbert his head and let him plot the way into the mountains.

"Find her, Elbert," he muttered. "You do that, and I'll make sure you get the five-star treatment the rest of your life."

They wound through the low hills and over the river

before climbing higher. A half hour into the ride, Jace knew where they were going—the lake. It was the only thing on this path. He still hadn't figured out Tara's plan—why she hadn't gone for help in the first place, or why she was heading for the lake and toward a wildfire—but he knew she had one.

Elbert kept a steady pace up the trail, and Jace kept an eye on the sky. It was growing more orange and darker the further west they went. He could smell smoke up here too. He prayed they wouldn't reach the lake, only to find a wall of fire coming at them.

Jace pushed the dark thoughts from his mind and concentrated on the trail. On the off-chance they weren't going where he thought they were, he didn't want to get lost.

But Elbert stayed on an unerring path to the lake. As he crested the hill and the water came into view, he heard a man shout.

He reined Elbert in, trying to keep him steady, as he determined where it came from.

A second shout allowed him to zero in on the far end of the lake. He gave Elbert a hard squeeze, and they took off toward the noise. As he got closer, he could hear Tara whistling in sharp bursts. The horse Jacobsen rode kept turning back the way they'd come every time she whistled. Without reins or a saddle, he struggled to keep the horse on task.

Good girl. Jace had seen the others use whistles to call the horses back to the barn. It meant feeding time. Elbert, of course, ignored it, because he ignored everything people wanted him to do. But the horse Jacobsen rode was as obedient as they came.

Jace put his head down and let Elbert become the silver streak he wanted to be.

Tara and the commander heard him coming. Both looked back at the sound of Elbert's hooves pounding over the dry ground. Tara grinned, but Jacobsen kicked his horse into action, trying to make the small mare ride away.

Yes, run, you bastard.

The commander's horse would never outrun Elbert. Jace streaked past Tara after Jacobsen. In seconds, he was alongside the man. Jace stood in the saddle, then lifted a boot free of the stirrup. Bringing his leg up, he turned and launched himself off his horse, tackling Jacobsen from his mare.

He tucked his body and rolled as he landed, as did Jacobsen. They both bounced to their feet, but before Jace could reach for his gun, Jacobsen pulled a knife from his boot and lunged at him. He deflected the blow, but the commander dropped the knife to his other hand and swung. The blade sliced through the front of his t-shirt, the tip grazing his stomach. Jacobsen came at him again, but Jace sidestepped, grabbing the other man's forearm and using his free hand to take the knife away.

Jacobsen bellowed and ran at him, using a similar maneuver to get it back. He swung it down toward Jace's chest, but Jace put a hand up to stop the downward momentum and used his free hand to deliver a solid punch to the commander's jaw.

He staggered back and Jace drew his gun.

"Freeze! It's over Jacobsen. Drop the knife."

The other man raised his hands, but didn't drop the knife. An evil smile spread over his face, crinkling the corners of his blue eyes.

Jace steadied his aim, unsure what Jacobsen's endgame was.

The commander's smile fell, determination in his eyes, and he flipped the knife so he was holding the point. At the same moment he tipped the knife back, Jace realized he intended to throw it at him, and fired.

The knife slid from Jacobsen's hand as a blood stain

bloomed on his polo shirt in the middle of his chest. His eyes rolled back, and he crumpled to the ground in a heap.

Jace slowly straightened and holstered his weapon. Staring down at the commander's lifeless form, he blew out a breath.

"Jace!"

He turned just in time to catch Tara as she leaped into his arms. She wrapped her legs around his waist, burying her face in his neck.

He held her tight, breathing in her scent. His hand shook as he smoothed it over the back of her head and around her jaw to bring her face up so he could look into her eyes.

"Are you okay?"

She nodded, tears trailing down her cheeks. "I'm fine."

"Good. I know you're probably not ready to hear it, but I love you, woman. You have no idea how scared I was to walk into your house and find Fetter dead, then see that blood trail leading toward the barn."

Her eyes grew round, but then a wide, sunny smile split her face. She cradled his head in her hands and leaned her forehead against his.

"I love you too."

She kissed him then. Jace felt all the passion and love in her heart in that one touch and did his best to show her how he felt too.

A loud, frightened whinny from Elbert broke them apart. They looked over to see him pawing at the ground, his eyes so wide the whites were showing.

Jace looked around, realizing it had grown darker and the temperature had risen at least ten degrees. His eyes shot to the ridge. Black smoke billowed against the dark orange cast to the sky.

"Shit, the fire's here. We need to go." He steadied Tara as she put her feet on the ground, then took her hand and led her toward his horse.

"Where's Brandywine and Winnie?" she asked.

He glanced around, but it was too dark and smoky to see much. Embers floated in the air now. "I don't know, but we need to get out of here now. They probably sensed the fire and took off. Elbert stayed because he's Elbert."

"No, Elbert stayed because he's decided you're his person and doesn't want to leave you in danger. But it doesn't matter. We won't outrun the fire, even on him. Not if he has to carry both of us."

Jace looked back at the ridge. The fire was now eating its way over the top, the dry grass and scraggly trees burning like they'd been doused in gasoline. He turned back to her, eyeing her, then the horse, and back again. He had a plan, but he didn't think she would like it.

She glared at him. "Don't even think about it. I'm not leaving without you."

He thrust Elbert's reins at her. "And I'm not willing to let you die. Get on him and go. As fast as you can."

She smacked his hand away. "No."

"Tara—"

"I'm not leaving, Jace, and that's final."

He growled, realizing that arguing with her was only wasting time. "What do you suggest we do, then?"

She pointed at the lake. "We go swimming."

TWENTY-FIVE

Tara held tight to Jace's waist as he brought Elbert to a quick halt at the edge of the water, where they skipped rocks the other day. After a moment of disbelief, he'd seen the merit of her idea, and they'd mounted the horse and rode the short distance to the easiest place Tara could think of to get the big animal into the water. The lake was shallower here, with a more gradual slope into the water. She hoped he didn't balk too much at the impromptu dip.

She swung her leg over the horse's neck and slid down, taking the reins and waiting for Jace to dismount. His boots sent up a little puff of dust as they touched the ground. She looked at the sky, watching embers float on the air currents created by the wildfire. She could hear it now. It had swept over the ridge and now roared down the mountain toward them.

"Come on, Elbert." She tugged on his reins and walked toward the water. He followed easily enough until they started to wade in.

"Jesus, that's cold," Jace said as the water lapped over their feet and hit their legs.

She agreed. Even with the warm summer temps, the lake stayed chilly thanks to its depth and snowy source.

"It's only a little chilly," she said, keeping her tone soothing as she tried to coax the silver horse away from the shore. "Come on, big guy. We need to take a little bath in this big pond until the fire passes. It'll feel good after your long run, I promise."

Elbert neighed and shook his head, but took another step forward.

"That's a good boy. Come just a little closer, buddy. We take our bath, then we can ride home and get you some nice treats."

His ears twitched at the last word.

"A big, juicy apple and some crunchy carrots. I'll even have Brady put a scoop of grain in your feed box. How does that sound?"

He tossed his head again, but walked forward. Tara pulled gently and waded out until the water was at her waist.

"We need to go a little further, Tara."

She looked away from the horse for a moment to gauge the fire. It now burned at the far end of the lake and was spreading around the shoreline on either side at a rapid pace.

"Come on, Elbert. None of us want to end up as crispy critters, even you, so let's go a little deeper, hmm?" She tugged on his reins. He resisted for a moment, eyes wild, but finally let her pull him further in until the water reached the point of his shoulders.

Tara sucked in a breath as the chilly water surrounded her. It was just under her breasts now, and it was *cold*.

The air around them grew hot, and the smoke thickened. Tara coughed.

Jace took off his shirt. "Take off your shirt. Get it wet and put it over your nose and mouth."

He ripped his tee down the middle. Dunking one half, he

tied it over his face, then dunked the other half and wrapped it around Elbert's nose.

The horse gave a low neigh and tossed his head.

"I know, bud. I'm sorry, but you need the filter."

Flames licked the vegetation only a hundred yards from them. Smoke billowed, making her eyes sting. Jace took Elbert's reins from her as he got more agitated. Tara ran her hands over his neck and shoulder, speaking to him in a soothing tone, doing her best to keep him calm. They kept his back to the fire, but he could still hear it and smell it, not to mention feel its heat.

She glanced back, eyes widening as she realized the flames were on top of them now. The shoreline burned only yards away. Elbert whinnied and reared, his feet kicking up water. Jace did his best to hold the horse. In the water, with the rocky bottom beneath their feet, he lost his footing, falling with a splash. He came up sputtering, but still had his grip on the reins.

They both murmured to the horse as the fire roared. Heat warmed Tara's body above the waterline, making her face feel like she'd spent the entirety of the hottest day of the year in the sun without sunscreen. Flames licked the air with a snap. The whites of Elbert's eyes showed bright in the dim light. He reared again, this time sending Jace flying face first into the water. The horse's hooves came down where he disappeared into the murk, and Tara screamed.

Elbert reared again and spun toward the shore. He caught sight of the fire and danced in the water, panic in every line of his body.

Jace popped through the surface. Blood sluiced down his face with the water, and he stumbled as he tried to stand.

She rushed to him, keeping an eye on Elbert, who now paced several feet away.

"Jace! Are you all right?" She reached out and grasped his arm to steady him.

He shook his head as though to clear it, and water droplets flew. "Yeah. I'm okay. I caught a glancing blow from one of his feet, but I'm all right." He pointed at Elbert. "We need to catch him. If he takes off once the fire passes, he might run for home and end up running right into the fire."

She nodded and let him go, both of them turning toward the frightened horse. They waded through the water, approaching him slowly, murmuring to him.

"Get between him and the fire, so he doesn't bolt once it passes," Jace told her. "I'm going to try to get his reins."

Tara kept her eyes on the horse, circling him until she stood between him and the shore, ignoring the flames now dangerously close. The heat pricked her scalp, making it itch.

She clicked her tongue, trying to get Elbert's attention. He stopped and looked at her, but didn't come any closer. She couldn't blame him. This close to the flames, she felt like her clothes would catch fire at any moment. Embers swirled around them through the smoke, sizzling as they touched the cold lake.

She took a few steps toward Elbert, still talking to him. His breath came out on harsh grunts, and Tara realized he'd lost the cover they'd put over his nose.

Behind the horse, she could see Jace come toward his left flank. She prayed hard as he reached out and touched Elbert's side, whispering to the horse.

Elbert's ears twitched, but he didn't skitter away. Jace took two steps, sliding his hand along the horse's side as he went, and snagged the reins.

The moment he had the horse secure, Tara whipped the cover off her face and used her teeth to tear a notch in the fabric and tore it down the middle. She tied one half around her face before approaching Elbert and draping the other half over his nose. He tossed his head, but stood still.

She ran a soothing hand over his neck as he continued to breathe hard. She hoped he could walk down the mountain. They all needed to get out of the smoke. Thankfully, he'd calmed some. The fire was moving on, leaving a trail of charred vegetation in its wake.

Together, the three of them splashed out of the lake. The water droplets dripping from them created steam as they hit the ground, which melded into the swirling smoke. Little patches of grass and some larger plants still burned here and there, but the main fire was headed away.

Tara leaned against Elbert's side, shivering from the cold lake water and the adrenaline leaving her system. She was about done with all the adrenaline rushes. The big horse shuddered beneath her touch as he, too, had an adrenaline dump.

Jace came up beside her and flipped open the saddlebag, pulling out a radio.

A relieved laugh slid past her lips. "I was hoping you'd bring one of those. Especially after we failed to do so Monday, when we all came up here."

He tugged the cover off his face, grinning as he twisted the antennae up. "I don't think any of us will forget it again."

"Probably not."

He brought the radio up to his mouth and pressed the microphone button. "Broken Bow, this is Travers. Do you copy?"

Tara held her breath as they waited for a reply. A few seconds later, the radio crackled.

"Travers, this is Broken Bow. What's your status, son? Over."

She almost wept in relief at the sound of her dad's voice.

"Tara and I are fine. Commander Jacobsen is dead. You need to be on the lookout for Brandywine and—" he paused, letting off the microphone, and looked down at her. "What's the other horse's name?"

"Winnie."

He gave a quick nod and pressed the button again. "Be on the lookout for Brandywine and Winnie. They took off when the fire got close. Elbert's with us. Over."

"The fire? Do you have an escape route? Over."

"It's already passed us. We went for a swim in the lake. Over."

"Bet that was a cold swim. Over."

They both huffed a short laugh. "That it was. We're going to hike over the ridge and will need a pick up on the highway in a few hours or so. Make sure Thomas is with them. Elbert inhaled some smoke. Tell Seb to get a hold of Declan and have him relay to the woodland firefighters that they need to douse the trees near the river with retardant. It'll be the best place to stop this beast."

"Copy. I'll send Thomas to meet you with a trailer on the road and call Sebastian. And Jace? Thanks for taking care of my little girl. Over."

Emotion clogged Tara's throat at the sound of tears in her dad's voice.

Jace took her hand and squeezed it. "She took care of herself. Travers out." He folded the radio up and put it away.

She leaned into him, savoring the feeling of being alive and with the man who had come to mean so much to her.

He wrapped his arms around her and pressed a kiss to the top of her head. When he pulled back a bit, she looked up, the cover slipping off her face.

"So, you want to tell me what your plan was? Why did you flee up here instead of going to your parents' house for help? And what happened once you got up here?"

She sighed, resting her forehead on his bare chest for a moment. "I didn't want to bring him to their house—or anyone else's—because I didn't want to risk him taking a hostage. I just pointed Brandywine away from the buildings and let her loose. My plan was to lose him on the other side of the ridge where the foliage is denser and maybe lead him toward the fire—without getting caught myself. But then you showed up, streaking over the ground like a bolt of lightning." She patted Elbert's neck. "Brady should have entered him in some races. I think that was the fastest I've ever seen him move."

"Well, he had a reason to turn on the afterburners today." He brushed at her cheek with his thumb, and she smiled, love burning in her veins as hot as the wildfire.

He smiled back and stared down at her. "What happened? I saw Fetter's body at the house."

She drew in a deep breath. "After we finished closing down the restaurant, Cassie dropped me off at home, so I could grab a few things."

His brows dipped in a frown at that, but she held up a hand to stymie the words she knew he wanted to say.

"It was a calculated risk. I was only going to be there for a few minutes. Just long enough to pack a few things before I headed over to Mom and Dad's. The window of opportunity was tiny, so Fetter must have been following me and none of us saw him. Anyway, I heard the door open and thought it was you, so I called out, only it wasn't you who showed up in the doorway. He wanted to know what I'd done with the artifact Sean took from him. Apparently, the flash drive wasn't the only thing he had on his unit. He took a gold comb from Fetter and stashed it in the bottom of his bugout bag. It wasn't at my house because I loaned it to Macy a while back. I had no idea it was a stolen artifact from the Middle East. I thought it was a present he never got the chance to give me.

"Anyway, I convinced Jared I buried it in the backyard in a fireproof box. I managed to get free and grabbed the shotgun in my closet. He didn't think I'd shoot him, but he didn't know me very well. My first shot just wounded him, but the second, I didn't miss. I was just getting ready to call you when Commander Jacobsen walked through the back door. He must have been following Fetter. I used the same ruse to distract him and managed to disarm him. It gave me enough time to get to my knives. My throwing skills are rusty, though. I aimed for his chest and hit his thigh. But it slowed him down. Enough for me to get to the horse pasture."

"Wait, you know how to throw knives? And how did you disarm him? He's a SEAL."

"You forget, my husband was also a SEAL. He taught me a thing or two, and I've never forgotten any of it. It helped that I took him by surprise. He wasn't expecting those moves out of a woman. Out of me."

She pushed her hair back. "Anyway, he rode after me, and when we got up here, I used the whistle trick to keep him at a distance, which drove him nuts. If it wasn't for the fire, I probably would have been over the ridge when you got here, but I could tell it was close by the look of the sky. I was planning my next steps when I saw you."

"Did he say why he did it?"

"Steal from the countries he was supposed to protect?"

Jace nodded.

"Money, of course. He caught Fetter and the others smuggling artifacts and told them he wouldn't turn them in if they cut him in on it. Sean found out, and they killed him for it."

Her face burned as tears threatened; these out of anger and frustration over the fact her husband died because the men who were supposed to have his back valued money over life.

Jace hugged her tighter. "I'm glad you got some closure and know what really happened."

She sniffed. "Me too. Now that it's all over, I can finally move on."

His grin was lopsided. "Oh, yeah?"

She smiled back and stood on her tiptoes to place a lingering kiss on his lips. "Yeah. Want to move on with me?"

"You have to ask?"

She giggled. "Probably not."

He pressed a fierce kiss to her lips, then pulled back, a wealth of emotion shining in his eyes. "I love you."

She beamed up at him. "I love you too."

"Come on." He stepped back and took her hand, keeping hold of Elbert's reins with the other. "Let's go find our ride."

By the time they reached the road, the sun had set. Tara's feet hurt from hiking over the rocky ground and she really needed a drink. Water first, then something stronger. It had been a hell of a day.

They broke through the tree line, and she almost cried at the sight of her brother, Thomas, leaning against the front of his truck, ankles and arms crossed as he waited on them.

He spotted her and straightened. Tara let go of Jace's hand and ran to her twin. He met her halfway and scooped her into a tight hug, heedless of her shirtless state.

"I'm so glad you're okay," he whispered into her hair.

She pulled back so she could see his face. "Me too."

He let her go just as Jace walked up with Elbert. Thomas turned his attention to the weary animal.

"Dad said he inhaled some smoke?"

Jace nodded. "We tried to put a cover over his nose. He tossed the first one off when he freaked out on us. It took us a bit to catch him and put another cover on."

Thomas took in their state of undress. "I take it that's where your shirts went?"

They nodded.

"My suitcase is in the truck if you want to grab something while I look him over."

Grateful, Tara stepped around him to do just that. She opened the back door and unzipped the bag on the seat, taking out two t-shirts. She passed one to Jace and pulled the other over her head.

They turned back to Thomas, who had tied Elbert to the trailer and had a stethoscope pressed to the horse's side.

"How is he?" she asked.

Thomas pulled one earpiece from his ear and looked at them. "He's a little wheezy, but not terribly so. I brought some oxygen with me. Jace, can you get it? It's in the storage compartment on the trailer."

Jace nodded and stepped away.

"How's the ranch? Did they stop the fire?"

Thomas nodded. "With the help of the river and a couple loads of that flame retardant, they halted the leading edge. It's still spreading sideways, but not as fast. It doesn't have the wind pushing it. Last I heard, they were going to attack the east flank, so it didn't take out the Nydert's crops." He straightened and stared at her a moment. "You sure you're okay? Seb told us what happened with Fetter."

Tara took a deep breath and tried not to picture the blood blooming on Jared's shirt after she shot him. "I'm okay, Thomas. Really. I'll probably have a few nightmares, but I did what I had to do to save myself. I'm just glad it's over."

Jace walked up, carrying the oxygen tank and the long conical mask attached to it. "We're all glad it's done." He held out the tank. "Did you know your sister knew how to throw knives?" he said as Thomas took the oxygen.

"What? No." He chuckled and shook his head, turning the nozzle on the tank and putting the mask over Elbert's nose. "I shouldn't be surprised, though. She used to be quite the daredevil."

Tara grinned. "I think you'll see more shades of that again now." But probably not for a little while. She'd had enough adrenaline for a bit.

Thomas rolled his eyes. "Wonderful. Be prepared, Jace."

Jace looped an arm around her shoulders, tucking her into his side. "Oh, I am. I can't wait to see what other surprises she has for me."

Epilogue

I*'m going to kill him.*

Tara hugged the toilet in the ladies' room at the reception hall. Her cornflower blue bridesmaid dress fanned out on the floor around her.

The outer door squealed as it opened, the noise of the reception reaching her before it swung shut.

"Tara? Are you in here?" London's voice echoed through the tiled room.

Her response was to heave more of her dinner into the commode.

"Hey, are you all right?" She stopped outside Tara's stall.

"I'm fine." She grabbed a handful of toilet paper and wiped her mouth.

"You don't sound fine."

The door squealed as it opened again.

"What's going on? Did you find her?" Macy said.

Tara groaned. "Let's just make it one big party. Is Rayna with you? You can all watch me puke."

London banged on the door. "Open up, Tara, or I'll go get your mother."

Not wanting an even larger audience, she reached up and slid open the latch. She glanced up to see the faces of her three closest friends smushed together to peer at her through the narrow opening. If she still didn't feel so weak, she'd laugh at the picture they made.

"This floor's not very sanitary, you know," Macy quipped. "Neither is the toilet bowl you're holding."

"Bite me." She rested her head against the wall. The cool metal felt good on her clammy skin.

"Are you sick?" Rayna asked.

"No, she's puking for fun," Macy said. "Of course she's sick."

"I hope it wasn't the food," London said. "I should go ask around and see if anyone else feels ill."

"I'm not sick." Tara lifted her head and opened her eyes, looking back at them. "I'm pregnant."

All three women gasped.

"What?"

"How long?"

"Does Jace know?"

The rapid-fire questions drew a smile from her. "Pregnant, London. That thing you're going to be soon if my brother has anything to say about it."

London blushed.

"I'm about nine weeks," she told Rayna. "And yes, Jace knows," she said in answer to Macy's question.

"You're nine weeks and we're just now finding out? I thought we had this discussion about not keeping things from each other." Macy's frown was fierce and matched those on London and Rayna's faces.

Tara sighed. "I know, but I was seven weeks along before I even realized it. With it being so close to the wedding, I didn't want to make the whole thing about me. I was going to tell you all when you and Seb got back from your honeymoon."

She looked at London. "I swear. I had it all planned out for our monthly girls' night."

She held up her hands. "Help me up."

They took hold of her and pulled her off the floor. Her legs shook a bit yet, but her stomach was staying put.

She brushed at the hair stuck to her forehead with her forearm. "Ugh. I was hoping this pregnancy would be like the last one and I wouldn't puke. I've been good until now. I think it was a combo of the heat in there and the rich food."

"Have you been very nauseous?" Rayna asked.

"Not too much. Some smells turn my stomach, but this is the first time I've actually thrown up." She walked to the sink to wash her hands and groaned when she caught sight of herself. "I can't go back out there looking like this." Jace would take one look at her and insist they go home.

"Splash some water on your face and fix your hair. You'll be fine," Macy replied.

Tara gave her a droll look.

Macy grinned, then rolled her eyes. "You look fine. A little pale, maybe, but you'll perk up. We'll pour some merlot—oh. I forgot. That's going to take some getting used to."

"But it's so exciting!" London wrapped her arms around Tara's shoulders and squeezed.

A happy grin spread over Tara's face. It was. When she realized she missed her period, a healthy dose of fear punched her in the gut, but was quickly replaced by a sense of wonder. She spent so long grieving the child she never got to hold, she hadn't let herself imagine what it would be like to have another.

Once it sank in, though, excitement took over. She'd called Jace home for lunch and surprised him with the pregnancy test. His reaction was everything she'd hoped it would be. He'd let out a loud whoop and spun her around. When he set her down, she'd seen tears shimmering in his eyes before he pressed a firm kiss to her lips.

They'd had a long talk that afternoon, too, discussing their fears about the pregnancy and beyond, both agreeing that they wouldn't allow those fears to color what should be a happy time. She was still a little apprehensive, but the anticipation made the nerves little more than a blip in her thoughts.

"I wish you said something sooner, so we could celebrate. Now, we're going to have to wait until after my honeymoon."

Tara smiled at her friend. "We'll still do what I had planned for girls' night. How's that sound?"

"It sounds good." London gave her another hug.

The door opened once more, the ear-piercing squeal filling the room. Jace stood in the doorway, a hand over his eyes.

"Tara, honey, you in here?"

"I'm right here. You can put your hand down; we're alone."

He dropped his hand away, a smile on his handsome face. Tara's heart two-stepped like it always did around him. Not just because he was gorgeous, but because he made her world better and brighter. She would be forever thankful to have him in her life. He'd pulled her out of her grief and shown her how beautiful life was again.

That charming grin vanished, though, when he got a look at her face. Concern drew his eyebrows together, and he stepped inside the restroom.

"Hey, are you okay? You look a little pale."

She smiled up at him. "I'm fine. Junior's decided to up the nausea game tonight, is all." She put a hand over the barely there swell of her abdomen.

Jace's eyes went wide at the mention of the baby, then darted around to look at their friends before landing on her again. Tara couldn't help but laugh.

"Relax, dear. The cat's out of the bag. London caught me

puking. She was ready to go have Seb interrogate the caterer about expiration dates and food prep methods, so I clued them in."

His shoulders relaxed and his smile returned. "Okay, good. I didn't want to spoil the surprise you had planned."

She stepped into his arms and placed a kiss on his jaw. "Nope, you're good. Now, how about we go find some more of that wedding cake? I need to get this taste out of my mouth, and I think I deserve another piece of cake."

He placed a smacking kiss on her cheek. "Your wish is my command."

"Oh, I like the sound of that," Tara said with a laugh.

He circled an arm around her waist and led her from the restroom. "Come on, ladies. I think we all need to have more cake."

"Hear, hear," Macy said. "The only thing that would make that better would be if it was laced with rum."

"Yeah, why didn't you have a rum-flavored cake?" Rayna asked.

"My wedding will have rum cake," Macy replied before London could chime in.

"Your wedding?" London said. "Who are you marrying?"

Tara smiled as she listened to her friends bicker. She tucked herself a little closer to Jace's side, grateful for him. His support and guidance had helped her to dig herself out of a hole filled with grief and see the sunshine again. And it was pretty damn nice.

Keep reading for a sneak peek _In Plain Sight,_ book 3 in the _Broken Bow_ series.

Thank you for reading Wildfire! I hope you enjoyed it.

Want to read an EXCLUSIVE and FREE book? Sign up for my mailing list. You can find the sign-up form on my website, ashleyaquinn.com. My list also receives sneak peeks of my latest work and access to exclusive giveaways. Also, please consider leaving a rating or review on Amazon and or Goodreads. It would be greatly appreciated!

Thanks again for reading!
- Ashley

~

Keep reading for a sneak peek at Book 3, In Plain Sight in the Broken Bow series.

IN PLAIN SIGHT

BROKEN BOW
BOOK 3

One

A cool wind whispered over Rayna Nydert's face and through her hair as she cut the engine on her utility vehicle. She glanced back at the wagon she towed. It was full of a dozen different kinds of tomatoes and peppers, and she still had more to pick. She needed to hurry, though. There was only about an hour of daylight left before the sun dipped behind the mountain and cast the valley into deep shadow.

Hopping out of the vehicle, she unhitched the wagon, leaving it parked next to the shed she used to store her harvest. She would unload all the crates later. Right now, she just wanted to get as much of the field picked as she could before it got too dark to see.

Rayna climbed back into the vehicle and backed it up to a second wagon, already loaded with empty crates, parked behind the building. She made quick work of hitching it up, then set off for the field. Once back in the rows of pepper plants, she cut the UTV's engine and climbed out. She took a crate from the wagon and got to work.

For twenty minutes, she made her way down the line of plants, the snip of her clippers the only sound other than the wind and the chirp of the evening birds. The peace was nice. It took the edge off the restlessness in her mind.

The last few weeks had been rough. It had been a couple months since she found out the man she'd started to fall for was a lying, manipulative, psycho who'd killed her best friend's husband when they were both part of the same SEAL team deployed in Afghanistan. Since then, Rayna had carried a hefty amount of guilt that she'd allowed him to get close to Tara. That she'd put her friend's life in danger. It had put a strain on her relationship with her friend. Tara kept telling her she didn't blame her, but Rayna blamed herself, and it was much harder to gain her own forgiveness. She'd always been hard on herself.

She glanced at the sky as she filled a crate, lifting it to carry it back to the wagon. One more row and she would have to head back in.

A muffled grunt made her pause just before she reached the back of the wagon. She glanced toward the rows of beans, where the sound came from, trying to see through the dense foliage and growing darkness. Something scuffed the dirt, and she heard another low grunt.

What the hell?

Setting the crate on the ground, she withdrew a shovel from the back of the UTV, mindful of all the craziness that had gone on lately. Between the serial killer who abducted one of her best friends and the crazy ex-soldier who lied to her about who he was, so he could get close to another one of her best friends, she wasn't taking any chances.

Heart thumping, Rayna moved through the rows of peppers toward the beans. She rounded the end of the row where she thought the noise came from, brandishing the shovel. Shock made her eyes round.

She dropped the shovel and hurried toward the young man curled up on the ground. Small, circular wounds dotted his arms, one of his eyes was swollen shut, and he cradled his dislocated left arm against his bare chest. Bruises discolored the skin around his wrists and marred his naked torso.

As she got close, he scrabbled backward.

"I'm sorry! I'll pay for what I ate. I don't want any trouble." He backed further from her, struggling to get his feet under him.

Rayna stopped and held her hands out. "Wait! Don't go. Please. You can eat whatever you want. I just want to help you. My name's Rayna. What's yours?"

He stared up at her through his good eye. "I'm sorry," he mumbled again. He crumpled into the dirt, as though his muscles couldn't hold him up anymore, and curled up on his right side in a fetal position. His dirty, blonde hair hung in hanks over his face.

Her mind whirled as she stared down at him. She'd never seen him before, she was sure of that, so where did he come from?

His eyes closed, and he moaned. Taking a chance, she took a few more steps toward him, then crouched near his hips. She reached out and laid a gentle hand on his thigh.

He jerked and started to scramble up, but pain from his dislocated arm had him falling back to the ground, moaning.

"I'm not going to hurt you," she said softly. "Let me help you up. I'll get you to the hospital."

His eyes snapped open, the whites showing with his fear. "No! They'll find me and make me go back. I just need to rest for a bit. I'll be fine."

"You need a doctor." *And a police officer, from the sound of things*, she couldn't help but think. "Your shoulder is dislocated."

"No hospitals."

His voice carried a strength that surprised Rayna. She stared down at him again, debating what to do. She couldn't leave him out here, but if she tried to take him to the hospital, he'd bolt.

Kind, dark eyes and a mischievous smile flashed through her mind.

Did she dare call Thomas? Would he even answer the phone if he saw her calling?

The boy moaned again, wincing. A fine shiver ran through him, making up her mind for her.

"Hang on. I have an idea." She stood and hurried back to the UTV, grabbing her jacket and her phone. Running back to the young man, she draped the jacket over him before pulling up Thomas' name in her cell.

"Please answer," she muttered to herself as she lifted the phone to her ear. It rang five times before it rolled to voicemail.

"Dammit." She sighed and tried again. And again, it went to voicemail.

Muttering curses under her breath, her thumb hovered over the home button, but she decided to try one last time. She touched the green phone icon once more and lifted the phone.

He picked up on the third ring. "I'm busy, Rayna."

"Thomas, please don't hang up. I know you don't want to talk to me, but I need your help."

There was a pause, and she could almost see his face as he processed that. A little crease would form between his brows, and he'd get a slight purse to his lips.

"Is one of your animals sick?"

"No. Look, I don't really want to explain this over the phone. It'll be easier if you just come over and see for yourself."

"Rayna..." The hesitation in his voice was clear.

"Please, Thomas. I wouldn't ask if it wasn't important."

She glanced down at the man again, who looked like he'd fallen asleep.

Thomas sighed. "Fine. I'll be there in a few minutes." He hung up without saying goodbye.

Tara released the breath she didn't know she'd been holding and turned off the phone's screen, putting the cell in her back pocket. She bent down and gently poked the man— more of a boy, really—on the hip.

"Hey. I have help coming, but you need to get up."

His eyes cracked open. "I told you, no hospitals."

"It's not a hospital. It's just a friend who can help. Can you get up? I have a utility vehicle parked a few rows over."

"You swear you won't take me to the hospital?"

"I promise. Unless my friend says you could suffer serious, permanent damage. Then all bets are off."

He stared up at her, weighing her words.

Rayna decided to sweeten the pot. "I have vegetable soup waiting in the slow cooker back at the house. Fresh baked bread, too. I think I might even be able to scrounge up some homemade chocolate chip cookies."

His eyes widened imperceptibly and his tongue darted out to wet his lips. "With milk?"

She smiled and nodded. "Of course."

Indecision lit his face for only another moment before he shifted and stood on wobbly legs. Rayna reached out to steady him and helped him toward the UTV. Once she had him settled in the passenger seat, she put the crate of peppers in the wagon, then hurried around to the driver's side and climbed in, starting it up.

She tried to make the drive back to the house as smooth as she could, but she knew the terrain jostled his injured arm by the pinch to his face. Even with his eyes closed and relaxed against the seat, he looked like he was in a tremendous amount of pain.

They came to a halt at the back door of her little log cabin, which was a few hundred yards from her parents' two-story, white farmhouse. She'd had the cabin built a few years ago after her produce business took off. She loved her mom and dad, but she needed her own space.

Rayna shut off the UTV's engine, then hurried around to help the young man out. She led him to the door, giving the knob a twist. Figuring he would be more comfortable in a chair he didn't sink into, she helped him to the dining table.

"I'm going to get you some water."

"Milk. Please," he said. "I'm so hungry."

She hesitated. "How about we let my friend take a look at you first? If you need surgery, I don't want to put any food in your stomach."

She could see the protest brewing, so she headed him off. "I meant what I said in the field. If he thinks your condition is serious enough that you need a hospital, you're going. We'll figure out the rest later."

He glared at her, but said nothing.

Rayna walked to the sink and took down a glass from the cupboard, filling it with water, then took it to him. He nodded his thanks and took a hearty gulp.

She heard the front door open and turned to look. Thomas walked in, his large frame filling the doorway. Her heart skipped a beat at the sight of him, like it had since they were teenagers.

His eyes landed on hers, and he stared at her for a moment before they shifted to the disheveled man sitting at her kitchen table. He walked further into the cabin, closing the door, a deep frown marring his handsome face.

"Rayna? What's going on? Who is that?"

She walked toward him, casting a glance at the boy before looking up at Thomas. "I'm not sure who he is. I found him in my field." She lowered her voice. "He's been beaten and burned. I think his left shoulder is dislocated. I also think he's dehydrated."

Alarm widened his eyes. He stared at the young man for a second, then looked down at her again. "Why did you call me instead of taking him to the hospital?"

"He wouldn't let me take him. Said that *they* would find him there and make him go back."

"Who's they?"

She shrugged. "I don't know. He wouldn't tell me his name, either. But he's in a lot of pain, Thomas. I did tell him if you thought he needed serious medical attention, he was going to the hospital whether he wanted to or not." She laid a hand on his forearm. "Please, just take a quick look at him. I know you're a vet, but I didn't know who else to call. He's scared and in pain."

Those lovely lips pursed as he regarded her. He nodded and stepped toward the stranger. "I'll look at him, but he probably really does need a doctor."

Thomas stepped toward the young man at Rayna's table. His blonde hair hung limp over his dirt-streaked face. Even from fifteen feet away, he could see the burn marks on the man's arms and torso, not to mention the wicked bruises on his left arm and ribcage. Someone had used him as a punching bag.

Anger burned in his gut that someone could do such a thing to another human being, but he pushed those thoughts away, so his expression didn't scare the man.

"Hi. I'm Thomas," he said, crouching down. "Can you tell me your name?"

The man looked up at him, weariness in the one light blue eye he could see. Thomas tamped down the shock as he got a good look at the man's face. If he was over eighteen, Thomas would eat his boots.

The kid studied him for a moment before replying. "Mason."

"Good to meet you, Mason." He gestured to the arm hanging at a funny angle at the boy's side. "Can you tell me what happened?"

Mason swallowed hard and shook his head.

Thomas bobbed his head. "How about these?" He pointed to the burn marks—which looked an awful lot like cigarette burns.

Again, Mason shook his head. "I don't want any trouble."

"Kid, I think you're knee-deep in it, whether you want to be or not." He rose. "I need to take a look at your shoulder. It's not going to feel good, but if I can pop it back into place, you won't need to go to the ER. Okay?"

Mason nodded and sat straighter.

Thomas looked back at Rayna. "Do you have a towel or something he can bite on?"

She walked over to a drawer by the stove and pulled out a dish towel, passing it to him. He rolled it into a log and handed it to the kid.

"Here. Bite on this so you don't break a molar."

The kid took the towel and put it between his teeth.

"All right, let's see what we have here." Thomas put his hands on the boy's shoulder, pushing lightly around the joint.

The kid grunted, but stayed still.

"I'm sorry. I need to see if there's any obvious fracture." He probed the end of the humerus as well as the clavicle, but didn't feel anything move that shouldn't.

"Well, the good news is, I don't think anything is broken, and it feels like it's only a partial dislocation. But we need to put that shoulder back into place."

The young man nodded and took the towel out of his mouth so he could speak. "Do it."

"I can try, but this works a lot better if you've got pain killers onboard. They help relax you and your muscles. How long has it been out of place?"

Mason looked down. "Three days," he mumbled.

Thomas crouched back in front of the boy. "You walked around with your arm like that for three days?"

The kid nodded, giving Thomas a brief glance before looking away again.

Thomas looked at Rayna in surprise. She wore a shocked expression as she stared at the young man in her kitchen. Tears shimmered in her violet eyes.

He turned back to Mason. "Why didn't you go to the authorities for help?"

The kid tried to shrug, but winced. "They don't help. I end up back where I started."

"Mason, how old are you?" Rayna asked, coming to stand beside them.

He looked at her through his lashes, then turned his gaze to the floor. "I don't know," he mumbled.

"What do you mean, you don't know?" Thomas asked, his voice soft.

Mason looked at him, a wealth of sadness in his eyes. "What's the date?"

"September 13th," Thomas said.

"Of what year?"

Shock rendered Thomas speechless for a moment. What had this kid been through that he didn't even know what year it was? He cleared his throat and croaked out the year.

The boy gave them his first genuine smile. "Then I'm eighteen."

"Does that mean I can take you to the hospital?" he asked,

hopeful. This kid could have a lot of underlying issues if he'd been held captive.

Mason's smile disappeared and some of the fear crept back into his eyes. "No. I'd still rather not go."

Rayna crouched beside them. "Mason, who did this to you?"

"I don't want any trouble," he repeated. "Please, just fix my arm and let me go on my way."

Thomas shared another glance with Rayna. Her eyes pleaded with him to help.

Dammit. He never could say no to her.

Taking a deep breath, he nodded. "Okay." He patted the boy on his leg. "Let's see what we can do about that shoulder. We'll talk about the rest later."

The young man nodded.

"Ray, I need a piece of cloth we can fashion a sling out of."

She nodded and stood, hurrying off to another part of the house.

"You some kind of doctor?" Mason asked when she disappeared.

Thomas smiled and stood. "Sort of. I'm a vet. But I have some EMT training. Yours won't be the first shoulder I've popped back into place. My brothers have had their fair share." He pointed to the dish towel the kid clutched. "Put that back in your mouth and do your best to relax. This will feel much better after I get it back in the socket." He prayed he would be able to pop it back in. With as long as it had been out, there was a chance the muscles had seized around it, and it would take some heavy sedation to get it back into place.

He put one hand back on Mason's shoulder, feeling for the ends of the joint. Rayna returned with a strip of fabric in her hands as he picked up the kid's arm.

"Okay, here we go."

He lifted the boy's arm higher, and the young man let out

a moan. Thomas applied some pressure, feeling the muscles resist. He massaged the muscle going over the joint, then pulled up and twisted Mason's arm. The kid's shout was muffled by the towel, then cut short as the joint slid back into the socket, bringing him some relief.

Mason pulled the towel from his mouth and slumped in the chair. "Thank you," he murmured.

"You're welcome." Thomas stepped aside, so Rayna could tie a sling around the boy's arm.

"Thomas, grab the bottle of ibuprofen out of the drawer by the fridge," Rayna told him. "And pour him a glass of milk."

He did as he was told and soon set four tablets and the milk on the table in front of Mason. The kid scooped them up and downed them with one big gulp.

"Do you want some food now?" Rayna asked the young man, patting him on his good shoulder.

Mason nodded. "Yes, please."

She looked at Thomas. "Have you eaten?"

He shook his head.

She walked around the half wall separating the dining area from the kitchen, and went to the cabinet by the fridge, taking down three bowls. Stepping over to the slow cooker, she removed the lid. Thomas walked up to stand next to her.

"What do you want to do about him?" he asked in a low whisper, glancing back at Mason, who sat on the other side of the half wall, eyes closed as he slouched in the dining chair.

"I'm not sure, but I know we can't turn him out. He's got no money, and he's injured. We might as well give him back to whoever he ran away from."

"Agreed."

"I guess he could stay here for a few days. I have a spare room."

Alarm bells clanged in Thomas' head. "I don't know if

that's such a good idea, Ray. You don't know anything about him."

"Oh, come on, Thomas. He's just a frightened child." Her whisper was harsh, and she glared up at him.

"That may be, but he's still a stranger."

"What do you want me to do, then? You can't take him home; there's too many people on The Broken Bow. Someone will wonder who he is and start asking questions. Until we know who he ran from, it's probably best he stays somewhere out of the way." She ladled soup into the three bowls, passing them to him as she went.

"I think so, too, but I still don't like the idea of you being here with him alone." He grabbed the last bowl and went to the silverware drawer.

Rayna took a loaf of homemade bread from the bread box and set it on a cutting board. Thomas took a butter knife from the drawer along with three spoons, then retrieved the butter from the fridge.

She sliced off several pieces of the bread and handed them to him to be buttered.

"Unless you know of a better place for him, I'm inviting him to stay," she said, setting the buttered bread on a small plate.

He took hold of her arm to stop her from walking away. "If he's staying, then I am too."

About the Author

Ashley started writing in her teens and never stopped. Her first novel, Smoky Mountain Murder, came out in 2016, and she has since published two more series and has plans for more. When not writing, you can find her with her nose stuck in a book or watching some terrible disaster movie on SyFy. An avid baseball fan, she also enjoys crafting and cooking. She lives in Ohio with her husband, two kids, three cats, and one very wild shepherd mix.

Website: https://ashleyaquinn.com

goodreads.com/ashleyaquinn

amazon.com/Ashley-A-Quinn/e/B07HCT4QST

ALSO BY ASHLEY A QUINN

Foggy Mountain Intrigue

Smoky Mountain Murder

Smoky Mountain Baby

Smoky Mountain Stalker

Smoky Mountain Doctor

Smoky Mountain K-9

Smoky Mountain Judge

The Broken Bow

A Beautiful End

Wildfire

In Plain Sight

Close Quarters

Scorched

Light of Dawn

Pine Ridge

Sweetness

Loner

Shark

Katydid

Homespun

9 781959 943051